# Traitors

A Novel

William Issel

Carleton Street Publications

In order for a worldview to spread, what it needs is
not full-time employees, but fanatical apostles.
**—Adolph Hitler, memorandum to Nazi Party leaders,
December 12, 1932.**

Blood and race determine the world of ideas of the German.
**—Ernst Bohle, *Gauleiter* of the Foreign Organization of the
Nazi Party, at the 1936 Party Congress in Nuremberg.**

Let us redeem our promises to Jewry and shame the devil of
Nazism, Fascism, and our own prejudices
**—Captain Orde Wingate, letter to
General Sir Francis Reginald Wingate, January 12, 1937.**

We regard with dismay the mushroom growths of fascistic
movements in the world today.
**—Elliot Burstein, Senior Rabbi, Temple Beth Shalom, in a
March 27, 1937 KFRC radio broadcast in San Francisco.**

Walt Whitman wrote years ago, America is a "nation of nations"
and therein lies our strength.
**—Eleanor Roosevelt, in a January 11, 1942
national radio broadcast.**

# Part I
# Saturday, May 9, 1942

## The United States Army tests the Harbor Defense Guns in San Francisco

### Ferry Building, San Francisco, 11:00 A.M.

Through the windows of his Hatzfeld Enterprises office, Charles Brown could see the boats docking and the passengers disembarking. The windows rattled every time the loud boom of the sixteen-inch harbor defense guns reverberated through the Ferry Building.

"We won't ever need to use these guns because the Japs will never invade San Francisco," Charles said to Catherine Lanham, the *Examiner* reporter sitting in the visitor's chair in front of his desk.

Lanham, a well-dressed woman with short brown hair, smiled ruefully. "Why did I have to schedule my interview on the day the army decided to test-fire the big guns?"

Charles shrugged. "The guns don't bother me." He took a cigarette from a silver case and offered her one, but she declined. He noticed her glancing at the Iron Cross emblem on the case.

"I'm here in connection with my article about what's doing now with the city's America First organization," she said. "Pearl Harbor put you guys out of a job, right? Since you are their president, I figured you were the person to interview."

He lit his cigarette. "I would have preferred us to stay out," he replied, "but the Japanese attacked us and the President and Congress had no choice but to declare war. I think we'll quickly defeat the Japs. When we do, Roosevelt and Churchill should make peace with Germany."

Lanham frowned. "But I thought FDR vowed to fight the Axis to an unconditional surrender. Since that is government policy, will your organization support that policy?"

He flashed a brief smile. "I can't speak for the organization," he said, "but I'll tell you what *I* think. Germany is our natural ally. While I do concede that Hitler's gone too far in some respects, and don't condone his excesses, I think we should be doing our best to educate the public about our true interests as a White Anglo Saxon nation. We have to defeat the Japanese empire, but it's a huge mistake to ally ourselves with Stalin and the communists."

Lanham was looking decidedly uncomfortable. She had stopped writing in her reporter's notebook. She picked up the leather carryall from the floor next to her chair and placed her notebook and pencil inside. "Do you want to say anything about your current activities?" she asked. "I notice you have held no meetings or rallies since December 7."

"We're necessarily quiet now," he replied. "Our point of view is not popular here in San Francisco. We will wait for an opportunity to regain our respectability. You haven't heard the last of us." He stood up and walked to the front of his desk. "I thank you for the interview but I won't be surprised if your editor refuses to print my sentiments."

He began to raise his right arm with his hand outstretched, but Lanham stood up, silently turned, and left his office without shaking hands.

Charles told himself not to be insulted by Lanham's rude departure. He remembered the words of his friend Alexander Campbell: "We need to talk up our patriotism now!"

Campbell was right, of course. But it was hard to accept that they needed to stop criticizing the government.

He met Campbell for lunch at Joe DiMaggio's Grotto and told him about his meeting with the reporter. As expected, his friend thought he had been too blunt.

As he walked back to his office along the Embarcadero from Fisherman's Wharf to the Ferry Building, passing the ships loading and unloading at the piers along the bustling waterfront, he thought about how he should mention his interview with Lanham at his afternoon meeting.

The Embarcadero and Market Street were filled with the noise of pedestrians, cars, and trucks. Streetcars were traveling uptown and downtown on the four tracks down the middle of Market Street. He could see Twin Peaks in the distance.

He crossed the cavernous first floor filled with men and women going to and from the ferry boats and walked upstairs to his office, where he caught up on some paperwork.


He was reading the *Chronicle* when he heard a knock on his door. He glanced at his watch. It was a bit early for his meeting, but he shrugged and called out, "Just a minute."

He stood up, took his suit jacket off his desk chair and put it back on. He straightened his tie and walked to the door.

"Hello," he said, smiling at the man with blue eyes and blond hair. "Come in! I didn't expect you but I'm glad to see you." The man returned his smile, said hello, and stepped into the office.

"Pull up a chair," Charles said. "Make yourself comfortable." He closed the door, walked back to his desk and sat down.

Instead of taking a seat, the blond-haired man walked to the front of the desk, took out a .38 caliber pistol from his suit jacket and pointed it at Charles.

"What are you *doing*?" Charles cried. He instinctively reared back in his chair and threw up his hands.

"Wait, what's going on?" he wanted to say, but the man shot him before he could speak.

**SATURDAY, MAY 9, 1942**

# Hatzfeld Enterprises Office
# Ferry Building, San Francisco, 7:00 P.M.

"Find the killer! And no leaks to the papers or anybody else!"

Tony Bosco smiled. "You don't need to shout, Chief. I'm standing right in front of you."

A former city police commissioner and the chief's special investigator for cases linked to national security, Tony was accustomed to Chief O'Reilly's temper. Yet shouting like this was out of character, even for a man who never beat around the bush.

"I don't need etiquette lessons, Tony," the Chief said, though his tone had mellowed a bit. "Find out who killed Charles Brown! When I asked you to take care of the Coit Tower murder you spent more time eating in Italian restaurants than tracking down the killer."

"That was a difficult case and you know it," Tony retorted. "Harlan Winthrop was killed somewhere else and his body dumped in Coit Tower." He pointed to the body in the desk chair. "Judging by the amount of blood on the chair and the wall behind him, Charles Brown was definitely shot right here in his office."

"There's one thing both these killings have in common, though," said Detective Sergeant Dennis Sullivan, a tall handsome man with round, wire frame glasses. "Both times the killers left dramatic messages."

Tony studied the hand-lettered sign the killer had hung around Charles Brown's neck. It read "Traitor" – in bold caps. Below, in smaller letters, was written "The Grynszpan Group."

"I don't understand this," the chief said. "Traitor? Grynsz-pan Group? What does it signify?" He looked at Tony, then at Dennis. "I know Charles Brown's work with the America First Committee made him controversial, but Charles Lindbergh and Father Coughlin support that group. *They* certainly aren't trai-tors."

"Grynszpan was the Polish Jewish student who murdered that German diplomat in Paris back in 1938," Sullivan explained. He was in his twenties, draft age, but the army deferred him be-cause of his police work.

"I remember it too," said Ruthie Fuller, a young Russian language teacher at Mills College in Oakland who did what she called "volunteer work" for the chief – an old family friend. He depended on her to be his eyes and ears at Communist meetings and rallies. "My friend Rachel was living in London then. She wrote me about how the Nazis used Grynszpan's killing of the diplomat as an excuse for their attacks on Jews all over Germa-ny and Austria. They called it *Kristallnacht,* the night of broken glass."

"Now I remember," the chief said. "That was when the Arch-bishop made a lot of us Catholics mad saying on that nationwide radio program that the Jews are our brothers."

Tony, who was also president of the city's Catholic men's or-ganization, said, "Chief, the archbishop didn't go that far, but he did say that Catholics have a duty to be sympathetic with the Jews."

"Don't be getting Jesuitical on me," O'Reilly barked. "What are we saying? This is some Jewish terrorist group named after that Grynszpan guy? Going around killing people in *my city* and hanging signs on the bodies?"

"That's what it looks like," Dennis said.

"But why Charles Brown?" the chief asked. "I don't really know anything about Jews, but killing Brown? That's a damned funny way to be religious. I don't want the public to get all riled up about Jews because of this."

"That's why you called us, isn't it?" Tony said. "You want to keep this quiet, like the Coit Tower case, if it does turn out that some Jewish terrorists are killing our leading citizens?"

"People are already nervous and jittery," the chief said. "Whatever that sign means, I don't want it in the newspapers. And since we're getting all religious, I'm giving you a commandment: find this killer and put him out of commission. If we don't clear this up quickly, somebody is bound to discover what happened and the papers will have a field day. Do you understand?"

"What about the body?" Tony asked. "Don't we need to find the bullets and do an autopsy?"

"It's obvious he was shot here. Our priority is to quickly clean up the mess and make sure this doesn't get to the press. I'll have my people dispose of the body in the city incinerator."

"Won't his family be worried?" Ruthie cried. "This seems cruel!"

The chief shook his head. "Ruthie, I told you during the other case – the public doesn't need to know everything. Brown's family will probably report him as missing. I had the cleaning lady who found the body driven to the Southern Pacific station in Oakland. We convinced her she'd be happier in a new home in Denver, Colorado. Hell, she's already happier, we gave her a nice bonus in fifty dollar bills."

Ruthie sighed.

"Keep me informed about your progress," the chief said and walked out.

Tony, Dennis, and Ruthie looked at one another for a moment. "I see a briefcase here," Dennis said. "I'll put the desk diary and anything else that looks useful inside it and we can look at it later. What are you thinking, Ruthie? You look upset."

"My friend Rachel's husband, Jacob, used to live in Palestine," she said. "He was an officer in a special Jewish police squad. Now he's the FBI special agent handling Nazi, Fascist, and Communist subversion cases in the city." She crossed her arms over her chest. "I don't care what the chief says, we need to talk to him. If anybody knows about this Grynszpan Group, it would be Jacob Weiss."

# Part II

# Three Years and Six Months Earlier

## October 1938 – September 1939

### FRIDAY, OCTOBER 21, 1938

## Orde and Lorna Wingate's Flat, Talbieh Neighborhood, Jerusalem

## British Mandate Palestine, 8:00 P.M.

"A Toast to our 'Hayedid' – Captain Orde Wingate, truly a 'Friend' to us and our cause!"

The dozen khaki-clad young veterans of the captain's Special Night Squad were gathered on the balcony of the Jerusalem flat. The Wingates lived on the top floor of a spacious two-story building with a view over the Kidron Valley. It looked like it was plucked out of the pages of *The Arabian Nights* and plunked down among other recently built villas. Jacob Weiss thought the neighborhood seemed a world away from the crowded Old City streets.

He had walked the two kilometers from the Damascus Gate by himself, feeling out of place – a broad shouldered muscular young man in a khaki uniform with pale skin, blond hair, and blue eyes. At well over six feet, even without his hat, he towered over the dark-haired, dark-eyed men and women in all kinds of civilian clothes going to and from their late model cars parked along the sidewalks.

But now he was in his element, with his fellow soldiers – Moshe Dayan and the other young Jewish fighters attending the going away dinner party. They raised their glasses and shouted three times, "To Captain Wingate. Hip, Hip, Hooray." Each cheer louder than the last. The captain and his wife smiled, bowing their heads in acknowledgement.

Wingate, a thirty-five-year-old intelligence officer, was leaving Jerusalem, reassigned to London with a promotion to major. But Jacob knew that his commanding officer was anything but pleased with the new posting. Jacob remembered when Wingate had called him and Dayan to his office, the day after he received his transfer orders.

"Sit down, boys," he had said, pointing to the chairs in front of his desk.

They walked into the small stuffy office, brushed off their uniforms and removed their hats. Drilling on the parade ground was hot, dusty work, and they were thirsty. Wingate poured two glasses of water from the pitcher on the desk and handed them to Jacob and Dayan.

"My superiors are removing me from Palestine. They can't abide my recruiting young men like you from the Haganah defense organization."

"That's crazy," Dayan said.

"Most of my fellow officers are captives of an Arab mystique. Worse, it was spread by my cousin, T.E. Lawrence. Now they're siding with the Arabs against the Jews."

"We've heard the charges against our squad," Jacob said. "They're calling us terrorists. I'm never sure how to answer those criticisms."

"It's simple," Wingate explained. "Zionism is our guiding star. God meant Palestine to be the true home of the Jews; that was the Christian tradition I grew up in. I believe in it still. Using any means necessary to defend Jews in Palestine cannot be called terrorism!"

"I agree, but you're an odd sort of British commanding officer for a Jewish force," Dayan argued. "That being said, we respect you more than I can say."

Wingate nodded, more to himself than at them.

"I've asked the two of you here because I can see you have great potential for leadership," he continued. "I'd like you to think about coming with me to London. I'll set you up with tutors to perfect your English and then you can move to the United States before the second Great War starts."

"What do you mean?" Dayan asked. "What second Great War? Why do you think another war will start soon?"

"There's no way Chamberlain's 'Peace in Our Time' nonsense will ever happen," Wingate said.

"Hitler's been allowed to steal part of Czechoslovakia, and he won't stop there. I read *Mein Kampf* – his goal is to take over all the vast farming lands east of Germany and wipe all Jews from the face of the earth."

"I haven't read his book," Jacob said, "but how do we know that what's in there will be what he tries to accomplish? Won't he have enough to do just to run his own country?"

"That would be comforting," Wingate said, "but he's an ego maniac and he'll keep trying to conquer, just like Napoleon did."

"But why go to the United States?" Jacob asked.

"If you stay here, you'll likely die in a shooting war with Arab terrorists. I don't see a shred of difference between Adolph Hitler and the mufti Haj Amin al-Husseini when it comes to Jew-hating. Boys, Hitler wants to rid *the entire world* of Jews, not just Europe."

Dayan was shaking his head. "I'm not going anywhere," he said. "I plan to devote my life to freeing us from the British."

"I understand," Wingate said. "You both know I think the Jews should have their own land and be independent. I'd like to fight alongside you to achieve that, but the higher-ups have decided that I'm a bloodthirsty Bible-quoting Zionist. Just when we're making progress the army has decided I'm training terrorists and sending me back to London."

Listening to the captain's impassioned rant, Jacob felt his stomach tightening and his pulse racing. He thought to himself that if he were English, he might agree that Wingate was a little crazy.

He took another drink of water. "Terrorist tactics have spread like a disease, Captain," he said. "The Nazis are using terrorism against the Jews in Germany and Austria. The Arab extremists are using terrorism to kill innocent Jews in Palestine. And when we defend ourselves, people turn around and accuse *us* of terrorism against the Arabs."

"I hate the idea that we might be using terrorist tactics ourselves, but what other option do we have?" Dayan said. "Just passively wait to be killed?"

Jacob felt his face getting hot. "Actually, I've been thinking about going to the United States ever since my family was killed outside the Edison Cinema."

Wingate made a disgusted grimace. "Khalil al-Sakakini called that murderer a hero!"

"I don't like to talk about it," Jacob continued. "Lots of people have suffered more than I have."

"After Hitler became Chancellor my dad said he saw the writing on the wall. He brought us to Palestine from Vienna. I'm an American citizen. I was born in San Francisco, where my parents owned a restaurant. But they lost so many customers during the Great War that they returned to Austria when I was two years old in 1920. My grandparents stayed in San Francisco."

Wingate got up and walked over to Jacob's chair. "Jacob, you never let on about any of this. I'm so sorry." He went to the other side of the room and picked up another chair. Instead of sitting back at the desk, he put it down next to the two young men and straddled it, facing them.

"My grandmother wrote to me that she's a widow now," Jacob continued. "She needs me to come to San Francisco and support her. I have a duty to take care of her. I'm the only remaining member of the American side of the family."

"Jacob, if you are a U.S. born citizen, you can go back to America and become a special agent," Wingate said. "You can work against anti- Semitism there. The FBI will like your training and experience in my squad and a recommendation from me will impress them. They're hunting down American home-grown Nazis."

"But, Jacob," Dayan said, "this country gave refuge to your family."

Jacob was silent for a while. "I can't stay. My grandmother is alone. I have to help her. It's what my parents would have wanted."

Wingate got up and started pacing around the room. "You boys need to think about how you can best make a contribution in the war that's on the horizon. If I'm right about what's coming, I think the best place for you is the United States. The Americans won't refuse you a military career because you're Jews.

"If you stay here, you could be killed in battle, or assassinated as you walk down the street."

"I expect the British army will probably refuse to allow Haganah members like you to bear arms and fight alongside the boys from Manchester and Birmingham. I'm afraid my Special Night Squad will be disbanded as soon as I leave Jerusalem."

A week had passed since they'd had the conversation with the captain. Jacob and Dayan said their goodbyes to Cap-tain and Mrs. Wingate with mixed feelings. They walked along the streets of the well-to-do neighborhood toward their quarters near the Damascus Gate. The full moon cast a silvery glow over the Dome of the Rock and the al-Aqsa Mosque in the distance.

"I won't hold it against you if you decide to go to London with the captain," Dayan said. "Especially if you help rid the USA of Nazis."

Jacob thought for a moment. "If the Captain is right, and Hit-ler really does want to rid the world of Jews, I will fight on the American front."

**SATURDAY, NOVEMBER 12, 1938**

## West London Synagogue
## Upper Berkeley Street, London, 11:00 A.M.

"Good morning," said the young woman next to him as they filed into the community room after the service. "You must be new, I don't recall seeing you before."

The previous Saturday had been warm and sunny, but Jacob figured it was the events of the last three days, not the rainy weather, that brought a standing room only crowd to services.

"I'm not a member of the congregation," he replied, "but I felt the need to be here today. I guess I wasn't the only one."

The woman had wavy brown hair and large brown eyes. He had to look down to make eye contact.

"My name is Rachel Bernstein," she said, extending her hand, her eyes twinkling with interest. Jacob took her hand in his and felt a jolt inside that surprised and startled him.

"I'm Jacob Weiss," he said. "Judging by your accent, you must be American."

She smiled. "Graduate student at the London School of Economics."

"That's impressive. Most girls don't like economics, do they?"

"Master's degree students don't appreciate being referred to as girls, Mr. Weiss," she replied. "But I'm happy to help educate men like you to the fact that women *can* find economics a field of interest."

Jacob reddened and made a slight bow, realizing he had

gotten off on the wrong foot. "I meant no disrespect, Miss Bernstein," he hastened to reply. "I guess you can be my teacher." He flashed a playful smile. "But I do hope you won't limit your lessons to good manners at Sabbath services."

Now Rachel was blushing. She cocked her head. "Why, Mr. Weiss! Have you gone so quickly from calling me a child to flirting with me?"

Jacob laughed, and they moved to the front of the queue. They each accepted a cup of tea and a biscuit from the volunteer at the refreshment table before finding a place below one of the windows, away from the crowds.

"Speaking of accents," Rachel said, "I can't place yours. As long as we're in the mutual education business, where are you from?"

"It's complicated. I was born in San Francisco but moved to Vienna, Austria, when I was a little kid. I grew up speaking German and English. When I was fifteen we moved to Palestine, where I learned Hebrew, Yiddish, and Arabic. But I've been around a lot of British English most recently."

"I can't believe this," Rachel said, more animated all of a sudden, "I was also born in San Francisco and graduated from the university at Berkeley. My adviser recommended that I study with Professor Hayek at the LSE. So here I am. But what a small world!"

"Rachel, I've never seen you so obviously enjoying a conversation," a voice behind them spoke.

Jacob turned and saw Rabbi Harold Reinhart, a slight professorial-looking man with thin hair and metal eyeglasses. He was making the rounds and greeting the congregation as they enjoyed their tea and biscuits.

"You are usually very sober and serious – the picture of academic probity. But today you're having a jolly good time. Can it be the attention of this handsome young lad, who I hasten to add is very welcome to our synagogue?"

"You'll never guess what, Rabbi," said Rachel, "and I'll ignore your naughty teasing. This is Jacob Weiss, from San Francisco, Vienna, and Palestine!"

"I'm also American, Jacob," said the rabbi. "I lived in Los Angeles and Sacramento before I came to London."

"I'm happy to meet you, Rabbi," Jacob answered. "I was very moved by the sermon, and so was everyone else, judging by the solemn faces I saw at the end. This is only the second time I've come to Saturday services, and what a difference between last week and this."

"We don't often have such a full house, it's true," the rabbi said. "But the events of this past week have put the world on edge, not just we Jews. My Christian minister colleagues have also centered their sermons this weekend on the need to respond to the terrible attacks on the Jews in Germany and Austria."

"You're from Vienna?" the rabbi asked. "I hope your people are all right."

"I have relatives in Vienna, and I haven't been able to get in touch with them," Jacob said. "I haven't been able to sleep that well the last several nights."

"The papers are full of stories," Rachel said. "Horrible pictures of broken windows, looted stores, burning synagogues. I couldn't stand to even read the articles about people being beaten, arrested, and even killed."

"I can't stop worrying about my aunts and uncles and my

cousins in Austria," Jacob admitted.

"I'm afraid we haven't seen the end of this," the rabbi said. "Several of us in the West End, even a Catholic priest, are especially concerned with the reports of the killing of children. We're organizing a demonstration at Trafalgar Square, and I hope you and your friends will join us. It was a pleasure to meet you, Jacob. I hope you will join us again."

He turned and walked to speak with another group. Neither Rachel nor Jacob broke the silence. "You mentioned you had relatives in Austria," Rachel said after a while. "Are your parents in Palestine?"

Jacob looked down at the tea cup and saucer in his hands. "My parents and sister died two years ago. Well, they were killed, actually. Shot to death in Jerusalem."

Rachel put her hand on his arm. "Oh, that's so terrible. I'm sorry, I didn't mean to pry. I shouldn't have asked. Oh, dear, what can you be thinking of me for being so rude. I'm…"

Jacob shook his head, "Rachel, please, it's all right. I don't mind. I've had to get used to talking about this and you haven't been rude at all. There's an undeclared war going on in Palestine. Terrorists among the Arab nationalists are trying to scare away Jewish settlers."

"But aren't some of the Jews also using terrorist tactics?" Rachel asked. "Some Arab students at the LSE are saying there are Jewish extremists in Palestine acting just like the Nazis."

"That's a lie," Jacob said, his voice louder.

"I should know more about what's happening there," Rachel said. "I spend so much time studying to keep up with my courses that I hardly ever have time to read the papers or listen to the radio. But in the canteen at the LSE yesterday and the day before, everybody was talking about the Nazi attacks. I feel helpless to do anything, but at least I could keep myself informed."

"I know what you mean. It's hard not to feel helpless. Speaking of your courses, I don't want to keep you from your studying if you have work to do."

"I suppose I should be on my way," she said. They put their tea cups on the table and walked out the door of the Neo-Byzantine building. The streets were wet but it wasn't raining. The sound of traffic on Edgeware Road, with its incessant honking of horns, greeted them as they turned the corner and walked toward the Marble Arch underground station.

She put her hand on his arm again. "I'm going to the library at LSE to study. Walk with me to the tube stop, why don't you? If you have the time, I mean. But then I haven't the slightest notion as to what you might be doing, Jacob. What is it you do, anyway? Were you a student in Palestine?"

"I lived in several places, most recently in Jerusalem. I left school when my parents were killed."

Jacob went silent. They walked on, each of them lost in their separate thoughts.

A loud horn blared, and Jacob jumped back on the curb to avoid getting bumped by a black taxi. He realized he had started to cross without looking in the right direction. They were already alongside Hyde Park and he hadn't even been aware that they were so close to Marble Arch.

"The Marble Arch station is just there," he said, "and you must need to go study. I hope I'll see you at services next Saturday."

Rachel smiled up at him, her eyes twinkling. He felt a momentary flutter in his chest and a catch in his throat. She was carrying her umbrella, and now switched it from her right hand to her left. She placed her right hand on Jacob's left arm.

"I have a better idea. Why don't you come to the demonstration against the attacks on the Jews? I'll give you my telephone number. Call me and we'll decide on a place to meet. Afterwards, we can go out for a pint, as they say here."

"So you even go to pubs and drink ale?" Jacob teased.

She looked up at him again with mischief in her eyes. "Oh, I've developed all kinds of new tastes here. Or, as my parents might say, bad habits. I actually prefer wine to beer. Italian Chianti is my favorite!"

"Well then, Miss Bad Habits," Jacob said, "I'll look forward to it."

## SATURDAY, NOVEMBER 12, 1938

## Oxford Street

## London, 12:30 P.M.

The Saturday shopping crowds surrounded him as he walked down Oxford Street to meet his new friend Paul Klein. Despite the tumult, Jacob felt lonely. For the first time since arriving in London almost two weeks ago, he was nothing more than a face in the crowd.

He'd met Paul onboard the *Dorsetshire*, the troop ship that brought them from Haifa to Portsmouth. Every day seemed packed with a constant stream of new people who wanted to talk and demanded his attention. Major and Mrs. Wingate had insisted that he join them for dinners at their table. He'd had no time to be lonely.

Here in this strange city, staying in a cold hotel room by himself, he found himself missing his family again. The weather outside today seemed to match his mood. A clouded, darkening sky hung heavy over the trees of Hyde Park, most of which were already bare. The few straggler leaves were brittle-looking and lacking color. The temperature had dropped, as if lowered by the coldness inside of him.

Jacob realized he wasn't prepared for the noise of London with its ubiquitous cars, big red busses and black taxis spewing smoke in every direction.

After using the Underground, he wondered how people didn't get claustrophobic going down the steep escalators. He couldn't imagine getting used to the awful smells and hot winds that came at him as he stood on the crowded platforms.

He noticed that most of the men on the Oxford Street sidewalks looked almost shabby, not nearly as well dressed as he was. He was reminded that masses of men of all ages were still out of a job or working for low wages. A few men his age in worn cheap clothing were giving him critical sidelong glances as they passed. He felt conspicuous and perhaps a little guilty about his good fortune. At the same time, he was happy to be warm in this dark, depressing city. He was also glad that Mrs. Wingate had taken him to a banker and a tailor the day after they arrived.

Jacob would always be grateful to the Wingates. They had stepped up and helped him sort out his affairs in record time after he told the major he wanted to accompany him to London. Actually, it was Mrs. Wingate who had helped him the most.

As soon as they arrived in London, she sat him down and made him explain the complicated financial affairs he had inherited after his parents' murder. Then she contacted the manager of their own finances. Now Jacob's modest but sufficient assets were in the hands of the same trustworthy London banker.

Mrs. Wingate went with him to see Mr. Brooks at Lloyd's Bank in Piccadilly. He assured Jacob that he could draw on his funds when he traveled to America, "or anywhere else you desire to go."

Afterwards, they had lunch at the Savoy, a grandiose establishment that made Jacob feel out of place in his Jerusalem best clothes. Mrs. Wingate seemed to agree. "The next thing we must do is see to it that you are not walking about looking like an overgrown ragamuffin from the desert. Winter is on the way, and you need a proper suit of clothes, as well as a coat and hat." When he protested that one of his new friends from the ship had told him about a place called Marks and Spencer where he could buy himself a ready-made suit, she sniffed. "Jacob, the matter is settled, I'm taking you to see Mr. Harry Benson on Bury Street." Two days later, he walked out of the Benson and Clegg shop wearing his new suit, topcoat, shoes, and hat. He carried an umbrella and a box containing his old clothes.

On the way to meet Mrs. Wingate at the nearby Buckingham Palace Gate that day, he had a thought. Major Wingate was an intelligence officer back in Palestine. He might approve the new outfit as perfect for spying on the Londoners.

That was three days ago. Now he was getting used to looking like a Londoner. At least Rachel and the rabbi didn't act like he was an imposter. As he walked to The Victoria, where he was supposed to have lunch, he wondered what Paul would say about his new look.

He saw him standing at the bar as he walked into the venerable wood paneled pub. Paul was shorter than Jacob with close-cropped brown hair and hazel eyes. He was wearing a blazer and trousers, not a suit. He had on an open-collar shirt in contrast to Jacob's tie.

"You seem to have turned into a young member of the gentry overnight," he said with a big smile.

"Never mind," Jacob answered. "Beneath these fancy togs beats the heart of a desert fighter." He winked. "So watch what you say, city boy!"

"Ha, ha, maybe so," Paul said, "but you're in my territory now, desert rat. If you don't behave I'll take you to one of the favorite ambush spots near the docks and leave you there. Then we'll see just how rough and tough you really are."

"Well now, boys," said the bartender. "Are ye going to order or do ye just plan to stand there jabbering all day?"

Paul ordered a pint of Fullers and a steak and kidney pie, and

Jacob said he would have the same. Jacob was beginning to like the English custom of drinking ale.

Paul paid the barman. "My city, my treat," he said. They waited until their beer settled and took their drinks to one of the few unoccupied tables.

"So, what have you done besides give away half your fortune to a tailor?" Paul joked.

Jacob laughed along with him. "So far I've seen Buckingham Palace and lunched at the Savoy with Mrs. Wingate. I saw the Tower of London with the major. The three of us walked along the Embankment, and we had dinner at Simpsons-in-the-Strand."

"My word," Paul said. "You've eaten enough beef and mutton to last you for the rest of the year! You told me on the ship that your Major Wingate rarely touched meat?"

"He hardly ate anything at all in Palestine," Jacob said. "He ate grapes, and he took bites out of onions and garlic that he hung on a string around his neck."

"That's hard to imagine," Paul said. "But I've heard of these odd characters with their health regimens. Did he force you all to follow his example?" He chuckled.

"Thank God, no," Jacob said, smiling. "And here he seems to eat like a regular person. At least he did at Simpsons."

Their steak and kidney pies arrived, and they tucked into their lunches. Jacob asked Paul about his own military service. "Nothing like your nighttime raids on terrorists," Paul admitted. "I was assigned to the military intelligence department in Cairo. Boring."

"The major had me do some intelligence work in Palestine. I had to dress up like an Arab and smear stuff on my face so I'd be inconspicuous. How could it be boring?"

Paul scowled. "I was stuck behind a desk or in the embassy library. You can't believe how boring *that* is. You're never doing anything more exciting than sharpening a bloody pencil!"

"Can you read and speak Arabic? I picked up some Arabic in the five years I was in Palestine – I know as much of it as I do Yiddish."

"That's the best way to learn a language," Paul said. "Mine was mostly schoolboy stuff. First at college and then at the School of Oriental Studies. I met my first American there, another Paul! An amazing Negro named Paul Robeson."

"I envy you being able to attend such a place, but maybe I can go to a good college when I go to America. I can afford it – well, I can if I don't waste my money on steak pie and beer and just eat grapes, onions, and garlic!"

They both laughed. There was silence for a few moments as they finished their meal. "I thought I'd take you to the Hyde Park Speakers Corner," Paul said. "It's nearby, you don't seem to have been there, and it's Saturday afternoon – the best day. It's not raining. There should be masses of people there."

They left the pub and noticed that the sky had brightened.

"Who are the speakers?" Jacob asked.

"Anybody can speak about anything. And sometimes on a Saturday, that's exactly what happens."

"Do you think anybody will make a speech condemning the Nazi outrages Wednesday and Thursday nights in Austria and Germany?" Jacob asked.

Paul studied his face for a moment, before nodding. "I wouldn't be surprised," he said.

## SATURDAY, NOVEMBER 12, 1938

# Speakers Corner, Hyde Park

# London, 2:00 P.M.

The conversation with Paul, and the pint of Fullers, had put Jacob in a better mood. London felt less cold and unfriendly. They crossed Bayswater Road, headed into Hyde Park, and walked toward Speakers Corner.

He wasn't used to seeing so many young women walking alone, or in twos and threes, talking and laughing, animated and carefree. He liked their colorful brown, red, and blue jackets and coats. Most of them were hatless – blonds, brunettes, and even a few redheads. It was a pleasant change from the dull costumes that hid the bodies and covered the heads of the Arab women in Jaffa, Haifa, and Jerusalem.

Thinking of Arabs, he realized with a start that when he went into the pub, he failed to check on the location of the exits. And since they left the pub he'd neglected to check to see if anyone on the sidewalk behind them looked familiar. Was he already forgetting the routine self-defense habits he had learned in his Haganah and Special Night Squad training? Major Wingate would not approve.

"You've gone quiet," Paul said. "I asked you a question back there and I guess you think I'm being silly. Or maybe you're preoccupied with something. You look like you're a thousand miles away."

"Oh, sorry, what did you say?"

"Well, it *was* silly, rather." He laughed. "I just asked how you liked being among real flesh and blood English girls again. But then I realized you've never actually had the pleasure, have you? Living in the Negev with the female servants of Allah hardly counts, does it?"

"Well, I confess I do like looking at the girls. But, no, I was thinking that I was getting sloppy and not paying attention to my surroundings. I haven't even been here two weeks and I'm already forgetting my training."

Paul had a puzzled look. "But we're in London! Surely you can let down your guard in the capital of the British Empire!"

"I suppose you're right," Jacob replied, "but they pounded it into us that you always need to be on the alert."

He described how two of his friends who had let down their guard had met a bloody gruesome end, how Fawzi el Kawukji's terrorists and his men attacked Kiryat Shmuel in Tiberias, how they even killed children. Some of their victims were still alive when they threw their stabbed bodies into the burning synagogue.

"My god," Paul cried, shaking his head. "Why have I never even heard of this outrage?"

"Probably because the British – listen to me, sorry – don't really care about the Jews and don't take their safety seriously enough. Who's to say that Kawaukji hasn't sent a team to London just because it *is* the empire's capital? From what we saw of him, he'd like nothing better than to see big headlines in *The Palestine Post* – 'Explosion in Piccadilly, ten Jews killed in Arab terrorist attack!'"

They walked in silence while Paul took in Jacob's outburst. "I'm sorry," he finally said. "I'm not against the Jews. But I've never thought that much about the fighting in Palestine. It seemed far removed from my station in Cairo. Now that I stop to think about it, I can recall a lot of Jew jokes and prejudice among the senior officers."

Jacob placed a hand on his friend's shoulder. "Forgive me. I don't mean to suggest that you and all English people are anti-Jewish. I seem to be ranting these days the way Major Wingate does."

"No, not at all," Paul said. "I can scarcely imagine all the things you must have seen, what you must have gone through."

He looked so distressed that Jacob felt bad for bringing up the subject. He decided he needed to be more careful. He didn't want to rant and rave, to risk putting off people he liked and who seemed to like him.

As they approached the Marble Arch and Speakers Corner, they began to hear vehement voices, cheers, and jeers as well as the more distant traffic noise from Park Lane. Several hundred men and women gathered around a half dozen or so speakers, including a woman, all standing on makeshift podiums. They lectured, pounded their fists into their palms, and leaned forward to wave their arms or point their fingers at their audiences. The audiences in turn loudly shouted their approval or disapproval, sometimes announcing in extremely impolite language that the speaker ought to be otherwise occupied.

The largest group, at least fifty men and women, obviously middle class and well dressed, listened to a very tall, fit and healthy looking handsome man in his late thirties or early forties. His dark brown hair was stylishly cut and his moustache carefully trimmed. Jacob had heard such well turned out and well-spoken men on the parade ground and in the lecture hall. He recognized English upper class breeding and education when he heard it. This man was obviously cut from the same cloth. Jacob couldn't hear what he was saying, but it seemed compelling. In contrast to most of the other groups crowded around speakers, this group seemed captivated and stood silently straining to hear every word.

Jacob was curious. "Let's get closer so we can hear what he's saying," he said to Paul.

"You're not going to like what he has to say. That's one of Oswald Mosely's men."

"Ha," Jacob barked, "you're right, I won't like it. But now I can blend in." He gestured to his new clothes.

Paul grimaced and hung back as Jacob made his way through the outliers in the listeners to a place in the middle of the crowd. He quickly felt his stomach tighten. The speaker was urging his rapt audience to congratulate themselves on living in a time when, at last, the Jews would be put in their place. Jacob studied the audience more carefully. They were nodding to each other, smiling their approvals. They enjoyed being part of this Jew-hating experience. One man, standing maybe fifteen feet away, wore a red armband depicting a circle with a white border. Inside was a white lightning bolt on a dark blue background – not a swastika but a close relative.

He realized that Paul was standing next to him and had gently grabbed his elbow. "Jacob," he whispered, "let's get out of here, this is making me nervous."

Jacob had to admit that this might be one of those times when discretion was the better part of valor. If anything happened to alert the crowd that he was a Jew, the odds were decisively against him.

As they walked away from Speakers Corner and toward the Marble Arch, they encountered a man about their age with an armful of pamphlets. He was holding up one of them. "Gentlemen! I saw you listening to that fascist. Please take one of these and learn the truth. It's only five pence. You look like you can afford it. The truth doesn't always come so cheap."

Jacob took the pamphlet and gave the man five pence without a word. As he and Paul walked toward Oxford Street, he looked at the cover and saw the title: "Sir Oswald Mosely and the Jews."

## SUNDAY, NOVEMBER 20, 1938
## Balderton Street and Oxford Street
## London, 8:00 A.M.

Jacob sat down at the little table in the small kitchen, putting both hands around the coffee cup to warm them up. *This is a cold place*, he thought. The single, small electric fire barely heated the apartment and you had to feed it coins every ten minutes to keep it going.

He and Paul Klein were roommates now, after accepting an offer from Paul's Uncle George to stay in one of his vacant rentals. They were a stone's throw from Oxford Street, and the Bond Street tube station was a five-minute walk. The United States Embassy was only a few blocks away. Jacob had inquired about getting his American passport and was waiting for his appointment. He was told to expect a long wait; the staff was overwhelmed by the large number of visa requests from Europeans in London trying to get to America.

Paul entered the kitchen wearing a topcoat over his pajamas, rubbing his eyes. He poured a cup of coffee and sat down. "My uncle should have told us how cold this place would be."

"We seem to have gone from one extreme to another," Jacob said. "From mind-numbing heat in Cairo and Palestine to bone chilling cold in London." He shot a glance out the window. "I miss sunshine. I don't think I could live in a place like this. It gets dark by 4:00 and stays dark until 8:00 the next day."

"This weather doesn't bother me," Paul said. "I grew up in London. But I'd better get dressed. We need to leave soon so we can meet your friend Rachel at Trafalgar Square."

The weak sun was just beginning to lighten up the sky as they walked out of their apartment house and headed toward Self-ridges department store, visible at the end of the street. The clock above the entrance read 8:30. Jacob was thinking that perhaps they ought to have taken a cab, but then he had another thought. Like many of the younger men out this early, they were hatless, wearing their army-issue boots, worn trousers, and jerseys under old winter coats that they had brought with them from Palestine and Egypt. Dressed this way, he could pretend to belong where he was, observe and listen in on the real Londoners. *That might work,* he thought, *as long as I don't betray myself by talking.*

Paul wanted to show off his native local knowledge, so instead of zig-zagging through Mayfair he insisted they walk along Oxford Street to Regent Street so Jacob could see the famous hotels and department stores. Every pub they passed gave off sickly sweet beery odors left over from the Saturday night crowds. Nobody paid any attention to them until they came to the entrance of the Oxford Circus tube station. There stood a London policeman. Jacob had studied the history of the force in his Haganah training. He'd seen pictures of their uniforms and traditional "custodian helmets." He knew the London police were established by Sir Robert Peel, hence their nickname "bobbies." This one was surveying the passersby. He had small deep-set eyes and a sallow narrow face. His head was too small for his body. His ears stuck out like little flags behind the chin strap of his helmet. He watched them as they approached and looked them up and down. As they passed, he shouted "Oy, chaps, where'd ye come by them boots, then? Come over here, you two."

Jacob and Paul were about ten feet past the bobby. They stopped and looked at each other. Paul put his left hand on Jacob's arm. "Let me handle this," he whispered. He turned to the bobby. "Are you speaking to us, officer?"

The man's eyes showed surprise, but his face was immobile. "I asked yer about them boots, didn't I? Them's not yer ordnary bloke's 'footware' now, don't ya know. What's a couple a troublemakers like yers doing with them, eh?"

"I'll have you know, my good man, we were issued these boots as officers in His Majesty King George's Army," Paul said in an unmistakable public school and Oxford accent. "They've served us well in Egypt and Palestine; now they're retired. I'll thank you to resume your duties, constable, and bid us a good day as we continue on our way."

"Why ye cocky young faker," the bobby said, his face now pink. He put his right hand on his baton and walked toward them uncertainly. "Yer ain't goin nowhere until I tell ye to, and let's see some identification if yer who ye say ye are. We're on the lookout for a couple a thieving Oxford Street no accounts and ye two fit the description."

Jacob's mind flipped him back to early October, when he had been leading a patrol searching for weapons. They were in a narrow street in Tiberias after the massacre of Jews in that city. They encountered an Arab policeman who challenged their right to be in "his" neighborhood. He was quickly dispatched.

Now Jacob felt as if he were outside his body, watching, as his head cleared and things slowed down. His fists clenched and he took a deep breath, ready to neutralize this pasty-faced policeman.

Paul broke the spell. "Officer, has no one taught you to use proper English when addressing a gentleman? I seem not to have heard you use the word 'please' and I'm waiting. But, mind you, I don't have all morning, so ask us politely or please get out of our way. We have an appointment."

"Oh, my good sirs," the bobby sneered, "please do show me your identity cards. I'd be ever so grateful, ye lordships."

They took their army and Special Night Squad identification cards out of the inside pockets of their coats. Jacob also handed him his London Police registration card. The bobby looked at them in surprise. His body seemed to deflate before their eyes. "My mistake, officers," he said, refusing to look them in the eye. After he handed back the ID cards, he turned on his heel and walked away without a single word.

## SUNDAY, NOVEMBER 20, 1938

## Regent Street, London

## 9:30 A.M.

As he walked into Trafalgar Square, Jacob saw hundreds of people milling around the base of the Lord Nelson column with its four giant bronze lion statues, one on each corner. He mulled over the conversation he had with Paul as they had walked down Regent Street.

It had started shortly after they left Oxford Circus. Paul point-ed out a long four-story building across the street that looked ex-tremely out of place, like several old buildings with peaked roofs stuck together. It had timbers showing on the outside. "Do you see that building? The one that looks like it's from King Henry VIII's time?"

Jacob had said nothing since their interaction with the bobby. He just looked across the street and nodded.

"That's Liberty's store. It was built using the timbers from two British navy ships. Women come from all over to buy specially-de-signed fabrics and clothing there. It's my mother's favorite store."

Jacob just grunted. "Is something the matter?" Paul asked. "You've said nothing for fifteen minutes. What's wrong?"

"Ah, Paul, I'm sorry," he answered. "The way that bobby de-cided we were thieves just by looking at us really got to me."

"Well, I can't blame him," Paul said. "It must be hard to tell a crook from someone just wearing their old clothes, right?"

"I'm surprised you're sticking up for him."

"Maybe you're mad at him and feeling sorry for him at the same time. Didn't you tell me a similar story on the ship? When you had to make a split-second decision about who was dangerous..."

"You're not even Jewish and now you're pretending to be Dr. Freud!" Jacob said. "Yes, I told you about my first patrol, when I was still in the *Notrim*, the Jewish Guards, before Captain Wingate organized the Night Squad."

His mind took him back. It was just getting dark. They were on patrol and walking up a narrow street in the Old Town of Nablus. He was with his partner Aaron, in their khaki uniforms and special tarbush hats with official insignias. They were carrying Lee-Enfield rifles on straps over their right shoulders. Rounding a corner and coming down toward them were two men about their age, both wearing keffiyes, carrying a large wooden box with rope handles between them. Jacob and Aaron unshouldered their rifles, and asked them for their identification. The tallest man said, "What are you doing here? We don't accept your authority!" They put down the box – it looked just like the boxes that grenades come in – and the man reached for something. Before Jacob knew what was happening, Aaron shot him. He hadn't even realized Aaron had sighted his rifle.

"The Arab was just reaching for his identification, right?" Paul said.

"Yes. The box was full of the soap they make in Nablus. It's lucky for me and Aaron that he was just wounded and not killed. We were never even reprimanded."

"Well, you were all very lucky that evening. Sometimes when I think about your work in Palestine I get envious, but at the same time it seems like you had a thankless, impossible assignment."

"What do you mean?" Jacob asked. They were in Piccadilly Circus. Lots of people were coming out of the tube station, all seemingly heading down Regent Street toward the Thames River in the same direction as he and Paul.

"Well, you were protecting the Jewish residents of Nablus, and Tiberias, and wherever you were patrolling, right? And the Palestine rebels were protecting their land. They thought the tens of thousands of Jews who came after the war were thieves!"

"But the Jews bought and paid for their land, and sometimes much more than it was worth. Just like my parents did. I can't see how you can take their side like this!"

"I'm not taking their side," Paul insisted. "I said they *thought* the Jews were thieves, not that they *were* thieves. Jacob, I don't want to make light of your feelings, but surely you can understand how this is complicated. How could it not be? And you must be upset about all of this yourself, or you wouldn't get so hot under the collar just talking about it."

Jacob knew Paul was right, but he felt tongue-tied. He had never forgotten how his parents always argued about moving to Palestine. His mother had mixed feelings about being part of Zionism because they were displacing the Arabs who'd lived there for hundreds of years. She taught him to put himself in the Arabs' shoes. Some of them were very poor and they were worried about the future. He was confused and conflicted.

Someone bumped into him. He looked around to see who it was and saw they were now surrounded by a mass of people surging toward Trafalgar Square. He wished Paul would stop talking, but he wasn't finished.

"You don't have to be Dr. Freud to see that you have mixed feelings about your service in Palestine," he said. "The Jews going to Palestine are looking for a place where they can be safe and secure. But some of the Arabs feel like the Jews are invaders, pushing them out of their homeland, right? I don't mean to excuse violence. Terrorists who murder Jews are killers and they ought to be punished. But aren't Jews who kill innocent bystanders also terrorists? I'm not defending Arab terrorists. But if you're the police, and you can't tell who is a killer and who isn't, you could hurt innocent people. You had an impossible job, Jacob. You should be glad to be out of there.

"By the way, speaking of patrols, we're coming to the memorial to the soldiers who died in the Crimean War."

He pointed to the impressive marble and bronze ensemble they were approaching. Jacob saw three bronze soldiers wearing tall shako hats from the 1850s, flags behind them and rifles at their sides. High above them atop a marble pedestal stood a female figure with arms outstretched, two victory garlands in each hand.

"Look," Jacob said, "over there."

Rachel was standing with another woman, both wearing red coats, next to the statue of Florence Nightingale, famous for caring for wounded soldiers during the Crimean War.

People were pushing by them as they stood greeting one another. Rachel introduced the woman next to her. "This is my friend Miriam Cohen."

"We'd better keep moving," Miriam said, "it's hard to stand here and talk with all these people going by."

"That's a good idea," Rachel said. She smiled, looked up at Jacob and took his arm. He was surprised at the strength of her grip. "With all these people, I'm going to make sure I don't get separated from you."

As they turned onto Pall Mall toward Trafalgar Square, now a short distance away, Jacob realized the crowd was the biggest he'd seen since he was assigned to keep order in Jerusalem one year ago.

**SUNDAY, NOVEMBER 20, 1938**

Trafalgar Square, London

10:30 A.M.

The river of people carrying Jacob, Rachel, Paul and Miriam along Pall Mall flowed into Trafalgar Square, where it subsided, filling only half the plaza. The sound of chatter filled the air.

They made their way toward the speakers standing on the base of the Nelson column. Jacob thought it was a perfect stage, with monumental lions on each side. A large banner, easily twenty feet wide, attached to two tall poles, was propped up against the bottom of the column. "SAVE THE CHILDREN" in large black letters ran across the top. "FIGHT THE NAZI MENACE" was written along the bottom.

In front of the banner stood a dozen men and women wearing long coats and hats. A woman wearing gloves gestured as she spoke into a standup microphone attached to a pair of loudspeakers positioned at the feet of the bronze lions.

"Look," Rachel said, straining to be heard above the crowd, "there's Rabbi Reinhart behind the speaker."

Everyone was listening intently to the speaker's high-pitched, well-modulated voice. "It's long past time that we reject the government's excuses for not allowing the victims of the Gestapo to come to Britain.

"The government says: We don't want to provoke more antisemitism. We don't want unemployed Britons to be jealous. We don't want to encourage other countries to unload their Jews on to us.

"Well, the three nights of pillage, plunder, and murder ten

days ago make it clear that we must act now or tens of thousands of innocent children will disappear forever!"

"Who is she?" Paul asked, impressed by the power in the woman's voice.

Miriam spoke up. "Eleanor Rathbone. Leader in the Women Suffrage campaign? Member of Parliament?"

"I've heard of her, of course," Paul said, "but I've never seen her before. My mum thinks she's wonderful."

"My friends and I worship her. Even though she's not Jewish, she opposed the Nazis from the very beginning. And a few weeks ago, she denounced the Munich agreement."

After Rathbone finished, they joined the crowd in applause. "I see the Marks sisters standing next to Rabbi Reinhart!" Rachel said.

"Well, *they* are Jewish, that's for certain," said Miriam. Jacob looked confused, so she told him about Elaine Blond and Rebecca Sieff, daughters of Michael Marks. "You're not English, but every Englishman in Manchester and London knows about the Marks and Spencer department stores."

"There's one right down Oxford Street near our apartment," Paul said.

Rachel explained that the Marks sisters were famous for their Jewish charity work. Rebecca Sieff was the president of the Women's International Zionist Organization.

Rabbi Reinhart announced the next speakers: Elaine Blond and Bertha Bracey. Blond strode to the microphone, her long hair pinned up. She motioned to a woman wearing a beret to join her.

"This is my friend Lola Hahn-Warburg," Blond announced.

"She recently escaped from Hitler's hell with her two children. Lola, would you say a word?"

"Ladies and gentlemen," she started, "I have come from a place where hundreds of thousands of men, women, and children have suddenly found themselves scorned, branded, and banned from society. You have no idea how terrible are the consequences of this Nazi barbarism for children. I have sat across the desk from a young man who became so shattered telling me about his parents' deportation he climbed onto my windowsill and tried to jump to his death."

The crowd reacted with a quiet but distinct murmur.

"Please, please," she extended both of her arms to the audience and leaned forward, "take seriously the depth of this inhumanity. Write or call your MP and the Home Secretary. Demand that they save the children."

The audience seemed stunned into silence. Jacob glanced at the people nearby. They were somber.

"We have to do something," said Rachel, who was standing next to him. She slipped her right arm under his left and held onto him tightly.

Bertha Bracey spoke next. She explained that she represented the Society of Friends, the Quakers. In her mid-forties, with thick brown hair tied back and wearing no hat, she said that she had been working with poor children and refugee children since the end of the Great War, but nothing compared to the horrible sights that she'd seen in the last ten days.

"Words are not adequate to tell of the anguish of the Jewish people today," Bracey said. "We need volunteers. You can make a difference."

Rabbi Reinhart prompted volunteers to contact the West London Synagogue. He said that the members of the emergency committee, including some of the day's speakers, would meet with the Home Secretary and the Prime Minister tomorrow. "We hope and pray that they will accept our proposal for a Save the Children program. But whatever they recommend to the Cabinet we need you to continue to demand that the government act, and act now. And we need your donations. Please do not delay. A life could depend on you. Thank you and God Save the King. This meeting is adjourned."

A pall of sadness seemed to descend on the crowd. People began leaving the plaza, filing past the two fountains, one by one, or in clusters of two or more, mostly silent.

"I think it will be hard to concentrate, but I have to study this afternoon," Rachel said.

"So do I," said Miriam, "but would everybody like to have lunch first? I don't know about the rest of you. There's a lot I want to talk about but I need to think about what I've heard here first. A walk to Bertorelli's on Charlotte Street will help clear my head."

They all agreed and started to leave Trafalgar Square, heading toward the National Gallery and Charing Cross Road. Off to his left, Jacob heard a sound that reminded him of the streets of Jerusalem in the summer – men marching, their hobnailed boots striking the street in unison.

"Here come the fascists!" Paul said.

Miriam followed up, "My god, they're not supposed to march in public!"

Twenty yards away, six men approached in formation, chanting as they came, "The Yids, the Yids, it's time to get rid of the Yids." They were dressed in ordinary street clothes, wearing long topcoats, hats, and caps. They had no banners or flags, but Jacob saw that the lead marcher on the right wore an armband identifying him as a member of the British Union of Fascists.

As they came closer, the leader pulled a two foot long piece of pipe from under his topcoat with his right hand. He shouted, "Looks like a couple of Jew bitches and their boyfriends. What should we do with these Yids? What do you say, boys?"

Paul started to walk toward the fascists, but Jacob stopped him. "Let me handle this one," he said.

The leader walked ahead and stopped about ten feet away. Jacob walked toward him. The fascist was almost as tall and thick as Jacob, but he looked to be all fat and no muscle. "Look, boys, the big Jew boy thinks he's tough," he said. "Do you think you're tough, Jew boy? What do *you* say, boys?"

"Don't you know you're supposed to say 'Heil Hitler' to your comrades?" Jacob said, his voice calm and unhurried. He raised his right hand and shouted, "Hi Littler," in a thick Austrian accent.

The fascist was confused. He hesitated, then switched the length of pipe from his right hand to his left. He clicked his heels together, raised his right arm and shouted out the Hitler salute.

Jacob grabbed the pipe out of his hand. With a swift downward motion, he struck the man's kneecap. As he fell to his left, Jacob hit him again. A strong backhand strike to his right knee brought the man crumpling to the ground.

Without hesitation, Jacob launched himself into the other five men, swinging his pipe left and right. Two of them went down, the others turned and ran back toward Haymarket Street.

Paul quickly followed Jacob, using his army-issue boots to deliver solid kicks to each of the downed men.

Jacob finally dropped the pipe and walked up to the leader. He grabbed him by his lapels, pulled him up and shoved him to his knees. The fascist screamed in pain. "Who the hell are you? I thought you were one of us! You might have broken my knees!"

"Listen carefully," Jacob said. "If you want to play at being a fascist thug, you'd better go to Germany." He thrust him down hard and he screamed again as he hit the ground.

A small crowd had gathered around them. A middle-aged man in a suit and tie with a topcoat and hat put out his hand as if to stop Jacob, but he drew back when Jacob looked him in the eye.

"I say, shouldn't we summon the police?" he said.

"I *am* the police," Jacob replied. He brushed past the man and walked with Paul to where Rachel and Miriam were standing. Rachel's face was white. She was holding on to Miriam.

"My God," Miriam said, "you put that fascist in his place."

Wide-eyed, Rachel moved away from Miriam. "But Jacob *attacked* him," she cried. "Shouldn't he have tried to talk to him?" She looked at Jacob and said, "You could have been hurt!" Her eyes glistened with tears.

"It's all right, Rachel," Jacob said. He put his right arm around her shoulders, gently pulling her close. She didn't resist. He felt her tense body relaxing. They remained like that for a minute, then separated. Rachel took his arm. "Let's go to Bertorelli's," he said and they all crossed the street heading up Charing Cross Road.

## SUNDAY, NOVEMBER 20, 1938

## Bertorelli's Restaurant, Charlotte Street

## London, 2:00 P.M.

The sky began to clear. Patches of blue allowed sunshine to lighten the façades of the four- and five-story gray-and-black buildings on either side of the street toward Leicester Square. They talked about the speakers at the demonstration. Rachel offered to talk to Rabbi Reinhart about becoming volunteers.

By the time they reached Charlotte Street, the sky clouded over again. Jacob thought it might soon rain.

When they reached Bertorelli's, the headwaiter greeted Rachel with a smile. "My favorite customer," he said. "And your friends, too! Welcome everyone. I have your table ready." As they sat down, he smiled at Rachel, "Shall I bring you a bottle of Chianti?" She said yes and he left them at the table.

Miriam pulled off her knit hat and her hair sprang up. She shook her head. Her thick, long, curly hair whipped back and forth. "Jacob," she said, "the way you took down that fascist thug, a person would think you're from Whitechapel – a member of the Yiddisher gang, or one of Jack Spot's men. Where'd you grow up, anyway?"

Jacob shared a look with Rachel. "Didn't Rachel tell you we were both born in California? In San Francisco?" He told them that he didn't really remember the city because his parents moved to Vienna when he was only two years old.

"What did your parents do?" Rachel asked. "You told me they were murdered, right?"

"Oh my God," Miriam exclaimed. "I'm so sorry, Jacob."

"They were killed in 1936, in Jerusalem," he said. "Three years after we moved there. My father decided to leave Vienna after Hitler began persecuting the Jews in Germany. He lived through how things got bad for Germans and Austrians, even if they were Jewish, in San Francisco after 1914. Especially after the United States declared war on Germany in 1917."

"He must have felt history was repeating itself," Rachel said.

"People stopped coming to their Vienna Hofbrau House restaurant in San Francisco. Somebody even broke the windows. My dad had to sell the restaurant and work as a carpenter. He took us back to Vienna as soon as he made enough money to buy the tickets."

"What did your parents do in Vienna?" Paul asked. "I don't think you told me about that on the ship."

"They opened a restaurant with one of my uncles. They called it California Haus. It was very popular. When they moved to Palestine my dad sold his share of the restaurant to my uncle. I'm afraid that something might have happened to my aunt and uncle and my cousins. I wrote to them, but they haven't answered."

"So you grew up in Vienna and Jerusalem, right?" Miriam asked. "I guess you learned to fight in Jerusalem, then. You'd have been too young to be out fighting in the street in Vienna."

"Actually, my birthday is in January," Jacob said, "but I never learned to fight on the street, like some East End gangster."

"You're acting like you're trying to keep your life a secret or something," Rachel teased. "If not the East End, then where did you learn to fight like that?"

"He does have secrets," Paul said. "Ask him about going behind the enemy lines and being a spy." He winked. "But don't believe a word of what he tells you."

"You're all acting like an interrogation team," Jacob answered with a laugh. "There's no secret about where I learned to fight. It was in Palestine.

"My teacher was Oleg Mazel, a Zionist born in Russia, a veteran of the Jewish Legion in the Great War. He was wounded fighting the Ottomans at the Battle of Megiddo in 1918. He trained us to use all kinds of weapons and we learned hand to hand combat."

"Here comes the waiter," Rachel said.

"What was your mission exactly?" Miriam asked after they placed their orders.

"Well," Jacob said. "After my parents were murdered I went through a difficult patch, as the English say. Eventually I volunteered for a new special Jewish police force."

"How was it special?" Rachel asked.

"Well, we went into the Arab communities – behind the lines, as it were. We dressed in Arab clothes and worked as undercover spies. We used informants to find out terrorist plans. We had to be able to quickly deal with the unexpected, so we used the OJA method – Observe, Judge, and Act.

"And speaking of OJA, here comes our lunch," he said, "so let's eat."

Paul refilled their wine glasses, and they grew quiet as they began to eat.

"So, you observed that fascist, judged that he was not a good fighter, and acted the way you did to take away his weapon?" Rachel asked eventually.

Jacob nodded, his mouth full. He took another bite of his *vitello al parmigiana*. When he didn't immediately reply, Rachel said, "I don't understand something. If you were part of a Jewish police force, did that mean you were policing the Jews living in Palestine? Or what? I thought it was the British soldiers who policed everybody in Palestine, Jewish and Arab and Christian."

"My understanding," Paul said, "and forgive me but this is from somebody who was shuffling paper in Cairo while Jacob was patrolling Nablus, is that our British forces needed assistance from local Jewish residents who know, as it were, the lay of the land. And also, the Jewish settlements had been demanding a role in the job of protecting their lives and property ever since the first Arab nationalist revolt almost twenty years ago. Right, Jacob?"

"That's it in the proverbial nut shell," said Jacob. "In the spring, Captain Wingate decided it was high time we stopped just waiting for the terrorists to attack. We needed to hit them hard in their own towns and neighborhoods. Teach them a lesson they wouldn't forget. Discourage them from making their murderous raids. That's where I learned to go into the enemy's own backyards to spy on them, figure out their next moves, and then attack them before they could launch more attacks on Jewish settlements."

Rachel looked puzzled. "But if that was only earlier this year, why are you here in London so soon after your training?" she asked. "Is the work finished? Will there be peace between the Jews and the Arabs now?"

Jacob shook his head. Paul looked down at his plate.

"I think the Arabs, at least the extremists, don't want to live in peace; they don't want to share the country," Miriam said. "They just want the Jews out of Palestine. The Grand Mufti of Jerusalem hates the British, the Communists, and the Jews. He's as bad as Hitler."

"Well, it's complicated," Jacob said. "The Arabs are divided amongst themselves, just like the Jews. Oleg Mazel thinks the British should leave and the Jews and Arabs should create a sort of United States of Palestine, like America after its revolution."

"What do you think of that idea?" Miriam asked.

"I agree," Jacob said, "but after all this terrorism, and some of it *is* our fault, the Jews' fault, I don't know. I don't know if there's enough trust between all the groups to even have a peaceful settlement. It might take a sort of civil war, with the winner just imposing a new constitution.

"Also, ever since my family was murdered, I've felt like I don't really have a home in Palestine."

The table was quiet. The waiter came with the check and they paid the bill. Paul, Miriam and Rachel looked somber. "I haven't talked so much in a long time," Jacob said. "I'm sorry, I don't really like to complain about my life. I know a lot of people have a lot more troubles than I do."

Rachel, who was sitting on Jacob's left, reached out and put her hand on his arm. "You haven't been talking that long. Are you really going to San Francisco?"

"I wouldn't have considered it except that my grandmother in San Francisco is all alone," Jacob said. "She wants me to help take care of her. There's no other family there, and she's seventy years old! Major Wingate thinks the FBI will hire me, and if all goes well I'll be able to fight back against anti-Jewish hate groups in the city where I was born."

"My parents want me to come home to San Francisco," Rachel said. "It seems so far away now."

Miriam said she needed to leave, so there would be time

to study. Rachel agreed. Jacob noticed that Rachel still had her hand on his arm, and he placed his right hand on top of hers. She looked up at him and smiled. As Paul and Miriam got up from the table, Jacob turned to Rachel and said, "Speaking of birthdays, I've been invited to a birthday party on the thirtieth. Would you like to join me?"

She smiled and cocked her head to the left, her eyes twinkling. "Of course," she said, "I love birthday parties!"

**WEDNESDAY, NOVEMBER 30, 1938**

## Vicarage Gardens, London

## 8:00 P.M.

Despite the chilly night air, Rachel and Jacob were feeling comfortably warm after their walk from the Kensington High Street tube station to Venetia Montagu's white painted row house. They gave their coats and hats to the maid who greeted them at the door. Major Wingate and his wife Lorna met them in the foyer and brought them into the drawing room. A portly man in a dark blue suit stood examining a landscape painting on the wall. He had his left hand behind his back and held a cigar in his right. He turned as he heard them come closer and they realized it was Winston Churchill.

"Here are our San Francisco people, Miss Bernstein and Mr. Weiss," Lorna Wingate said. "She's studying with Professor Hayek!"

"I quite enjoyed San Francisco," Churchill said to Rachel, homing in on her as if she were the only person in the room. "One didn't lack for good brandy in San Francisco!" He laughed heartily at his own joke. Rachel started to reply but Churchill kept talking, sounding as though he were giving a speech in Parliament. "Mr. Hearst was not there, of course. He had already entertained us in his rather bizarre castle. But his man Neylan, a splendid fellow, gave me a tour of the newspaper offices, followed by a fine luncheon at your Palace Hotel. I dare say it was him, not Mr. Hearst, who talked me into writing for your *San Francisco Examiner*."

He took a puff from his cigar. Rachel took advantage of the pause. "My father reads the *Examiner* every day, and I can remember seeing your articles in the paper," she said. "He will be thrilled when I tell him I actually came to your birthday party!"

"I'm the one to be thrilled," Churchill replied, "it's not every day that I get to meet such a lovely young lady. And imagine, a pretty young thing like you, a student of the esteemed Dr. Hayek!"

"Rachel, come and meet our hostess," Lorna Wingate said, taking Rachel by the elbow and leading her away.

"And this is Jacob Weiss," Wingate said to Churchill. "He was born in San Francisco, but he's been living in Palestine. Jacob was one of the two best NCOs who fought in my Special Night Squad."

Churchill turned to Jacob. "My boy, I did some fighting when I was your age. If the major is giving you such high praise, I'm honored to meet you. I'm not colonial secretary any longer, but allow me to say that the Empire owes a debt of gratitude to men like you."

"The Empire," Wingate said, "has so far failed to treat Jewish soldiers like Jacob with the respect that we give to our English boys. I've urged Jacob to return to America. When it comes time to fight Hitler, he can do so in the American army. The British army will discriminate against Jacob for being Jewish much more than would ever happen in the United States."

A maid came up to them with a tray of Champagne glasses. They each took one. "I would have stayed in Palestine," Jacob said, "but I have an elderly grandmother in California who asked me to come take care of her. My parents and sister were killed by Arab extremists in Jerusalem."

Churchill's voice deepened. "I completely understand, young man," he said. "I see a time when we shall have to fight to protect *our* families and *our* countries. Because of Mr. Chamberlain, as I said on the floor just the other day, we have suffered 'a total and unmitigated defeat' at Munich."

Rachel came up to them with Venetia Montagu, who was wearing a floor-length black dress that showed off her slim figure. She wore a rope of pearls around her neck. Rachel said, "Some of my friends at the LSE are hoping that we really will have 'Peace in our Time,' but you don't agree, Mr. Churchill?"

"My hope is that we have only lost a battle, not the war that will undoubtedly be forced upon us," Churchill answered. "Young man," he said, turning to look Jacob in the eye, "I would be happy to have you as our ally against that madman Hitler."

Venetia Montagu held out her hand to Jacob. "So you are the outstanding young American that Major Wingate has been praising so highly?" she said.

Jacob took her hand and noted her confident smile and comfortable manner. He smiled. "Well, the major has a habit of exaggerating things, as you may know."

"Oh, dear!" Venetia Montagu said, throwing her head back in faux shock, accompanied by an equally phony cry of alarm. "Who could imagine such a thing as Major Wingate exaggerating something?"

Lorna Wingate smiled at her. "It's a good thing that you and my husband share an equally unshakable belief in the Zionist project. If it weren't for that bond, I can't imagine you would willingly endure his unremitting enthusiasm by inviting him to dinner. You know he talks of nothing else. It's quite a religious principle with him!"

Venetia Montagu ushered the guests into the dining room. They enjoyed a dinner of leek and potato soup, followed by pheasant, roast beef, and a chocolate birthday cake. Churchill, who had praised the quality of the Claret, was now enjoying a snifter of brandy as the rest of them sipped their after-dinner sherry.

"Chaim Weizmann was meant to join us," Venetia said, "but he decided to make one of his spur of the moment trips to Jerusalem. He asked me to give his regards to you, Winston, and also to you Orde."

"You youngsters from California would be interested in what Chaim said the other day to Malcom MacDonald," Churchill said. "You know, the Secretary of State for the Colonies. After the government refused to allow 15,000 children, victims of *Kristallnacht*, into Palestine."

"Yes, he said he would fight the government from here to San Francisco," said Wingate. "He's even threatened to boycott the conference on Palestine scheduled for next month. I'm afraid, though, that Chaim does not always turn his fighting words into actions."

"I know your Zionism is part of your fundamentalist Christian beliefs," Jacob said to Wingate, "but lots of Jews are opposed to Zionism, not supporters of it."

"My parents in California think that Zionism is bad for the Jews," Rachel said.

Before Wingate could reply, Venetia Montagu said, "That was the position of my late husband Edwin, poor soul. He's been gone almost fifteen years now. He called Zionism 'a malicious political creed.' He said it played into the hands of anti-Semites all over the world. All right, they would say, if Palestine is your national home, then would you please get out of our country and go to Palestine!"

Rachel nodded. "My dad says exactly the same thing. He claims he's not an American Jew; he's a Jewish American. He says the Jews are not a nation at all. So if they're not a nation, they don't need a national home. There's a Jewish religion, he believes, but not a Jewish nation. And not even all Jews are that religious. My family only goes to the synagogue on the high holy days."

Orde Wingate seemed about to make a point, but Churchill spoke instead, his voice almost a growl. "My dear young friend, we simply cannot go back to 1917 when Venetia's husband condemned Britain for ensuring 'a national home for the Jewish people' in Palestine."

Wingate's face was clouding over with anger. He pounded his fist on the table. "I've spoken to Chaim," he said, "and while I respect him, I think he doesn't understand that the Arabs will never agree to a peaceful settlement. I agree with Jabotinsky. Years ago, he knew there has to be a military solution – protect the Jewish people already in Palestine and future Jewish settlers from Arab resistance with an 'Iron Wall' of military might."

Jacob felt like a student in a room full of teachers, but he spoke up. "I've been on the streets of Jerusalem, Jaffa, and Nablus, and I've seen with my own eyes that the extremist Arabs want the Jews to leave forever. They murdered my family, so I should know."

There was a collective murmur of concern at the table. Jacob fought to stay in control of his voice. "I used to want vengeance, but I don't feel that way anymore. When I saw an innocent Arab about my age get shot by mistake, I changed my mind. Both sides have to reject terrorism and live side by side peacefully. New Jewish settlers have to live somewhere that won't result in Arabs being forced out of their homes."

Wingate jumped in. "Mr. Churchill, speaking of new settlers, there's a great need right now for relaxing entry to more settlers. Instead, the government is actually putting more obstacles in the way."

"At least the government has allowed ten thousand children to come to England," Rachel said. "Jacob and I have volunteered to help when the first group arrives from Germany next week."

Venetia asked Rachel how they were planning to help with the *Kindertransport,* and Rachel explained they had signed up to volunteer with Rabbi Reinhart of the West London Synagogue.

"Oh, that's where I was married," Venetia said, "but I'm not a faithful Jew. I converted because my husband's family insisted, but I'm not a religious person."

Jacob explained that since he spoke German he would be a translator and Rachel would help out the smaller children. She had experience working with preschool age children at Temple Beth Israel in San Francisco.

Venetia stood up and said, "Well, this has been delightful, but Winston has another appointment tonight at the Café Royal. We must allow him to be on his way."

Churchill finished his brandy, stood and said, "I must leave this wonderful gathering to attend a party for me planned by my dear wife Clementine. I console myself with the knowledge that the Royal Café has a most satisfactory wine cellar." He walked over to Jacob, who was standing next to Rachel. "Young man," he said, "you may not be aware but I'm half-American, and I always enjoy meeting fellow Americans!" He shot a conspiratorial look at Rachel and Jacob. "Please contact me should you ever imagine that your admirer Winston might be of assistance."

**FRIDAY, DECEMBER 2, 1938**

## Liverpool Street Station, London

## 1:00 P.M.

Jacob wondered how he would be able to find Rachel in the crowded and cavernous railway station. It was almost dark inside. The only light came through the skylights high above the platforms. It was filtered by the foggy air outside, the steam and coal smoke coming from the trains, and the effluence produced by hundreds of cigarette, cigar, and pipe smokers. His eyes itched and his throat burned.

He had arrived early so he was passing the time drinking coffee, watching the travelers come and go and admiring the station's Victorian engineering. There was a combination of grace and strength in the steel columns that soared up to the web of steel framing that held the skylights. A huge marble memorial covered an entire wall, listing the names of some 1,000 railway employees who gave their lives "for king and country" during the Great War.

Was Major Wingate right? Would he soon be fighting in another Great War?

His thoughts turned to Rachel. He wondered why this was happening. Especially since the Trafalgar Square demonstration, whenever he would start thinking about the future and the steps he needed to take next, he found himself thinking about Rachel. There had never been a woman who had affected him the way she did. He told Paul after the demonstration that he wasn't sure he liked how this happened without his even willing it. At the same time, he looked forward to seeing her each time they planned to meet.

He found himself missing her. The last time was after they said goodbye the night of the birthday party. They'd decided to take a cab from Kensington High Street station to Rachel's flat on Westbourne Gardens. He paid the cabbie and after they agreed to meet at the station the day the children arrived, they said goodnight. She surprised him then when she reached up to his neck, gently pulled his head down, and kissed him. Jacob wondered if she had surprised herself, because she walked to the door without a word, gave a little wave, and entered her flat. He already missed her during the forty minutes it took him to walk from her Bayswater flat to his Balderton Street apartment.

"Train number 44 from Harwich and the Hook of Holland is arriving at Platform 3!" The announcement was difficult to hear over the cacophony of human and mechanical noise. Jacob headed for Platform 3, hoping that wherever Rachel was, she would do likewise and meet him there. He passed an empty cordoned-off space with large signs announcing "Reception Area." A dozen men and women stood by the entrance.

As he moved toward the "No.3" sign on an archway over the entry gate of the platform, he realized he was in a group of mostly women; older, middle aged, dressed in brown, gray, and black coats and hats. The crowd slowed as they passed through the gate one by one.

Jacob waited in line to speak to a woman who sat behind a table. He wondered if his being one of the few men accounted for the suspicious look in the eyes of the uniformed London policemen who stood next to the table.

As he neared the head of the queue, Jacob realized he recognized the woman at the table. It was Elaine Blond, one of the speakers at the Trafalgar Square demonstration. He gave his name, and she checked him off on a list on her clipboard. She handed him a name tag and told him to hang it around his neck before informing him that his job was to help the children off his assigned train car. He was to line them up and bring them to the reception area to meet their hosts. He asked her if she had checked off Rachel Bernstein. "Why yes, there she is," she said after consulting her list. She looked up and smiled. "Young man, I would imagine our volunteers today have offered to help us for a variety of reasons. But I'm not sure I want to encourage handsome young giants to consider this an opportunity for romantic interludes!" Jacob felt himself redden. Before he could reply, Elaine Blond winked, laughed, and said, "Off with you now! My colleague down the platform will tell you where to stand."

Jacob could hear the sound of the incoming train entering the shed and discharging steam as it applied the brakes. Another woman gestured to him to keep walking further. He passed seven, then eight, then nine women before he saw Rachel almost at the end of the platform. She noticed him too and did an excited little jump. Then, she came toward him, said hello and surprised him with a hug. "The children will be here soon," she said. "I'm so excited. We are assigned to the same train car – I'll be by the front door and you'll be in the back. I'll see you after we take the children to the reception area."

Her final words were drowned out by the noise of the approaching train. First, the engine slowly passed them. Then came the cars.

Sulfurous smoke and steam filled the air. They could see the faces of children through the windows.

When the train stopped, Jacob helped the children down the stairs and told them to line up behind him. They all wore large cards around their necks with their names and photographs. Most looked scared and tired. A handful, mostly teenage boys,

affected nonchalance and expressed an air of superiority. Whether very young or teenage, they all carried small suitcases and
purses or briefcases. For the smallest girls, especially, handling
their luggage was obviously a trial. Jacob found himself being a
railway porter as well as a child monitor.

They were all dressed up in coats and hats or caps, looking
like they were going to Synagogue or a fancy dress party. Most
wore warm clothing, but some were obviously not prepared for
London weather.

The next hours went by in the blink of an eye.

•

He remembered the noise of the station, the excited and sometimes worried chatter of the children, the jostling of volunteers as
they herded them to the reception area, the back and forth of the
Refugee Children's Movement staff with the host families.

It was nearly 7:00. He and Rachel were waiting for the steak
and kidney pie they had ordered at The Victoria. Jacob was
drinking Fullers, and Rachel a glass of Chianti. He had felt his
heart warm when, upon leaving the train station, she took his
arm and said, "Jacob, let's go to our pub. I'm starving." By the
time they arrived, he was hungry too. He realized this was the
third time he and Rachel had come to The Victoria. Paul had
been with them the other times. She had called it "our pub." Jacob wondered what that meant.

They were sitting side by side in the snug. Rachel told him she
liked the privacy. She enjoyed the quieter space offered by this
small well-appointed room with velvet cushions on the seats. She
took his left hand, held it on the table top and whispered, "I'm
glad to be here safe and sound with you." Jacob saw that she had
tears in her eyes. "I feel so sorry for those children," she said.

Jacob could relate. They had traveled from Germany to Holland on a train, ferried to Harwich on a boat, and were then put on another train to London. The little ones especially seemed terrified. One little girl was so exhausted she just broke into tears until Rachel picked her up and soothed her.

"Most of the people I saw seemed glad to meet their child," Jacob said.

"Yes, but what about that horrible woman who threw down her papers and name tag, and huffed out of the reception area when she didn't like the looks of the child she had been assigned. I can't even imagine how shocking that would be for the child!"

Rachel turned quiet. The waiter brought their dinners, and they started eating. "I found myself fantasizing about what it would be like to bring that one little girl to my home and take care of her," she said. "Of course, it's just fantasy. I don't have a home. And we're not even married yet, so..." She stopped, her face reddening. Without looking at Jacob, she took a large gulp of the Chianti.

Jacob waited. His heart seemed to stop beating. He realized he was holding his breath. *Did Rachel just say what I think she said?*

He took a deep breath and then a drink of his Fullers. He turned his head toward her as she turned to him with an impish look, bursting out with a loud musical laugh.

"Well, Jacob, today's number one translator," she said. "I guess nobody needs a translator to understand *this* girl's unconscious mind, right?"

### FRIDAY, MARCH 17, 1939

## Bertorelli's Restaurant, Charlotte Street, London, 2:00 P.M.

The first yellow daffodils of Grosvenor Square were bathed in warm sunlight as Jacob and Paul left the American Embassy heading for the restaurant in Fitzrovia. It would be a memorable day for both of them.

After a wait of more than three months, Jacob had finally picked up his passport. A messenger had delivered Paul's orders to report to army headquarters in Cairo.

The good cheer brought about by the clear blue sky was off-set for Jacob after he read the day's *Manchester Guardian.* An article headlined "Gestapo Busy in Prague" detailed the first day of Nazi occupation: 10,000 alleged Czech criminals were taken from their homes and offices to concentration camps. Another article announced that "Jews Reject the Palestine Plan" recounting how the Jewish Agency refused to endorse the government's whittling away of the rights of Jews. Not only would the numbers entering Palestine be cut, future Jewish immigration would need the consent of the Arab majority. Major Wingate and his wife were already back in Jerusalem.

Jacob imagined how the major would be ranting and raving about this latest setback to the Zionist cause. Paul seemed to share his bad mood, so they said little as they made their way to Bertorelli's.

Jacob found himself smiling and felt somewhat renewed when Carlo Lastrucci, the headwaiter, reached out and shook their hands. "On a day like this it feels like spring will soon be here," he said. "Your young ladies are waiting for you at the table!"

They greeted Rachel and Miriam and sat down. "Well, Carlo," said Miriam, "I don't know if we should ask for Chianti again, or maybe Champagne this time. This is a happy day and a sad day."

"Tell me the occasion," Carlo answered, "and I'll recommend the best choice."

"Oh, Carlo," Miriam said, "I'm sad for myself. Rachel, Jacob and Paul are leaving me here in London all alone. But I'm happy for them."

"I'll bring you Prosecco," the headwaiter said, winking. "Champagne? That's for a French restaurant. I'm sad I won't see you all anymore, but Miriam, you will come see me, won't you? Maybe it's not so bad living in London, no?" He looked across the room. "The professor over there told me a long time ago what the famous Dr. Johnson said: 'If a man is tired of London, he is tired of life because everything you could want is here.'"

"You're such a philosopher," Rachel said. "I'm going to miss you."

"I'm sure we're all sad," Paul added. "When you think about it, if it wasn't for our being able to get together here, the last several months would have been even more difficult. At least that's true for me."

Carlo nodded, smiled, and left to get their drinks. He returned carrying a tray with four glasses and a bottle of Prosecco. He poured their drinks and left after taking their dinner orders.

"Before we take a drink," Jacob said, "Rachel and I have an announcement to make. We're getting married."

Miriam jumped up suddenly, her curly hair jouncing and a big smile on her face. "Rachel, you big sneak. You never told me. And here I thought we were best friends. But really, I knew all along this was going to happen." She picked up her glass, raised it and said, "Three cheers for you, Rachel and Jacob." They all took a drink and Miriam sat down.

"Strange as it seems," Jacob said, "if it wasn't for Hitler's Nazis marching into Prague we might not be announcing our engagement today. But with things getting so uncertain we decided we didn't want to wait."

"Have you set a date?" Paul asked.

"Maybe on the *Queen Mary*!" Rachel said, laughing. "Do ship captains marry people?" Everyone laughed.

"Seriously, won't you wait until you get to San Francisco?" Paul asked. "Jacob, don't you need to get there to take care of your grandmother?"

"My grandmother wrote and told us she was pleased that I'm coming," Jacob answered. "She's happy about Rachel and told us that we should take advantage of being in New York to see the East Coast. She's not ill, and it's not like there's some kind of medical emergency."

"We're going to spend six to eight weeks in New York City, visit the capitol in Washington, D.C. and go to Boston to see the 'Cradle of Liberty,'" Rachel added.

"I wish I could go with you," Miriam said. "I'm worried the Nazis will attack us, now that they have taken over Czechoslovakia so easily."

"Oh, Miriam, I feel worried about you," Rachel said. "It's because it seems like the world could be at war anytime soon that we want to get married now. The future seems so uncertain."

"We can get married at the New York City Hall," Jacob suggested. "Then later we can have a regular Jewish wedding with

Rachel's family and my grandmother. We leave Sunday and five days later we'll be taking a walk in Central Park."

"My relatives offered to find us an apartment to rent in their neighborhood," Rachel said. "They live just a few blocks from Central Park and the famous Metropolitan Museum of Art."

"What about you?" Rachel asked Paul. "What are your plans?"

"I'm going back to Cairo the same way I came to London, on the *Dorsetshire*," he told them. "I'm looking forward to it. I put in for a transfer from General Staff to Military Intelligence. I haven't heard yet whether my request was successful, but with luck I'll be able to see some action instead of sitting in an office all day."

"I'm going to miss you all, especially you, Rachel," Miriam said. "Studying won't be nearly as much fun now, but at least I only have three months left before I'm done with my master's degree. You made arrangements to complete your work in America, right?"

"Yes, I only have to write my thesis. I can send it to the LSE by mail. As long as they receive it by the end of term in June, I will be finished. Well, presuming they accept it, of course."

"Didn't you tell me you were going to have a job doing something with a synagogue in San Francisco?"

Rachel nodded. "Yes, Temple Beth Israel wants me to work with the refugee children who are starting to come to San Francisco because of the war in China. They like that I've been working with the West London Synagogue."

"What about you, Jacob?" Miriam asked. "Are you going to go back into Jewish police work? I don't suppose they have anything like the Special Night Squad in America."

Paul barked out a laugh. "Ha! Jacob shouldn't be trusted to

answer such a question truthfully," he said. "After all, he was one of Major Wingate's best spies. You never want to trust what a spy tells you."

Before Jacob could reply, Carlo came to the table, clasped his hands and said, "I'm so sad but you have made me happy each time you came to see us. I always enjoyed your enthusiasm and hearing your laughter. Let me bring you our special dessert. It's on the house!"

He brought the Zabaglione, which they followed with glasses of Grappa. After they paid the bill, Carlo embraced each of them, teary-eyed. "Don't forget Bertorelli's," he said. Jacob wondered if he would ever see Carlo again.

**MONDAY, SEPTEMBER 4, 1939**

## Federal Bureau of Investigation Field Office
## Foley Square, New York City, 1:00 P.M.

More than four months had passed and Jacob still woke up every day with a feeling of guilt. Not that his grandmother was complaining, nor Rachel's parents, for that matter. They had all written to say how excited and pleased they were when they received the telegrams from the newlyweds.

They had gotten married at City Hall in April. They lived next door to the Park Avenue Synagogue on East 87th and Madison, and Rachel worked in the synagogue's preschool program. Jacob found it an idyllic existence, but he was plagued by the nagging sense that he was derelict in his duty to care for his grandmother.

Jacob's guilt got worse when she'd called long distance the previous day. She had heard the news on the radio. "Jacob," she said in a quivering voice, "what's going to happen now that England and France have declared war on Germany? Are we going to have to go to war too?"

Over coffee and bagels that morning, Jacob told Rachel that it might be time for them to stop putting off their move to San Francisco. "How would you feel about leaving your job here with the child care program?"

"I've never considered it more than temporary," she answered, reminding him that Rabbi Seifert was keeping a place for her in Temple Beth Israel's refugee children program.

She got up, came over to his side of the table, sat in his lap and snuggled up to him.

"Being here with you is like a dream come true. On the other hand, San Francisco is my home and I'll be happy to return. But will the FBI allow you to transfer to San Francisco after only three months as a probationary special agent?"

Jacob remembered the conversation as he sat waiting for his appointment with his boss. After taking the subway from Lexington and East 86th to Foley Square, he had gone straight to the office of the Special Agent in Charge, asking for an appointment. "It's an urgent family matter," he told Maggie O'Malley, the boss's secretary.

Edward Wedgwood, in a regulation FBI suit and tie, bounded into the room. "Mr. Weiss, what can I do for you? We haven't had the pleasure of a one-on-one meeting, but I've heard nothing but good things about you." He opened the door to his private office and motioned to Jacob to precede him. He sat down behind his desk and said, "Have a seat, Mr. Weiss. Maggie has put your file right here, but why don't you start by explaining why you wanted to see me?"

"I'm hoping you will allow me to transfer to the field office in San Francisco," Jacob said. "I'd rather be here in New York City, but my elderly grandmother is out there all by herself.

"I'm her only family in the United States. My parents and sister are dead. My uncles and aunts all live in Europe. At least I hope they are still alive."

Wedgwood looked up from the file he had been paging through.

"What do you mean?" he asked.

"I haven't heard from them since that *Kristallnacht* business last November. They could be dead or in camps. I just don't know."

"My relatives in England are also in Hitler's sights. He's a madman. He's targeted us with terror attacks and sabotage here, too. We're still uncovering his spy network on the East Coast. We were unprepared for how extensive and successful it has been."

"Right," Jacob said. "It was finding out about that spy network that clinched my decision to apply to be an FBI special agent. Major Wingate gave me the idea before I left Palestine, but I sent in my application right after my wife and I saw *Confessions of a Nazi Spy* on 86th Street."

"Mr. Weiss, if I had a dollar for every young man who walked into an FBI office and tried to sign up after that movie came out I'd be a rich man!"

Wedgwood laughed. "J. Edgar Hoover should pay Edward G. Robinson a bonus. But not all those would-be special agents have your experience and recommendations."

"Thank you, sir," Jacob said.

"Young man, Major Orde Wingate's four page single-spaced letter describing your undercover work in Palestine is very impressive. Winston Churchill's recommendation was so impressive Hoover wanted to meet you in person."

Wedgwood looked Jacob in the eye. "But I have a question. What would you say to someone who questioned your motives for wanting to fight Nazi terrorists? You're a veteran of Wingate's outfit. Wasn't it disbanded because your squad was itself using terrorist tactics?"

"First I'd defend Major Wingate against that lie, and then I'd say even if it was true, who'd be a better choice to fight terrorists and spies than a former terrorist and spy?"

Wedgwood waited a beat, nodded, and said, "Good answer, Jacob." He smiled. "I'm going to call you Jacob, okay?"

"Of course, sir. I never expected to meet Director J. Edgar Hoover," Jacob said, "and I'm grateful that he allowed me to be appointed as a special agent."

"According to your file, the director set up a special intensive six-week training program for you based on your record in Palestine. This memo," he held up a page, "says your scores on your British training were outstanding. I'm guessing the Bureau was so impressed, they gave you that special individual training program. The first one in the Bureau's history!"

"Well, I couldn't have done it without my wife's help. She went with me to Washington, D.C. and tutored me in the hotel room. If she hadn't helped, I don't know if I could have finished *reading* all the material on American laws and regulations, let alone passing the exams."

"According to your file, you earned one of the highest grades on record on those paper and pencil tests. The others went to American schools and colleges, even law schools!

"Plus, your performance at our shooting range here at Foley Square puts you into the highest marksmanship class. Where did you learn to shoot like that?"

"My dad loved to hunt and belonged to a rifle club in Vienna. He always took me hunting and to the rifle range. And when I joined the special Jewish police in Palestine, Oleg Mazel taught me how to use a variety of firearms."

"I saw in your file that you put down Jewish for religion, so I'm not surprised you did so well on those tests. And, of course, we need more Jews in the New York office. I'm not all that pleased that you want to leave us, Mr. Weiss."

"I don't want to, really, but I feel it's my duty," Jacob said.

"I understand. My people came over here on the Mayflower, but most of the Wedgwood clan stayed in England and are there still. If Hitler bombs England the way he's bombed Poland, they will surely be in harm's way."

He got up from the desk. "All right, Jacob. I've read through your file and I also see that you're married, you don't smoke, and you don't drink alcohol except for an occasional glass of beer or wine. I like you, I have to admit."

He sighed. "We'll miss you here, but the San Francisco field office is short of special agents who speak foreign languages. According to your file, you can speak German, Hebrew, Yiddish, and Arabic. If you spoke Italian, that would be even better. Since you're not working in an ongoing investigation here, I'm going to approve your request." He closed Jacob's file and smiled. "Go home," he said. "Tell your wife to start packing."

# Part III
# May 9 – May 16, 1942

SATURDAY, MAY 9, 1942

# The Weiss Home, Webster Street, Fillmore District, 9:00 P.M.

"Jacob! Wake up! Somebody is hammering on our front door," Rachel cried. "Who could it be this late? They'll wake the baby!"

Jacob had fallen asleep on the sofa reading the *San Francisco News* after dinner. Now he was instantly awake. He took his .38 caliber FBI-issue pistol out of the shoulder holster hanging on a coatrack in the hallway, checked it, and walked to the door.

The loud knocking suddenly stopped. Jacob heard voices. A man's voice said, "Mr. Weiss, this is the police, we just need to talk to you. Please open the door."

Then, he recognized the voice of Ruthie Fuller. "Jacob, it's Ruthie! We just want to talk to you about a case. Tony Bosco and Dennis Sullivan are with me. Can we come in?"

He lowered the gun to his side and opened the door. Ruthie saw the .38 and breathed a sigh of relief. Jacob asked them to come in and waved his hand for them to go into the dining room. After returning his gun to the holster, he followed and motioned for them to sit at the table.

"What's the matter with you, Ruthie?" he demanded. "Commissioner, I know who you are. Actually, you're on our ABC list of 'potentially dangerous' Italian-background people at the Bureau. Why didn't you call us? You guys can't just show up at somebody's house at night and pound on their door like the Gestapo!"

Rachel came into the dining room. She was wearing a bathrobe, looking worried. "Jacob, calm down or *you'll* be the one to wake up little David. But Ruthie, Jacob's right. Why didn't you call? And what's this all about?"

"We have to move quickly on a case so the papers don't get wind of it," Tony Bosco said. "Ruthie thinks you can help us, and if Ruthie trusts you both to keep this quiet, that's fine by me.

"We came straight from meeting with Chief O'Reilly at the scene of a murder. He gave us strict orders to investigate it and keep it quiet. We didn't want to call from a telephone booth, or take a chance that you wouldn't talk to us."

Jacob nodded. "You're a friend of the mayor, right?"

"Yes," Tony replied. "Last month, Ruthie and Dennis here worked with me on another case for the chief. Now, you could say, he's drafted us again."

Bosco described the details of the murder and the note attached to the body.

"Have you heard of this Grynszpan Group?" Ruthie asked.

Jacob shook his head. "No, I've never heard of it. I've been here over two years and I have good informants. If this group were active, I think I would know. Of course, they could be new to the city."

Rachel had been standing and listening, leaning against the dining room wall with her arms crossed. "I have a question," she said. "Who would name a group after Grynszpan? I don't know any Jews who think he's some kind of hero."

"That's a good point," Ruthie said.

Jacob agreed. "Everyone I know thought the shooting of Ernst vom Rath in Paris was a self-indulgent act. It gave Hitler and Goebbels an excuse for two nights of murder and mayhem." He turned to Tony. "Zionist assassins? I thought I left all this behind in Palestine. You said that the sign read 'Traitor' – that suggests some extremist Jewish group might have considered him a turncoat. Was he even Jewish?"

"I don't know if he was Jewish," Dennis said. "You can't tell just by his name. He could have changed it."

"Well," Jacob said, looking from Ruthie to the two men, "this sounds like it could be complicated. Since the murder is obviously related to national security, I'm going to insist it be an FBI case. I'll get permission to lead the investigation and you guys can work with me. Not the other way around."

Bosco wanted to reply, but they heard a wailing cry coming from a room down the hallway off the dining room. "This is what I was afraid of," Rachel said. "I can't tell for sure if that's a hungry cry or a scared cry. He could have been frightened and woke up. I hope not. But I have to go to him. Please excuse me."

Bosco gave a look to his colleagues, then turned to Jacob. "I'm sorry about waking your baby, but I felt like I needed to move on this right away. It sounds like you aren't aware of any group like this."

"No," Jacob said. "But I don't like the sound of it."

**SATURDAY, MAY 9, 1942**

## St. Emydius Church

## 286 Ashton Avenue, 9:00 P.M.

Father Frit Haber knew he was in trouble when he came out of the confessional and saw the man standing by the statue of St. Joseph – the patron saint of the dying. They were the only people in the church this late.

"Who are you?" said the priest. "Do you want me to hear your confession?"

"My confession?" the man echoed. "Maybe my confession will be heard one day. But I'm afraid it will have to be heard by another priest. I'm here to do a job, Father. I'm gonna take you for a little ride so you can enjoy the view."

The monsignor felt a cold shiver as the man took out a pistol and, without a word, motioned down the side aisle toward the doors. They dipped their hands into the holy water font and both made the sign of the cross. They walked outside, stopping at the top of the stairs.

"We're gettin' in that Hudson Terraplane," the killer said, motioning to a black four-door sedan parked in front of the church. He opened the front passenger side door, gesturing to Father Haber to get in.

He got in the driver's side. He made a three-point turn to travel west on DeMontfort, then turned left on Ashton Avenue and right on Holloway. They passed a dozen middle class houses built for streetcar commuters before the Great Crash. The hills to their left looked like wasteland. Father Haber almost never came to this part of the city, what most people called "the outside lands." He'd come out to give confession to a parishioner who'd recently relocated to the Ingleside district. He realized now that the parishioner was his very own Judas Iscariot.

The man turned left on Ramsell Street and drove past empty lots up the steep northern slope of Merced Heights. He stopped the car near the corner of Shields and Arch Streets and turned off the engine. "Let's go for a little walk, Father," he said. "There's just enough moonlight to get a nice view of the lake and the ocean."

He took out the gun and motioned Father Haber to cross the street. They walked up a path to a three-acre hilltop with a one-story house built of stone and bricks, with a garden and a small shed. A few trees shielded it from the west winds.

"The family that owns this little farm is out of town, so we'll have the entire hill to ourselves," the killer said. "I kinda thought you'd like the view. Do you really believe in God, Father? Do you actually think there's life after death?"

"My faith in God is strong," Father Haber answered. "I don't know why God has sent you on this mission, but I'm not meant to understand such things."

"You're not even curious? Don't you think this is unfair? Here you are, dedicatin' your life to Christian charity and all that. And here I am."

The priest gestured toward Lake Merced in the distance and the sand dunes and ocean beyond. "You don't understand. You and I? We're insignificant, but God is everywhere and all knowing. He loves us and forgives our sins. Look down there. All that was created by God. And over there is man's work inspired by God." He gestured north toward the El Rey Theater with its 150-foot-high Art Deco tower and the houses clustered together in Monterey Heights and Mount Davidson Manor.

He turned to say more, but the killer lifted the pistol and shot him in the forehead. The priest fell, dead before he hit the ground.

●

The killer went back to the Hudson and took a canvas tarp out of the trunk. He walked back up the rocky hill past the garden, the chicken coop, and the small herd of goats to where the monsignor's body lay on the ground. He unfolded the tarp and placed the body on it, tying it securely with a rope. He carried it back to the Hudson, folding it to fit so it wouldn't be seen from outside the car.

As he drove back to North Beach he was careful to keep within the speed limit. He drove over Twin Peaks, down Market Street, and then up Montgomery to Columbus and to Washington Square.

He waited until no cars were passing on Columbus Avenue or Filbert Street. Nobody was walking in Washington Square or anywhere nearby that he could see. He carried the body across the street to the church and went inside. He took the body up the main aisle, laid it on the floor at the base of the altar, and unwrapped it. He left the monsignor's arms outstretched, then took a sign out of his pocket and put it around the priest's neck.

SATURDAY, MAY 9, 1942

# The Rathskeller Restaurant, California Hall, Polk Street, 9:00 P.M.

Dr. Albert Smith was annoyed. Though the beer was excellent, as usual, and his special booth had been ready, Kurt Cassel was twenty minutes late. Albert did not like to be kept waiting. He decided to give Cassel five more minutes. Tall, blue-eyed, well dressed, in his forties, Albert looked like many of the men in the restaurant, except for his short military haircut. The wood-paneled room with its colorful murals of German folk culture was filled with the friendly chatter of German-speaking patrons.

Albert was about to leave when he saw his brother-in-law across the room going from table to table, peering at the guests. Finally, he looked across at the booths that lined the wall of the dimly-lit basement restaurant. Albert raised his hand and Cassel came toward him.

A tall, heavyset middle-aged mostly bald man, Cassel slipped into the booth and sat across from Albert. He pulled a crumpled handkerchief from his pocket and wiped his sweating face. "It *is* you!" he said.

"Of course it's me, you *dummkopf,* you're twenty-five minutes late!"

"But I was here right on time, Herr Doctor Smith," said Cassel. Albert knew that his brother-in-law disliked being reprimanded. He also noticed that Cassel looked shabby. His suit looked like something from one of the second-hand stores on Howard Street. Albert put up with him because he'd made himself indispensable to the work of the organization.

"I took a quick look in here," Cassel complained, "and I didn't see you. The lighting is low, after all. Then I went outside thinking you wanted to meet at the entrance to the building. When you didn't show up there, I came back downstairs. It's a good thing you waved. I hardly recognize you. You've gotten one of those G.I. crew cuts!"

"Never mind my haircut," Albert snapped.  He raised his arm and gestured to the waiter to come to the booth. "Bring us two Burgermeisters and two Sauerbraten, with extra *Rotkohl*."

The waiter took away Albert's empty glass. He quickly returned with two bottles and two glasses. He put them on the table, bowed, and said, "Here you are, Herr Smith."

They each poured their beer and took a drink. "What do you have to report?" Albert asked.

Cassel wiped the beer foam off his mouth, then looked at his hand as though unsure of what to do with it. Finally, he picked up a napkin and wiped off the back of his hand before reaching inside his suit coat and pulling out a large envelope folded in half.

"Don't hand me something here, in public, you fool," Albert growled.

"Well, you wanted me to take pictures and make drawings, didn't you?" Cassel retorted. He put the envelope back in his jacket. "What should I do with them then? I spent a lot of time doing what you wanted." His face got red, his eyes narrowed and his brow furrowed.

"Calm yourself, Cassel. If you didn't act like a fool I wouldn't call you a fool. We are in a public place. People are always watching."

"I don't like being called names, Doctor." He sat up straighter and adopted a serious look. "I know you were a *Hauptsturm-führer* back in the old country, but we're in America now. There's no SA here and you can't talk to me like I'm a lowly *Sturmmann*."

Noting his flushed face and the way he was slurring his words, Albert thought Cassel must have stopped at one of the bars on McAllister Street near his City Hall office before walking up the hill to California Hall. Albert decided to humor the man.

"My dear Herr Cassel. I appreciate your volunteering to do your duty to the Fatherland," he said. "You must forgive me if I failed to show you proper respect. I'm still not used to these American ways of speaking and I apologize if I upset you. You must understand, however, we need to be discreet.

"I can say also, I was very pleased when you first told me you wanted to help our people back home. The organization was impressed by your work in San Pedro and Mare Island last May and June. Of course, we rewarded you handsomely, don't you think?"

"I'm not complaining," Cassel said. "And don't forget that warehouse job I took care of in March. This here was an easier job – no guards to worry about, no danger of blowing up or burning myself up along with the target." He laughed. "Nothing to do but drive around taking pictures and making my drawings."

The waiter came to the booth with a large tray filled with their dinners. Cassel asked him for another bottle of Burgermeister.

After eating several bites, Albert wiped his mouth carefully with the corner of his napkin. He took a drink of beer. "When I asked what you have to report, I was hoping you would tell me what you discovered. You can give me the envelope later. We can go into the toilet before we leave and make sure no one is there to observe us."

Cassel was wolfing down his Sauerbraten like a starving

man, occasionally stopping to wipe his hands on a large cloth napkin he had tucked under his chin. When he finished, he took another drink.

"I went to the Presidio, where the army has its headquarters, and also to Fort Mason and the Armory in the Mission District. Oh, and I also went out to the Hunters Point shipyard construction site."

"Did anybody question your being there?"

"Not once!" Cassel said, looking pleased with himself. "That's because of my City and County of San Francisco identification card."

"That's quite surprising," Albert said. "The Americans must think they are safe even after Pearl Harbor! What utter stupidity."

"All these places are under construction. They're being expanded. I told the guards I needed to inspect the new generators, control panels, electrical motors, and the electrical wiring that's going in at those facilities. My ID card shows that I'm the city and county electrical code inspector. I carried my camera right out in the open on a strap around my neck. Nobody even asked me why I needed a camera."

Albert finished the last of his dinner and drained his beer glass. "Herr Cassel, this is an excellent report. Excellent news. I expect you've made your usual detailed drawings, so we know exactly where the electricity for all these operations can be turned on and off, correct?"

"Yes, sir, that's correct." He patted the side of his suit jacket. "And the photos here are up to date as of last week."

"Such good work, Herr Cassel."

Albert reached across the table and the men shook hands.

Cassel smiled with obvious pleasure in being complimented. "And the tools and materials for our operations?" Albert asked. We can't just quietly accept President Roosevelt's expulsion of all our diplo-mats from America. And we have to keep up our work despite this new wartime reality."

"Safe and sound." Cassel smiled even more broadly. "First of all," he started, but before he could continue Albert put his right hand up, palm toward Cassel, and said, "We don't need to discuss the details here, Herr Cassel, but this is good news. Are you ready for tomorrow?"

"Yes, I bought a new telephoto lens and I have ten rolls of film. Plus, I even bought us a case of Burgermeister, your favorite!"

**SUNDAY, MAY 10, 1942**

# The Yacht Club and San Francisco Bay
# The Marina, 8:00 A.M.

Albert parked his Packard station wagon in front of Kurt Cassel's house on San Carlos Street. It looked out of place among the battered older cars, mostly Fords and Chevrolets. Cassel was waiting by the curb. Around his neck he had a camera with a very long lens. A wooden case of beer bottles sat on the street next to him.

Albert exited the car, unlocked the rear compartment, and Cassel put the case of beer in the back. "Your house needs paint," Albert said as they closed their doors. He turned the key and started the car.

"I know," Cassel said. "My wife complains about how bad it looks, but I tell her it fits right in with all the others." Albert drove up 18th Street and turned right on Valencia.

"The Depression's over," he said. "When are you going to get out of this slum and put your wife in a nicer house?"

"I can't afford it," Cassel answered. "The medical bills after her accident were expensive. I never lost my job like a lot of people, but the city doesn't pay me that much!"

"Wait a minute," Albert said, "I gave you $1,500 from the organization when you agreed to help us. That was an exceedingly generous sum. I figured it was more than enough to pay Hannelore's medical bills and move her to a better neighborhood."

They were driving up Van Ness Avenue. Cassel was looking out his window at the 1941 Cadillacs on display as they passed the showroom. He turned toward his brother-in-law with a hangdog expression but his eyes flashed defiance. "Well, I had some debts to pay off, too. By the time I paid everybody there wasn't enough left to move."

Albert felt a surge of anger. Now he was convinced that the rumors about the man's visits to the gambling parlors in the Tenderloin were true. He was squeezing the steering wheel, making his knuckles white. He told himself this was no time to indulge his feelings, but he recalled the conversation with his sister at the Easter Day family dinner. He asked her about what looked like a bruise on the side of her face. She said she had hit her head. The rickety back stairs of their house were wet and she slipped and fell.

Two years ago, she had broken her leg – another accident, she had said. That time she was allegedly rushing to cross the street with groceries and tripped on the curb. Perhaps, Albert thought, but the family gossiped about Kurt Cassel: his fondness for the horses at Bay Meadows, his appetite for Burgermeister, and especially his notorious short temper.

Albert seethed inside, but forced himself to focus on the day's business. By the time they reached Marina Boulevard his pulse was back to normal. He pulled up to the curb alongside his berth at the Yacht Harbor.

The Harbormaster happened to be walking by and said, "Good morning, Dr. Smith, it's a fine day for boating!"

Scarcely looking at him, Albert mumbled a reply and bent over to unlock the back compartment. The Harbormaster waited for a minute then turned and continued on his way.

"I'll get the beer," Cassel said. He picked up the case and followed Albert. They walked onto the gangplank leading to the boat dock and the berths. Albert locked the gate back up and they headed over to his boat, a thirty-eight-foot cruiser with the name *The Horst Vessel* in large black letters on the white-painted stern.

Cassel put the beer into the cabin as Albert prepared the boat for departure. "I'm surprised you didn't change the name of your boat after Pearl Harbor," he said. "Aren't you afraid somebody will complain you have a Nazi hero's name painted on there?" He ducked into the cabin and came out with two bottles of beer. He sat down on one of the pull-down chairs in the stern and drained them in two long drinks before dropping them over the side into the water.

"If somebody complains, I'll change it," Albert replied, "but most Americans don't even know who Horst Wessel was." He started the engine as Cassel untied the lines to the dock.

Albert backed the boat out of the berth, then cruised slowly out of the small harbor. He set a course for their first stop, to photograph the ship repair docks at Hunters Point – a spit of land at the far southeastern limits of the city.

"I haven't been out on the bay since Pearl Harbor," Cassel said. He belched loudly. "Look at all these ships! I haven't seen this many since that big dock workers' strike."

"The ships couldn't unload so they had to just sit there until the strike was over," Albert explained. "The Communists were behind it. If there was a proper government, a National Socialist government, those Commies would never have gotten all that power."

"*Jawohl mein Führer*," Cassel loudly said. Then he did something he would often do at family gatherings. He covered his upper lip with the first two fingers of his left hand, raised his right arm, and shouted out, "Heil Hitler!" Albert found it deeply offensive but Cassel thought it was funny and never missed an opportunity.

"You should have more respect for the *Reich*," Albert said. "The *Reich* would never allow somebody like me to get away with the operations we have carried out here! Four months after Pearl Harbor and we can still cruise all around freely. The Congress still hasn't made military ports like this into prohibited zones."

"Maybe you should have more respect for the US government," Cassel said. "Be grateful that they are so incompetent!" They both laughed.

Albert slowed the engine to allow an Oakland-bound ferry boat to pass in front as it left the Ferry Building. They resumed speed as they went under the new Bay Bridge, high above them. "You can hear those Key System trains all the way down here," Cassel said, shouting to make himself heard. "I have to use the head!"

When he came back out of the cabin, Cassel had another two bottles of beer hanging between the first two fingers of his right hand.

"Ugh," he said, grimacing. "This is disgusting. I didn't know the slaughter houses down here in the Bayview worked on Sunday. The stench is sickening." He drank the beers quickly, belched, and dropped the empty bottles on the deck. He went into the cabin again and came out with two more.

As they passed the old Bethlehem Steel plant, Albert throttled down the engine to lessen his boat's wake. Several rowboats were anchored nearby. Fishermen from the Dogpatch district were sitting quietly, waiting for their day's catch.

Cassel drank one of the beers and threw the bottle into the bay. Then he noticed one of the fishermen shaking his head. He dramatically stood up, clicked his heels together, raised his arm toward the fisherman in a Hitler salute, and sang out the beginning of a Nazi anthem in a loud voice: *"Die Fahne hoch, die Reihen fest geschlossen."* He stopped and reached down for the other bottle.

"Cassel," shouted Smith, "sit down and shut up. *Mein Gott im Himmel*, you damned fool, the last thing we want is somebody to notice us!"

As Albert watched in horror, the fisherman put down his fishing pole and stood up in his boat, the third finger of his right hand extended. His boat rocked but he seemed not to care. "Fuck you, you damned Nazi bastards!" he yelled. "Fuckin rich sonsabitches in your fancy fuckin cruiser. Go to hell!"

Albert turned the wheel to the left, accelerated, and headed the boat out into the bay toward Oakland at high speed. They quickly left the fisherman and the other rowboats far behind. The boat slapped the surface of the bay, and the spray showered Cassel in the stern. He was having trouble holding on as the boat accelerated. He had one hand on the rail and the other on a bottle of beer.

"Goddamn you!" Albert yelled. Cassel took a long drink, belched, and yelled back, "Goddamn *you*, you nervous Nellie! I was just having a little fun. That guy's probably a Commie. What do you care, anyway, he can't do anything to you!"

"You damned *dummkopf*, the name of my boat is there for anybody to see!"

"Well, if anybody's a *dummkopf*, it's you, *mein Führer*. You're the one who painted the name on the boat! Besides, he'll forget all about it." Cassel took his left hand off the rail to reposition himself while lifting the bottle for another drink.

Just then, Albert realized he had to correct his course in order to continue to Hunters Point. Without slowing, he turned the wheel sharply to the right. He heard a loud "Hey!" and when he looked back, he saw Cassel lose his footing and fall over the side into the water.

Horrified, Albert lowered speed, turned the boat around, and cruised back to where he thought Cassel had fallen out of the boat. There was no sign of him. He put the boat in neutral and felt it rocking in place. He waited, staring at the water, and heard the sound of beer bottles rolling slowly back and forth across the deck.

### SUNDAY, MAY 10, 1942

## Saints Peter and Paul Church

## 666 Filbert Street, 10 A.M.

Jacob Weiss parked his Graham alongside Washington Square, across the street from what North Beach residents called "The Italian Cathedral." Tony Bosco excused himself from a small group of priests and came down the stairs to greet him. "I bet you didn't expect to hear from me this soon, did you?"

Jacob gave Tony a look, shook his head and followed him into the church. A hint of incense filled the air. Sunlight filtered into the space from skylights and two rows of stained-glass windows along the east and west walls. Jacob was not Catholic and he was a big man, but he felt small in the huge church with its high ceiling and imposing marble altar. He felt as though he was in the presence of something mystical. The feeling was short lived.

He followed Tony up the middle aisle to the base of the altar, where a black canvas covered a shape on the floor. Tony pulled back the tarp to reveal a body on its back with arms outstretched. The man was dressed in a black suit with a Roman collar. His eyes were closed. He had a thoughtful expression and a handsome face spoiled only by the bullet hole in his forehead.

"The custodian opened the church at 7:00, and the lady who puts flowers around the altar discovered the body around 7:30," Tony said. "They closed the church and cancelled today's ser-vices."

"This guy looks familiar," Jacob said. "I'm sure I saw his picture in the papers recently, but I can't remember his name."

"This is Father Fritz Haber," Tony explained. "He was in

charge of the after school Italian classes for kids in North Beach."

"Wasn't that the program that Eddie Sarno accused of being a front for the Mussolini government? According to the *Chronicle*, you were responsible for that school." Jacob thought back to how Sarno had been waging a newspaper offensive against Tony, saying he was the leading Fascist agent on the West Coast.

"Yes, indeed. Sarno's been attacking Father Haber as well as me lately," Tony said. "But I can't see Sarno doing this. His paper is full of attacks on me and the so-called Clerico-Fascists, but killing like this? I just can't see it."

The two men turned as an almost bald heavyset man in a dated double-breasted suit walked up to them, hat in hand. He was sweating. A line around his head showed where his hat had been. He wiped his face and head with a handkerchief. "I walked up here from the Hall of Justice," he said, sounding out of breath.

"That's not even a mile," Jacob joked. "You'd better shape up, Herb, there's a war on."

Herbert Doran was the police department's lead medical examiner. Jacob knew he was younger than Tony, but his weight and balding head made him look a lot older.

"What are you, some kind of Kraut health nut?" Doran said.

Jacob shook his head, annoyed. He was tired of being called a Kraut because of his accent. "When you've recovered from your hike, Herb, maybe you can take a look at the body," he said. He gestured at the hole in the priest's forehead. "That looks to me like a .45, but you're the expert."

Doran bent over, took out his glasses and peered at the bullet hole. "It's a .45 almost certainly." He straightened up.

"Give me a hand," he then said, "I want to turn him over." Jacob and Tony pulled the tarp all the way off and rolled the body over. Jacob had seen his share of corpses, but he was shocked once again by the damage a bullet in the forehead could do to the back of a head.

"One thing is for sure," Tony said, "Haber was shot somewhere else. There's almost no blood on the floor here."

"Looking at this exit wound, it's clear that we have no way of knowing where the bullet might be. There's no point in looking for the slug here in the church. And what about this?"

Tony gestured to the sign around the priest's neck. He picked it up and showed it to Jacob.

They read the handwritten message. At the top, in capital letters: "TRAITOR." At the bottom of the page: "The Grynszpan Group."

"Why would anyone accuse this priest of being a traitor?" Doran exclaimed.

Jacob's face clouded up. "Are you sure this couldn't be Sarno's doing?" he asked Tony. "You said he's been calling out you and Haber for being fascist collaborators, traitors to America."

Tony shook his head. "I don't know. I just can't see him as an assassin."

"I have to get back to the FBI office," Jacob said. "I have a meeting that will take up most of the afternoon. We don't have Sundays off since Pearl Harbor. After that I'll contact a couple of my informants. But what about Sarno?"

"We can at least pay him a visit at home this evening," Tony said. "See how he reacts to these two murders. I'll pick you up at your house after dinner, at say 7:00?"

### SUNDAY, MAY 10, 1942

## Saints Peter and Paul Parish Office

## 666 Filbert Street, 11 A.M.

Tony walked next door and rang the bell for the parish office.

"Mr. Bosco," said the young priest who answered. "What terrible things are happening!"

"The times are indeed terrible. I need to use the telephone." He walked past the priest to the secretary's office. "Mrs. Righetti, I need to use the phone and this needs to be a private conversation, if you don't mind."

A woman in her late forties, with graying black hair pulled back in a bun, pushed her round wire-framed glasses up, bounced up out of the chair where she had been typing something on church letterhead, and smiled at Tony. "Of course. I'll go wait in the dining room; come and get me when you're finished. I'll make you an espresso and give you a nice piece of brioche I bought this morning at Victoria Pastry. I know how fond you are of brioche."

Tony thanked her and called Chief O'Reilly at the Hall of Justice. He told the chief about the sign on the body and that Jacob Weiss had agreed to work with him on the two murders.

"Weiss? From the FBI? All right, but did you tell him this needs to be kept quiet?" the chief asked.

"He knows that, don't worry."

"I'm assuming you have enough time for these cases, now, since the Italian consulate is closed?"

"Well, all my work with the Italian consulate is over, ever

since they closed down after the declaration of war. But I have other clients. And Weiss might not always be available exactly when I need him. You need to assign Dennis and Ruthie to both cases, so they can back me up all the time."

"You've got a point. Come to think of it, you'd better get down to the Hall of Justice and get signed out with a badge and a police special. You can't be too careful these days."

"You know I hate guns. But you may be right about that. I'll walk down there when I finish talking to the people here at the Saints Peter and Paul office. Have your secretary get me a badge and call the boys in the armory. I'll stop there later this afternoon."

Tony hung up and walked to the dining room where Mildred Righetti was knitting, a basket full of yarn on the table next to her. "I'm making sweaters for the boys overseas," she said, "it's the least I can do. You sit right down, Tony, and I'll get you that espresso and brioche."

While she was gone, Tony imagined how his wife Flora would react to his coming home with a .38 police special under his suit coat. He didn't look forward to it.

Flora was bound to object, saying guns killed people. She'd bring up the story of her cousin Giuseppe, the anarchist. A black sheep in his family, the twenty-one year old went around boasting how he always proudly carried both a knife and a gun. He also boasted about how much he hated "the capitalist swine Giannini."

On a hot August day in 1935, on the tenth anniversary of the execution of their heroes Sacco and Vanzetti, Giuseppe and another anarchist comrade walked into the Santa Rosa branch of Giannini's Bank of America waving their pistols and demanding the cash.

Unfortunately for them, they had also bragged about what

they were planning to do. Two Italian American security guards were waiting for them. They used 12-gauge shotguns to send Giuseppe and his accomplice to early graves. Flora had insisted that Tony ask the archbishop for permission to bury Giuseppe in the Catholic cemetery. After a heated discussion, she finally admitted that her atheist cousin would have rejected both a funeral mass and a Catholic burial.

Tony decided he wouldn't even tell Flora he would be carrying a handgun. When Mildred Righetti returned with his espresso and brioche, he asked her if she knew about the murder of Father Haber. She answered that she did and she found it baffling.

"Everyone loved the monsignor, Tony," she said. "Especially the children who attended the Italian classes after school."

"Did you ever hear anything, from anybody at all, that was negative? Criticisms, complaints, anything?" Tony asked.

"No, not a thing. He was popular with everybody since he first came here about ten years ago."

Tony thought back to that time: it was just after the Mussolini regime sent its black shirt thugs into Turin and all the towns and villages of the Piedmont region to shut down the Catholic youth clubs. Several dozen priests went into exile to avoid being killed or imprisoned. Haber was originally from Bavaria, but he loved Italy and had lived in Northern Italy for years. It was his mother's home.

"That's right, Mildred, I remember meeting him at the train station in Oakland and riding the ferry back to the city," he said. "I brought him here for a welcome dinner."

"I remember that dinner, now that you mention it. Flora was here with you, wasn't she? It seems like just the other day that she and I were saying how impressed we were with the monsignor's English! Flora told me that he sounded like an English gentleman."

"He had a private tutor," Tony said, "German was his native language, but he spoke fluent Italian, French, and English. The Haber family is wealthy. They spared no expenses for their two children. Fritz told me that their English governess took him and his sister Maria to Italy every summer when they were growing up."

"I didn't know about that," Mildred said. "Well, maybe he spoke what they call 'the king's English' but you know he never put on any airs or anything like that." A moment passed, and her chin started to shake. "Oh, dear," she sobbed. "I'm sorry, Tony, all of a sudden I'm feeling very emotional." She stood up and picked up his empty espresso cup and plate. "Please excuse me, I'll take care of all this. It was nice to see you, Tony, and give my best to Flora." He stood up, said goodbye and watched as she walked, head held high, into the kitchen.

Tony returned to the office and called the Hall of Justice again, asking to be connected to Dennis Sullivan. Sullivan answered on the second ring. "Tony, I just had a call from the chief about the second Grynszpan murder."

"Right, and since I'm going to need all the help I can get now, I want to tell Ruthie about the new development. Is she working at the art school today, or is she teaching over at Mills College? I'm down at Saints Peter and Paul. If she's at the art school I thought I'd walk over and alert her."

"Yes, she's working over there today. The Russian language class she was teaching at Mills College ended last week. She's not expecting you; she'll be pleasantly surprised."

### SUNDAY, MAY 10, 1942

## California School of Fine Arts
## 800 Chestnut Street, 12:00 P.M.

Tony left the parish hall, walked to Columbus Avenue, then went three blocks to Chestnut Street and up the hill to the California School of Fine Arts campus. The courtyard, usually filled with young men and women at this time of day, was empty except for two female students deep in conversation on one of the benches.

He walked into the office, noting again the absence of men, and stood at the counter like a student. He watched as a twenty-something woman with long brown hair and green eyes at one of the two desks conducted an animated telephone conversation. A moment passed before she looked over at the counter and noticed Tony.

"I have to go now, Nancy, we'll talk later," she said. She hung up, got up from the desk and smiled at Tony, her green eyes full of excitement. "Tony, what a surprise? What brings you here?"

Tony thought back to Easter week, when he'd first met Ruthie after Chief O'Reilly had assigned her to work with him on the Coit Tower murder case. He'd told Flora he was convinced that closing that case quickly was in no small part due to Ruthie's connections in the local communist community, of which several members were her close personal friends. Not to mention her boundless energy and insights into human nature. Now she had become a part-time Russian language teacher at a women's college in Oakland in addition to her part-time job as a secretary at the art school.

Ruthie called in another young woman from the next-door office to take her place at the telephone. She and Tony walked out into the courtyard and sat down together at one of the benches. "It's time for my lunch," she said pulling a sandwich wrapped in a large cloth napkin from her carryall. "Tell me what's going on."

While Ruthie ate, Tony described the murder of Father Haber. "I don't have any leads at all, but I can't imagine he would be in the sights of a Zionist assassin, can you?"

"I've never heard him mentioned one way or another by any of my friends."

"That's what I heard from Mildred Righetti at the church, too. I'm going to talk with the pastor at some point." He told her that the pastor drove up to Pittsburg to talk with some Italian Catholics, fishermen and their wives, older men and women worried about getting put in camps because they never became American citizens.

"Is that really a possibility?" Ruthie asked.

"I'm afraid it could be, but we just don't know at this point. I've been talking to the archbishop, trying to get him to write to the Attorney General and the President. If they put some pressure on General DeWitt, maybe he'll leave the Italian citizens alone. He likes to think of himself as a patriot because he's locking up a bunch of old Italians in their 60s and 70s. Some of their sons are already in the army and navy. It's shameful."

Ruthie shook her head, saying nothing.

"But I'm going on and on here, Ruthie." Tony got up from the bench. "The main thing I wanted to say is that I need you and Dennis, along with Jacob Weiss on both these cases."

"Sure, Tony. I finished grading my Russian class student papers last week, so I have lots of time. And if necessary, I can get one of the students here to sub for me if I need to be away from the office."

Ruthie folded her napkin, put it into her bag, stood up and said goodbye. She went back into the building. Tony walked out of the courtyard and started down the hill to Columbus Avenue.

When he got to the Hall of Justice, Dennis Sullivan was waiting for him in their office in the basement. Dennis gave Tony the paperwork he'd filled out, and they walked upstairs to the chief's office. Maggie, his secretary, handed Tony a badge and the application to carry a handgun signed by the chief.

Kenneth Bryant, the uniformed sergeant in charge of the armory department smiled at them as they approached the desk. "Commissioner Bosco, I thought you were retired!"

"Kenny, I thought you were retired, too," Tony said.

"Ah, I've still two years to go, Commissioner. Then it's moving full time to Monte Rio, where the hardest job I'll have is pulling the starter rope on my outboard when I go fishing in the Russian River. In the meantime, what can I do for you?"

Dennis handed Bryant the paperwork and the sergeant looked it over. "I won't ask you why you need one of these because you probably won't tell me anyway," he said. He laughed at his own joke.

"I'd prefer the four-inch barrel," Tony said. "Less weight to carry around."

"Coming right up."

Bryant left them at the counter and walked back into the room filled with shelves and cabinets. He put a shoulder holster rig, a Colt .38 police special, and a box of bullets on the counter. His blue eyes crinkled in his red face as he smiled and said, "Come back when you run out and I'll sign out another box."

**SUNDAY, MAY 10, 1942**

## The Weiss Home, Webster Street,

## Fillmore District, 5:45 P.M.

Jacob entered his house and hung up his hat on the rack by the front door. He unstrapped his shoulder holster and hung it up too.

"Jacob," Rachel said from the living room, "don't get too comfortable. Tony Bosco called about a half hour ago. He's coming by to pick you up to go interview Eddie Sarno."

She walked into the entry hall holding a copy of *Time* magazine. A portrait of Nazi Admiral Erich Raeder glared from the cover, blood dripping from the twisted cross of a huge black swastika in the background.

"Tony told me he's more and more concerned about being accused of fascist sympathies," Rachel said. "Sarno is still publishing articles saying that his work with the after-school Italian language classes made him a Fascist agent."

"Yeah, but he seems tough," Jacob said. "He'll put up a good fight."

"When I asked him why you were going to Eddie Sarno's house, he joked about how the FBI was listening to his calls and he'd tell me everything when he saw me."

"That's not a joke. Tony's been accused of being a fascist fifth columnist. Hoover ordered us to open and read Tony's mail and tap his home and office telephones. I objected, but the boss told me we need to humor the director. Anyway, the charges are baloney. He will be exonerated."

"I suppose you can't just disobey Hoover," Rachel said. "Tony's wife must be very upset about this. You know, we wives have to stick together."

"Rachel, you're the top, really." He pulled her close and kissed her. "The house always seems empty on the days when David doesn't run to meet me at the door. Is he staying at *Oma's* house this afternoon?"

"Yes, she'll bring him over soon. How about some coffee before you go?"

"I'd love a cup," he answered. "And it's a relief to get out of that harness for a few minutes. I'm feeling more upset than I have for a long time. This Grynszpan Group has stirred up all kinds of memories from Palestine."

## SUNDAY, MAY 10, 1942

## The Sarno Home, Foote Avenue,
## Crocker-Amazon District, 6:30 P.M.

Tony said little for the first ten minutes as he drove his Buick Century down Webster, across Market, and then south on Guerrero. Jacob didn't try to lighten the mood. They crossed Army Street and headed southwest on Alemany. In the distance, the Southern Hills and San Bruno Mountain still wore their deep green color from the rains of the winter and early spring. They passed colorfully painted, cheaply built houses lined up on the street like cereal boxes on a supermarket shelf.

"Where the devil are we going, Tony?" Jacob asked him. "I assumed Eddie Sarno lived in North Beach, but at this rate we'll be in Daly City before long."

"Eddie Sarno goes on and on about being one with the working stiffs, but he bought one of these new houses out here," Tony explained. "He drives an almost-new car back and forth to his office in North Beach, like any other middle class commuter, almost seven miles each way. He wears a suit every day just like you and me, and he eats lunch with the editor of the Communist paper at Vanessi's and the Riviera." He frowned and turned right from Alemany onto Foote Avenue, where he parked in front of the fourth house.

"My, my," Jacob laughed, "I didn't know you liked him so much."

"I don't begrudge a man wanting to improve himself," Tony said, "and I'm not being envious of his house. He knows I'm not a fascist and attacks me for being a lackey of Mussolini because I'm 'a bourgeois Catholic fascist sympathizer.' That's hypocritical. I have a hard time forgiving him."

Across the street, the driver's door opened in a black Plymouth Special Deluxe convertible. It was   Dennis Sullivan. Tony saw Jacob look at Sullivan. "I asked Dennis to meet us here. I wanted to have an active duty SFPD man with a badge with us when we talked with Sarno."

Dennis came up to them. "Tony, what's the story about Eddie Sarno? All you said on the phone was you wanted me to meet you here at 7:00."

"We found the body of Father Fritz Haber in the Italian Cathedral with another Grynszpan note. Sarno attacked Haber in his paper for being a Clerico-fascist. I can't see Sarno as a killer, but we have to at least check him out."

Sarno's place stood in a row of stucco-front new houses. They varied in trim, but all had garages below, living rooms with windows that looked out onto the street, dining rooms, two bedrooms, kitchens, and bathrooms above. Tony led the way and Jacob and Dennis followed him up the dozen stairs.

They rang the bell, a two note chime sounded, and soon they heard footsteps. The door opened and they saw a girl about thirteen years old, with dark brown hair in pigtails and a skirt and sweater too old for her years. She looked at the three of them appraisingly, turned her head and shouted over her shoulder, "Daddy, there's cops here."

Eddie Sarno came up behind the girl. "Marie, go inside." She left him at the door. He was wearing an unbuttoned white dress shirt without a tie. Tony was surprised at how small he looked without a suit coat, maybe five eight, with narrow shoulders. His wavy dark brown hair was, as usual, uncombed and gravity-defying, making him look like an orchestra conductor.

"What the hell are you guys doing at my house? Tony Bosco? Your Irish thug sidekick? And this Kraut FBI man? You have a hell of a nerve coming here."

"Hello, Eddie," Tony said. "We just want to ask you some questions. May we come in?"

"Do you have a warrant? Why should I let you in my house? We're about to have our Sunday dinner!"

Dennis's voice was flat. "Fifteen or twenty minutes in your living room, Mr. Sarno, and then we're gone. Or you ride twenty minutes with us down to the Hall of Justice and we ask you our questions there."

"I'm sorry if we've come at an inconvenient time," Tony said, "but it couldn't be helped, and we have a case that may concern our national security. I'd think that a patriot like yourself would want to cooperate with the authorities."

Sarno looked at Tony, a crooked smile forming in his face. "*Ma, certamente, Signor Consigliere da Sindaco Rossi!*" He bowed theatrically and gestured for the three men to enter. They followed him past the entry to a living room on the left. Sarno gestured for them to have a seat and they sat on the sofa, facing him.

A short woman with a thin face, brown eyes and black hair in a braid that was wound around on the top of her head walked into the living room. She smiled and her eyes lit up in a friendly way. Sarno looked at her from his leather armchair but didn't introduce her.

"May I bring you gentlemen coffee?" she asked. Sarno waved his right arm up at her as though shooing away a fly. "They're not staying long, and they don't need any coffee. Go back to the kitchen, Mary."

Tony shook his head in disapproval of Sarno's treatment of his wife.

"We will keep this as short as possible," he said. "Father Fritz Haber has been murdered and there was a 'Traitor' sign on the body. Your editorials condemning me and Father Haber, the Catholic Church, and the *prominenti* are full of charges that we're traitors – fascist fellow-travelers."

"Listen, *Consigliere*," Sarno exclaimed, "never would I encourage assassination! I'm not some bloodthirsty anarchist. I hate Catholics and Fascism, but I'm never supporting a priest killer."

"Do you know anyone so determined to punish a bunch of alleged traitors they would assassinate a priest?" Jacob asked.

"We're not crazy killers," Sarno said. "That's insulting us Italians!"

Tony stood up, then Jacob and Dennis. They walked with Sarno to the front door. "Here's my card, Eddie," Jacob said. "Please call me if you hear anything that you think would help us get to the bottom of this. And please keep this under your hat. We don't want it to get around and possibly weaken morale, all right?"

"Of course, *Dottore*." He ushered them out and closed the door.

•

Sarno walked down the hallway to the telephone niche and dialed EXBROOK 5420. On the third ring a woman with an accent answered. "This is Sarno," he said. "We need to meet tomorrow. I just had a disturbing visit. Come to Joe DiMaggio's Restaurant at 12:30 and I'll tell you about it."

**MONDAY, MAY 11, 1942**

## The Archbishop's Mansion

## 1000 Fulton Street, 10:00 A.M.

Jacob kissed Rachel and the baby goodbye and walked up the hill from their house on Webster Street to the imposing three-story mansion. He had first seen it when Rachel took him to Alamo Square Park after they arrived in the city back in 1939. She told him how, when she was growing up, she imagined she would someday be a French princess and the mansion would be her home.

A tall, thin young priest dressed in a black suit with a Roman collar opened the door. His red hair looked freshly combed and his pale complexion was flushed. He looked right and left, up and down the street, and then motioned Jacob inside. "Good afternoon, Agent Weiss," the priest said after locking the door.

Jacob shook his hand replied, "It's good to see you again, Father Rourke. Let me guess, you've been running in Golden Gate Park again."

"You've not lost your special agent skills, I see," Rourke replied with a laugh.

"I've never been here during the day before," Jacob said. The sun was streaming into the spacious entry hall through the colored glass windows, setting the wood paneling aglow.

"I guess you'd say it's a miracle the earthquake and fire of 1906 spared this house."

"Oh yes," Rourke said. "On days like this we like to say God has gifted us with heavenly surroundings in which to live and work. But I dare say, if you are coming to see us again, the subject is not God's grace but man's fallen nature. Go right on upstairs, Agent Weiss, Father Oppenheimer is waiting for you in the library."

Jacob was tempted as always to take the stairs two at a time, but he reminded himself that he was here on business and represented the Bureau. The Director would not like to hear complaints about inappropriate behavior by one of his special agents in the house of an archbishop.

Jacob found Henry Oppenheimer, S. J., standing in front of the fireplace in the wood-paneled library. He was blond like Jacob, and nearly as tall, but there the resemblance ended. The Jesuit sported a reddish-blond beard, and his girth betrayed his love of rich food and red wine and his dislike of physical exercise. He moved toward Jacob. As was his practice, he opened his arms for an embrace, followed by an Austrian-style air kiss on each cheek.

"My dear good friend," Oppenheimer boomed. "It's always a pleasure to see you. How are your beautiful wife and your little one?"

How strange were the ways of the world. Here he was, a former resident of Vienna, back in the city of his birth. When he arrived to take up his duties as a newly-minted FBI agent, the Special Agent in Charge noted that he looked German and that his command of German and Yiddish, Hebrew and Arabic made him a great asset. He promptly put Jacob to work keeping track of Jewish and Catholic extremists on the Left and the Right. By Pearl Harbor, Jacob's network of informers kept him up to date on a motley crew consisting of what the FBI considered "potentially dangerous persons" – from Jewish members of the Zionist Betar group to Catholic veterans of the defunct German Bund who now supported the America First Committee.

Jacob thought about how surprised his boss would be if he knew that one of his confidential informants had become a close personal friend. Henry Oppenheimer was born a Jew in Vienna and then converted to Catholicism. Ordained in Rome, Oppenheimer was now the archbishop's unofficial ambassador to the city's Jewish community. For the sake of privacy, they sometimes met at the archbishop's house, not at the Chancery Office on Franklin Street.

"Rachel and David are just fine," Jacob said. "David walked for the first time last week, down the hallway in our house. Rachel sends greetings."

He told Oppenheimer about the late night visit of Tony Bosco and his two assistants, and informed him about the murders and the signs placed around the necks of the victims.

"We have to keep this confidential," Jacob said.

"Of course, of course," Oppenheimer said, "and I'm glad you came to me right away. I've never heard of any Grynszpan Group. The name has never come up in my monthly meetings with Rabbi Zalich."

Jacob knew that the priest met regularly with the city's two Zionist rabbis about anti-Semitic organizations and possible threats to the Jewish community from Catholics in hate groups like the Christian Front.

"I still meet with Rabbi Seifert, too," Oppenheimer said. "We haven't let down our guard. Your director announced back in January that the FBI put all the Nazi spies in prison. But as I told the archbishop, those spies were on the East Coast. There could still be spies out here. Have you ever noticed how California and the West Coast get ignored? It's ridiculous. And besides, it's not only spies who are Jew-hating Hitler sympathizers!"

"I agree," Jacob said, "I remember what you told me the last time we met. The Catholics who love Father Coughlin won't stop *their* pro-Nazi and anti-Jewish work just because Coughlin was told to stop all *his* political work."

"Not to mention the German Bund," Oppenheimer replied. "Sure, it's officially disbanded, but I'm ashamed to say I've recently run into some nasty Catholic Bundists here in San Francisco. They're still true believers."

"What about Jewish extremists?" Jacob asked. "Do you think this group killed Brown because of his America First work? But what about Father Haber? Why would anybody consider him a traitor?"

"If I were you, I'd go talk to Seifert and Zalich," Oppenheimer said. "Since you're Jewish, you might get more help from them than the typically Catholic special agent would! I can see why you came to me first, but since I've never heard of this group, it can't help to turn to the leading Zionists in San Francisco."

"I don't like to think that any Zionists here would have organized an extremist group," Jacob said.

Oppenheimer nodded sympathetically. They walked out of the library to the stairway. The large multicolored stained glass dome above filtered the sunlight, giving the space a feeling of harmony and peace. As they started down the stairway, Jacob noticed a white-haired older priest watching them from the doorway to the second floor parlor. He had raised eyebrows and a scowl on his face. Oppenheimer saw him, nodded, and simply said, "Monsignor Fuchs."

In the foyer Oppenheimer walked Jacob to the door. In a lowered voice, he said, "Speak of the devil, that's one of Father Coughlin's fans, the infamous Monsignor Fuchs. The archbishop has put him where he can't do any more harm, and I'm surprised to see him here today. But never mind. Please keep in touch, give my regards to Rachel, and let me know what you discover. And when do I get to visit with your little David again?"

**MONDAY, MAY 11, 1942**

## Joe DiMaggio's Restaurant
## Fisherman's Wharf, 12:30 P.M.

Luisa Arzano brushed past the host and sashayed into the dining room. Eddie Sarno, a smoldering cigarette in his hand, stood up to greet the woman with the lustrous long black hair as she approached his table.

The host caught up with her and pulled out the chair across from Sarno. "Mr. Sarno is having scotch and soda. May I get you a drink, Madame?"

"Bring me a glass of Asti Spumante, a serving of fried oysters, and some sourdough bread to start with."

As the man scurried away, Eddie flashed a crooked smile. "You attracted more attention when you came in than I did, and I'm on the front pages of the newspapers almost every week!"

"Maybe the city's leading anti-Fascist is becoming old news."

Eddie chuckled. They toasted the memory of her husband George, dead from an accident on the docks three weeks ago, then sipped their wine and enjoyed the oysters. Luisa told Eddie about her two sons joining up and leaving for basic training in the army.

When the waiter returned, they ordered dinner – salmon for Eddie and abalone steak for Luisa. "Eddie, I'm tired of sitting around reading the news," she said. "I hate the Japanese, the fascists, and the Nazis as much as George did, but I don't know what to do. I've never done volunteer work, and I'm not cut out to be planting victory gardens."

Eddie tipped his head to the side and smiled. "If you really want a job, I can always use a hand in the office. Are you handy with a typewriter?"

She raised an eyebrow. "You're joking, right? What makes you think I want to be a lousy typist when the Japs might invade San Francisco and my boys are prepared to die fighting the Axis?"

She bent over, lifted her large leather purse into her lap and opened it so Eddie could see the .45. "You and George were always complaining about the fascists in City Hall. Well, why the hell don't we do something about them?"

Sarno's face turned white. He looked around the room nervously. "For Christ's sake, Luisa, put that away. What's got into you? I hope it's not loaded."

"It wouldn't be much good to me if it weren't loaded, would it? I never figured you for a windbag. I thought you were a man of action who knew how to get things done. Maybe I was wrong about you."

Eddie frowned. "Tony Bosco and the FBI agent Jacob Weiss came to my house. They told me about a murder – Father Fritz Haber. You shouldn't be talking to anybody about 'doing something' about local fascist sympathizers, let alone carrying around a loaded gun. And I don't like to swear at ladies, but where the hell do you get off accusing me of being a bag of hot air?"

She gave him a condescending look. "If you're a man of action, prove it. George and I went all over the city with you making speeches against the mayor when he ran for reelection. It was three years ago, but it feels like just the other day. We never stopped calling Rossi a fascist. Him and his police commissioner and a bunch of others."

"C'mon, Luisa, that's politics," Eddie said. "That kind of

stuff was good for our side. We didn't beat Rossi, but we got a lot of votes from folks who wanted City Hall to serve the working class. We might win next time. I never believed that Angelo Rossi and Tony Bosco or any of those other guys were really fascists."

"Well, if you don't think they're fascists, why did *La Voce del Popolo* and the *People's World* publish those stories? You said you had proof that they were working for Mussolini and the Axis side. That seems pretty damaging."

Eddie chuckled. "I know all about those stories," he said. "It's pretty funny to see Jack Tenney's anti-subversive investigating committee using *our* phony stories to accuse the mayor and his pals of being fascist sympathizers."

"I read that in the *Chronicle*, Eddie. And they subpoenaed you to testify against them, isn't that right? So are you going to tell the world you don't really believe that Bosco and Rossi are fascists?"

"Luisa, you're a hard woman. Do you want me to say that I'll tell that committee the truth?"

Luisa shook her head but said nothing. She concentrated on cutting and eating bite-size pieces of her abalone steak. She took another drink of the Sauvignon Blanc they'd ordered to accompany their main courses.

"Do you think this committee will actually get rid of Rossi?"

"Well," he said, "if the testimony against them seems strong enough, the army will order them to report to those camps for people who are security risks. If that happens the city will have to replace the mayor."

"That's a hell of a lot of 'ifs.' I can think of a much better way to get rid of those guys and all their fascist pals."

"This is 1942, not 1900," Eddie said coldly. "You're not Gaetano Bresci, and Mayor Rossi is not King Emanuel. You can't go around talking like this. You never know who might be listening!"

"I'm not some crazy hysterical woman, Eddie. You don't need to worry about me."

"Do you think George's death and your sons leaving for the army might be too much for you?" he asked. "Have you considered seeing a doctor? I'm worried about you."

Luisa was looking past Eddie, watching two men in dark suits standing at the entrance of the dining room waiting to be seated.

"Don't look now, but speaking of the devil, two of the people who really *do* need to worry about me just walked in."

Eddie couldn't help himself and looked over his shoulder to see a priest and Tony Bosco himself taking their seats at a nearby table. The priest caught Eddie's eye and nodded in a friendly way before sitting down, shaking out his napkin, putting it on his lap, and speaking to the waiter. Eddie nodded back and turned his gaze to Luisa.

"Tony Bosco and Father Crespi?" he asked. "Why should they be worried about you?"

"You've written angry editorials about those two. You said that they should never have left Italy and come here to indoctrinate our children with the superstitious nonsense of the Fascist-collaborating Catholic Church."

"I did write that," he admitted. "I happen to believe in free thought and I oppose Catholic dogma. That doesn't mean I'd wish any harm to Bosco and Father Crespi."

Luisa tipped her head to the left with a crooked smile. "Just like I said before: all talk and no action."

**MONDAY, MAY 11, 1942**

# The Archbishop's Mansion
# 1000 Fulton Street, 5:00 P.M.

Henry Oppenheimer could not help thinking that some of the priests who attended the archbishop's afternoon sherry parties behaved as though they were celebrants at a liturgical event. He watched with the detached amusement of a transplanted Jewish convert the bowing and scraping of the elderly, mostly Irish American priests clutching their drinks as they clustered around the archbishop.

Henry was telling Bishop Ignatius O'Donnell that he disagreed with the army's evacuation of the Japanese residents of the city. "I have a friend who's an FBI agent. He told me that J. Edgar Hoover strongly opposed moving the Japanese and putting them behind barbed wire. According to Hoover they are not a danger to our national security. The FBI already knows who is a 'potentially dangerous person' in every city and county in the nation."

People said O'Donnell was too young for the job of Auxiliary Bishop, but he looked the part: ramrod straight, tall and fit, with strong Celtic features and gray eyes. "I thought the president made that decision and the army is just following orders," he said.

"That's true, Bishop O'Donnell. The president is the Commander in Chief of the Army, and the army's doing what it's told. My point is, this is forcing all these men, women, and children out of their homes and businesses when the FBI told the president it wasn't necessary."

"I didn't realize that. I wonder why he didn't listen to the FBI? If Hoover turns out to be right, then the government will have committed a terrible immoral action that will harm tens of thousands of Americans of Japanese ancestry."

Monsignor Peter Fuchs, a glass of sherry in hand, had left the group around the archbishop and come over to stand next to O'Donnell and Henry. His face was flushed from the sherry and his white hair needed trimming. He shook his head slightly and frowned at the bishop's comment. A thin man in his sixties who had served in a variety of assistant pastor positions, he was now assistant to the Chancellor. His office was next to Henry's on Franklin Street. Fuchs turned to Henry, waiting for his answer.

"My FBI friend says that the word around the Bureau is that FDR has prejudices like everybody else," Henry said. "He thinks the Japanese are an untrustworthy race. The same with the Jews. He has a few close friends who are Jewish, but he's prejudiced against them on the whole, especially the ones from Russia and Poland."

O'Donnell's expression went from inquisitive to skeptical. Henry felt a subtle change in the atmosphere. "That's a pretty damning statement to make about our president, don't you think? What's the evidence for this? Or is it just FBI office gossip?"

Henry was about to reply that Jacob Weiss had told him about a memo describing the president's views but Monsignor Fuchs cut in. "Father Oppenheimer, doesn't your Jewish background disqualify you from being a judge of President Roosevelt? And anyway, having a president who protects us from our enemies is something to cheer, not criticize."

"Yes, of course," O'Donnell said, "but it's troubling to hear that the president may be prejudiced against the Japanese or the Jewish people. That kind of bigotry is contrary to our faith."

"Well, Bishop O'Donnell, I'm older than you," Fuchs said.

"I remember when you were still a seminarian, wet-behind-the-ears. Then you went to D.C. and came back with your Ph.D. and all these liberal ideas. When the pope tells me that the Japs and the Jews, and the Negroes for that matter, are my brothers I'll start treating them as part of our Catholic family."

He puffed. "The Negroes are the worst. They're flooding into the city and bringing all their bad habits with them. They're a blight. As far as I'm concerned, we should keep being suspicious of all of those people."

O'Donnell gave a disapproving look to the monsignor. "We've already discussed your views about our new neighbors," he said. "You need to do some serious praying to overcome your un-Christian prejudices. I'm surprised and frankly shocked at your lack of compassion toward the Japanese."

The archbishop's steward, Louie Lowe, walked into the library and rang the bell for dinner. Bishop O'Donnell and Father Oppenheimer turned and walked toward the dining room without a word. Monsignor Fuchs was left by himself. He waited a moment, frowned, and followed them.

**TUESDAY, MAY 12, 1942**

## Federal Bureau of Investigation Office
## 111 Sutter Street, 9:00 A.M.

Jacob enjoyed the two mile walk to the office every day. It cleared his mind for work after the all-consuming routine at home. First getting themselves and David out of bed and dressed. Then family breakfast. Then the baby into the buggy, the buggy down the stairs, the kiss goodbye to Rachel and the boy. Then Rachel went on to her job at Temple Beth Israel after she dropped the boy off with his great-grandmother. Jacob was proud of his *Oma* after hearing her noisily object the previous day to one of their Jewish neighbors who had criticized the new Negro residents moving next door.

As he walked past the imposing granite City Hall with its famous high dome he wondered how his boss would react to his working with Tony Bosco and his crew on the Charles Brown and Father Haber murders. His thoughts were interrupted by the metallic screech and clatter of the two "iron monster" streetcar lines, the honking of cars and trucks, and the effort of avoiding slow moving pedestrians who got in his way as he strode down Market Street to Montgomery and Sutter.

After getting out of the elevator he walked straight into Ned Piper's office and found his boss standing alongside his desk, freshly shaven, with his black hair parted and neatly combed. "What a pleasant surprise," he said, his large brown eyes full of humor. "As you know, you're one of a select group of agents who doesn't need an appointment!"

Jacob laughed and they shook hands. "Thanks, Ned. I'm not a Greek, but I come bearing gifts today. He will be here at 9:30!"

"That's a pretty dumb joke," Piper said, smiling, "but you have my attention. Who exactly is this gift and what's the occasion?"

"Tony Bosco, the former police commissioner," Jacob answered. "Charles Brown and Father Fritz Haber were murdered. Chief O'Reilly wants the murders kept out of the public eye and he's assigned Bosco and his two assistants to deal with the case. Bosco asked me for help, but I told him that the Bureau needs to take over the case. He and his people could be our consultants. Tony came to our house in the middle of the night about the Brown murder."

"I know Bosco, of course," Piper said, "but this is a hell of a can of worms to dump on my desk first thing in the morning! Why in God's name would I want two city homicide cases? And how come I'm hearing this from you, and not O'Reilly?"

Jacob explained the "Traitor" signs and "The Grynszpan Group" signatures.

"I haven't heard of this group," Piper said.

"Me either, but it seemed to me that anything remotely connected to national security should be the business of the FBI, not the SFPD. I told Bosco to meet me here so he could talk to you directly."

"And here I am," Bosco said, walking into Piper's office. He made an elaborate bow like a character out of a Shakespeare play.

Noreen Scanlon, the SAC's secretary, was standing next to him looking frazzled. "I told him he needed an appointment," she complained, "but he just barged right in here as if I didn't even exist."

"That's all right, Noreen," said Piper, "this man is one of us. Our humble office is nothing compared to the grandeur of Mayor Rossi's throne room in City Hall, where the Commissioner can usually be found." He grinned. "But he's always welcome here."

Noreen left the room and they sat down, Piper behind his desk, Tony and Jacob in the chairs facing him. "What mischief have you gotten yourself into this time?" Piper said to Tony. "Since when are you going around making night time visits to the residents of our fair city like Arturo Bocchini and the *OVRA* secret police?"

"*Capo della Polizia* Bocchini, *requiescat in pace,* has gone to meet his maker," Bosco replied. "Don't worry, as long as my friend Angelo Rossi is mayor, nobody in the city of St. Francis will be allowed to use fascist policing tactics."

"C'mon, Tony, I was kidding you," Piper replied.

"Ned, my assistant Ruthie Fuller is a friend of Jacob's wife Rachel," Tony said. "Ruthie told me about Jacob's remit, so we went to see him first thing after seeing the body of Charles Brown. Jacob seems to think you will be comfortable taking over these cases and keeping them out of the papers."

Piper turned from Tony to Jacob, the humor gone from his eyes. He looked at Jacob. "Don't you have a lot on your plate already? Can you take the time for this business?"

Before Jacob could answer, Piper turned back to Tony and said, "Tony, I know about your close relationship with the mayor, but are you on good enough terms with Chief O'Reilly to string him along this way? Or do you plan to tell him that you've handed this off to the FBI? If so, you are a braver man than me!"

Tony put both hands in the air, palms up, and shrugged with eyebrows raised and a crooked smile. "When I was an immigrant kid in North Beach learning English, back before the big earthquake, one of my favorite phrases was 'what he doesn't know won't hurt him.' Between us, that would seem to apply in this situation, *non e vero*?"

"I don't speak much Italian," Jacob said, "but as we used to say back in Vienna, *Alles gut.*" He turned to Piper. "And if you give this the go ahead, boss, I will get to work."

"I know the chief pretty well," Tony said. "What he wants most is not ever having to even *think* about this case. Jacob, if you take the lead, Ruthie, Dennis and I will help however we can."

Piper turned to Jacob. "You've been taking care of this part of the business since you arrived, over two years ago," he said. "As our director likes to say, 'I have the utmost confidence in you,' so go at it." He got up and shook the hands of Tony and Jacob.

Before letting go of Tony's hand, Piper looked him in the eye and at the same time grabbed Jacob's shoulder with his left hand. "Whatever you do, boys, don't forget to first check in with Franklin Street."

Tony laughed at hearing Piper invoke the local saying. Before anyone proceeded with a civic matter, they needed the approval of the Catholic Church's office on Franklin Street. Jacob laughed too. "I already did you one better," he said. "I checked in with *Fulton Street!*"

**TUESDAY, MAY 12, 1942**

## Federal Bureau of Investigation Office
## 111 Sutter Street, 10:00 A.M.

Ned Piper finished his morning coffee and handed the cup and saucer to Noreen Scanlon. "Thank you, my dear," he said. "Do I have another appointment this morning?"

"Yes sir, its Angus Ferguson," she answered. "You cancelled his appointment last week and he's been pestering me to see you. He told me he has another complaint about something Agent Weiss did."

*I'm getting sick and tired of Ferguson*, Piper thought.

He wasn't alone. Almost all of his colleagues disliked the man's overbearing manner.

"I wish he would retire and move permanently to his house at Lake Tahoe," Ned muttered to himself.

He sighed. "All right Noreen, send him in and I'll see what he wants."

A ruddy-complexioned man in his fifties, his craggy features composed in a frown, his gray eyes smoldering, walked in and sat down without being asked. His swept-back long graying hair matched his long, unruly eyebrows. He crossed his right leg and rested the ankle on his left knee.

"Well, Fergus," Piper said, knowing that his agent hated the nickname his colleagues had chosen for him, "what's this I hear of another complaint about a colleague?"

"I'll not mince words, boss," Ferguson said, his Scottish accent still noticeable three decades after leaving Edinburgh. "Last week somebody came to me and told me he spoke to Weiss about wanting to volunteer information about subversive activities in North Beach. He says Weiss told him to get out of his office, saying FBI agents are not gossip columnists. Weiss said, quote, 'Who do you think I am, Hedda Hopper or Walter Winchell?'"

He leaned forward in an almost-aggressive manner.

"Boss, we're in a war. We need all the information about subversives that we can get. I know Weiss mostly handles Nazi and Communist stuff, but he should have referred that walk-in person to me, since I've done some work on Italian fascist subversion. It looks to me like he's getting lazy."

"All right, Fergus, duly noted," Ned said. "Now it's your turn to take note. It's my job to decide whether my agents are doing their jobs or not. Give me the name of this person and his telephone number. I'll talk to him and hear what he has to say."

## TUESDAY, MAY 12, 1942

## Foster's Cafeteria

## 555 Sansome Street, 11:00 A.M.

Foster's was filled with young men and women when Jacob walked in. Half the men were in uniform. He realized that Tony Bosco had a good point when he suggested the popular cafeteria as a good place to "hide in plain sight."

He saw Ruthie first. She was a striking stand-out in any crowd – movie star beautiful, with long brown hair, large hazel eyes, and red lipstick that matched her beret.

Jacob approached their table. "I guess even the FBI can find Foster's on Sansome Street," said Dennis Sullivan. Ruthie laughed, seeming to indulge him. Jacob got the impression they were more than just partners. He made a mental note to ask Rachel if something was going on with them.

He walked to the other side of the table and stood in front of Dennis. As they shook hands, Jacob held on. With a straight face and a serious tone, he said, "Now that the city is on wartime footing, the government has issued a strict order: no more FBI jokes will be allowed." He released his hold and sat down. A moment passed before Dennis's face relaxed and he laughed, followed by Ruthie and Tony.

"I've arranged things with my boss so I can make the Charles Brown and Father Haber cases my priority," Jacob said. "You all saw Brown's body, but apparently O'Reilly has already had it cremated. You told me Saturday night that you saw two bullet wounds, right?"

"That's right," Dennis answered. "The pattern of blood on

the chair, the floor and the wall made it clear he was shot at close range while sitting at his desk. The killer must have been standing right in front of him."

Jacob asked if they had checked for bullets at the scene.

"The wall behind the desk showed no evidence that the shots made it through the body," Dennis said. "I think the chief was foolish to be so worried about covering up the murder, but both bullets must have gone into the furnace with the corpse."

"I agree," Jacob said. "Did you find a pocket diary? And what about his wallet?"

Dennis shook his head. "All we have is this." He reached down, picked up a briefcase, and handed it to Jacob. "I put everything that might possibly be useful in here."

"I met Brown once, during the big strike," Tony said. "I spent a lot of time at Mayor Rossi's office then. Brown was one of the businessmen who demanded the mayor ask Governor Merriam to send in National Guard troops to load and unload their cargo."

"That was way back in '34, wasn't it?" Jacob asked. "I know a lot of San Franciscans think the so-called Big Strike was a turning point for the city, but we need to focus more on what's going on right now. Brown was involved with the America First Committee. Was there anything in his desk relating to that organization?"

"No, nothing," Dennis said. "And he had no filing cabinets or a closet in the office where he could have kept records."

"What about his house?" Ruthie asked. She turned to Dennis. "Maybe we have to search it like we did that other case last month."

"You need to do that, of course," Jacob said, taking Brown's diary out of the briefcase. He turned to the page for Saturday,

May 9. "But first of all we need to go talk with the person he appears to have had lunch with on Saturday, Alexander Campbell. Here's another appointment for that day, at 2:00..." Jacob stopped mid-sentence, staring at the page. Dennis and Ruthie waited a moment. "What's the matter, Jacob?" Ruthie eventually asked.

When he looked at them, the color had gone out of his face. "According to this, his 2:00 meeting on Saturday was with Jacob Weiss. I never made any appointment with Charles Brown."

"Well we can check to see if there's another person with your name in the city directory," Dennis said.

"And if there isn't," Jacob said coldly, "then that would make me a possible suspect."

**TUESDAY, MAY 12, 1942**

# San Francisco Catholic Archdiocese Office
# 1100 Franklin Street, 12:00 P.M.

Tony parked his Buick Century in front of the Chancery Office.

"There's a wooden sign here on the curb that says 'No Parking. Reserved for Archbishop. SFPD'," Jacob said.

Tony got out and started walking to the front door so Jacob followed.

"I know that," he said. "I'm allowed to park in the archbishop's place."

He told Jacob he frequently visited in connection with his Catholic men's organization. And since Italy declared war he'd made several trips every week to take calls from Italian Catholics who were worried they'd be sent away like the Japanese.

"People on your 'ABC List' of potentially dangerous persons in case of war," he explained. "One fisherman had his boat impounded and was sent to a camp."

"I don't handle that list, and I'm not involved in roundups and detentions of Italians," Jacob said in a sharper tone of voice than he'd intended.

"It's nothing personal," Tony answered. "The chief told me and Mayor Rossi we're on the list. I think if Angelo and I were scheduled for detention, we would have been informed by now."

Jacob didn't answer. They opened the imposing oak door with its prominent hand carved cross and walked up the stairs to the foyer. Guido Molinari was standing in his usual spot at the head of the stairs.

"Gentlemen," he said, smiling. "I'm always glad to see you, but I never dreamed you might show up together someday!"

Guido was taller than Jacob, with wide shoulders, a bull neck, a large head, and thick wavy black hair. Jacob recalled the day, before the baby was born, when he and Rachel were visiting the DeYoung Museum in Golden Gate Park. Rachel had stopped to give him a little talk about the life-size copy of Michelangelo's David. "This guy looks just like Guido, the guard in the Catholic archbishop's office," Jacob joked. "But he's not wearing his classy suit." Rachel laughed. "You certainly know how to spoil a girl's mood," she'd said.

"The archbishop's not here, gentlemen," Guido said. "He's making a visit to St. James High School this afternoon. They're having a ceremony for the boys who are graduating early so they can join the army."

"Speaking of the army," Jacob said. "You told me you were joining up. What's happening with that?"

"Ha," he said, "Tony here knows all about that, don't you, Commissioner." He turned to Jacob and said, "Tony's the director of my draft board, number 100. I already passed my physical. I'm classified I-A and I'm ready to go. As soon as my auntie gets here from Chicago to help take care of my momma and poppa, I'm off to basic training. I can't wait."

"Good luck, Guido," Jacob said, moving close and giving him a bear hug. "I'll miss our trips to the shooting range down in Sharp Park. If I don't see you before you go, remember to obey your officers, and make every shot count! Come on, Tony, let's let Guido get back to work."

"Ciao, signori," the giant said and walked back to the head of the stairs. Jacob led the way past the framed portraits of monsignors, bishops, and archbishops of yesteryear to Henry Oppenheimer's office. Their footsteps echoed on the polished wooden floor of the high-ceilinged hallway. The door to Monsignor Fuchs's office was open. They could see the white-haired priest at his desk, talking on the telephone.

Tony knocked on the door with a brass plate that read "Father Henry Oppenheimer, S.J." They heard, "Come in," in a clear firm voice and walked into the office. Tony started to close the door but Oppenheimer said, "You can leave it open, this little office will get stuffy otherwise, especially if there are two of you filling it with hot air."

"Father," Jacob said, "you're the second person today I had to warn about the new government rule against making fun of the FBI."

"Right," Tony said. "The same goes for making fun of your humble police commissioner."

"Okay, Father, kidding aside," Jacob said, "you suggested I talk with Rabbi Zalich about the case Tony and I are working on. We're going to do that this afternoon." He turned to Tony and smiled. "The FBI can be full of surprises," he said. "I hope you didn't plan anything else today."

"So how can I help, gentlemen?" Oppenheimer said, leaning forward in his desk chair.

"Here's what we need," Jacob continued. "Because we want to find out who Charles Brown has been seeing in the last several weeks, we need to contact the leading people in his America First Committee. And, for that matter, people in other groups you're aware of that Brown might have been involved with."

"Charles Brown was a busy man," the priest said. "Before he became the president of the local America First organization, he was active in the Friends of the New Germany and the German Bund."

"I seem to remember that," Tony said, "didn't he and Dr. Albert Smith organize that big pro-Nazi meeting in '38 that the Bund put on in California Hall?"

"I've heard all about that night, the riot and the arrests," Jacob said, "but it was before I came to San Francisco. What about in the last few years?"

"If you want details, you've come to the right place," Oppenheimer said. "Do you see that cabinet over there?" He pointed to an oak five-drawer filing cabinet next to a bookshelf by the window.

*No wonder the room gets stuffy,* Jacob thought. The desk, the two chairs he and Tony were sitting on, the bookshelf and the filing cabinet filled the cramped space with scarcely any room left over.

"You are welcome to avail yourselves of anything in there that attracts your attention. The top drawer will be particularly interesting, I wager. I'd prefer you use the materials here, as I haven't made copies of anything."

"Excellent," Jacob said. "Tony, can you have Ruthie and Dennis come by later? Father, will that be a good time for them to sit down and make us a list of people we need to interview?"

"Yes, that will be fine," Oppenheimer said. "I'll be waiting. If they come about 5:00, they can work in my office. I'll take a walk down to my usual place on Van Ness Avenue and have myself a cup of tea while they carry on."

Tony laughed. "I bet you were happy when Prohibition ended and you could resume your afternoon High Tea ceremony!"

Jacob and Tony thanked Oppenheimer and they all stood.

Jacob turned toward the door and was surprised to see Monsignor Fuchs quickly turn away from where he was standing next to the door frame. Without a word, Fuchs entered his office and shut the door.

**TUESDAY, MAY 12, 1942**

## Matson Building and Chambord Apartments
## Market Street & Sacramento Street, 1:00 P.M.

Dennis and Ruthie showed their police badges to Alexander Campbell. He smiled at Ruthie. "I didn't know Chief O'Reilly had started hiring girl detectives," he said.

Ruthie frowned and looked at Dennis, then back at Campbell. "I'm just doing my part for my country," she answered flatly. "We're wondering if you know anything about the whereabouts of Charles Brown."

Campbell, a tall balding man in his fifties, sat behind the desk in his spacious wood-paneled office at the foot of Market Street. A large painting of a clipper ship in full sail hung behind his desk. Bookshelves lined one wall, and a large American flag stood in one of the corners. Dennis thought he'd never walked on such a plush carpet in an office before.

"I haven't seen Charles since Saturday," Campbell said. "We had lunch at Joe DiMaggio's on Fisherman's Wharf. He told me he had an appointment that afternoon. The last time I saw him, he was walking back to the Ferry Building. Did you check with his wife?"

"Yes," Ruthie said. "She called the police this morning. They live apart – she's in Los Angeles. She called him on Saturday and Sunday and there was no answer, which she said was unusual. When she tried again this morning and he still didn't answer, she called us."

"How did he seem when you had lunch?" Dennis asked. "Was he upset or worried?"

"Well, now that you mention it," Campbell said, "he was upset about something, but I didn't get the sense that it was serious."

"What was upsetting him, did he tell you?" Dennis asked.

"Yes, he felt insulted by a newspaper reporter who interviewed him about our America First Committee. According to him, she was offended by the views of our organization, so she left in a huff and didn't say goodbye."

"And that was it?" Dennis asked. "He was upset about something that had already happened, not worried about the future?"

"Yes, quite," Campbell said. "He's not a nervous Nellie. He's not even been that worried about the war. Nor for that matter am I. We both believe it's only a matter of time before we send the Japanese navy to the bottom of the ocean. And after that, well, we'll see. But I'm rambling here. The point is Brown didn't strike me as worried about anything when we said goodbye."

"Speaking of the America First Committee," Ruthie said, "do you know where we could get a copy of the membership list? We thought we might contact the board of directors and see if anyone could help us locate Mr. Brown."

"I wish our local chapter was as imposing as you make it sound," Campbell replied. "It wouldn't be right to call it a 'one man show' but on the other hand it was in a real sense Charles Brown's baby. There can't be much in the way of records, but I imagine whatever there is would be in his office, or possibly in his apartment up on Nob Hill. He moved there when he sold the house in St. Francis Wood after his wife moved to LA."

Campbell stood up and walked around the desk to where Dennis and Ruthie were sitting. "I'm sorry I can't be of more help, but that's about all I know," he said. "I have to leave for a meeting at the Southern Pacific offices down the street."

Dennis and Ruthie thanked him and shook hands. They all walked together to the elevator. A map of the Hawaiian Islands was engraved on the shiny brass doors. The elevator operator, a uniformed young woman said, "Good afternoon, Mr. Campbell." They rode down to the ground floor and walked through the gleaming high-ceilinged marble entry hall and the glass doors with shiny brass fittings into the bustle and noise of Market Street.

As they crossed Market Street heading for the California Street cable cars, Dennis said, "Ruthie, you handled that guy beautifully."

"It's just a white lie, right?"

She smiled and started running to catch the cable car that was just about to start its trip up Nob Hill. "Come on!" she shouted and Dennis ran after her. They reached the car just in time. Ruthie took the last outside seat and Dennis stood on the platform in front of her. The conductor rang the bell and the car jerked forward. Dennis had to hold on to the pole with both hands to keep his balance.

The cable car clattered along on its way, a gradual rise and then a steep climb, up the east side of Nob Hill. Dennis hopped off when it reached the top at Mason Street, and waited as Ruthie climbed down. They found themselves surrounded by men in army and navy uniforms, and well-dressed women, going into and coming out of the Fairmount and Mark Hopkins Hotels. They walked down Mason Street past the three-story brownstone Flood mansion to Sacramento Street, where they turned to go to Charles Brown's apartment.

In the Chambord Apartments, they took the elevator to the third floor, where Brown's apartment was located. Dennis used his lock pick set to open the door.

"This gives me the willies," Ruthie said as they walked inside. "It seems like just the other day we broke into another apartment in this very same building."

"Yes, but this one is nothing like Harlan Winthrop's. Look at this! There's hardly any furniture."

The living room had a small sofa, an easy chair, and a small bookshelf. Two landscape paintings hung on the wall. A Persian carpet covered most of the hardwood floor. Down the hall, the bedroom was as bare of decoration as the living room, with just a bed, a dresser and a painting of a landscape with a village in the background. The second bedroom appeared to be Brown's office, with an oak desk and a matching chair and filing cabinet.

Ruthie began inspecting the contents of the filing cabinet. "They're mostly empty," she said. "The files all seem to deal with his business – Hatzfeld Enterprises."

Dennis was looking through the desk drawers. "Here we go," he said, taking out a large black leather ledger book with gilt-edged pages. "Here's a book with names and addresses." He handed it to Ruthie, who turned to the first page. At the top was written in large letters, "America First." She flipped through the pages and saw names, addresses, and telephone numbers.

"We have what we came for," she said. "Let's get out of here!"

**TUESDAY, MAY 12, 1942**

## Temple Beth Israel, Geary Street, The Fillmore District, 3:30 P.M.

"Mrs. Weiss, have all the children been picked up yet?"

Rachel Bernstein Weiss turned her head and saw Rabbi Seifert, a heavyset disheveled man with wild graying hair. He was standing at the door to the auditorium of Temple Beth Israel, wearing suspenders and a shirt with the sleeves rolled up.

"Yes, Rabbi," she answered. "I'm just checking the stage to make sure nothing was left behind at the afternoon assembly." She held up a cardigan sweater. "I nearly always find at least a jacket or a sweater. The children are always in such a hurry to go home I'm surprised that so few things end up in the lost and found box."

Rachel became the director of the Beth Israel nursery school shortly after she and Jacob moved to San Francisco, filling in temporarily after the previous head retired. Her plan was to stay only long enough for the congregation to hire a professional, then continue on for her Ph.D. in economics at Berkeley. But the rabbi talked her into staying on as acting director, after which she became pregnant. At first, she was happy to be a full-time mother, but by the time David was walking, at fourteen months, she was getting restless.

"Rachel, I was hoping against hope that you would want to come back," Rabbi Seifert had said when she approached him. Jacob and her parents encouraged her to accept the position as permanent director, with a handsome raise in salary. Jacob's *Oma* was so excited that she would be David's everyday caregiver that she clapped her hands in pleasure.

So Rachel decided to put off the idea of doctoral work in economics following up on the topic of her master's thesis with Professor Hayek. That could wait, she thought, until the war was over. There was little time to reflect, in any case. They were nearly overwhelmed with the numbers of Jewish children who had recently arrived in the Fillmore and Golden Gate Park Panhandle neighborhoods. Some spoke fluent English, but most spoke very little. They mostly spoke German, Yiddish, Hungarian, or Romanian.

"You mentioned that you and Jacob wanted to talk with me about something after school today," Rabbi Seifert said. "When do you expect him?"

"He should be here in about thirty minutes," Rachel replied. "He called me from Temple Beth Shalom, where he was talking to Rabbi Zalich. He's bringing Commissioner Tony Bosco with him, if that's all right. They're working together on something and Jacob and I have an idea we want to talk to you about."

"Commissioner Bosco?" Seifert said. "Why would he want to talk to me?"

"I'll let Jacob tell you," Rachel said. "Let's wait for them in your office." They walked down the hall and went into his comfortable office.

Bookshelves lined two walls. There were framed engravings, a leather sofa, an easy chair, and a table with four chairs alongside the rabbi's desk. "Take a seat, Rachel, and fill me in with what's going on with the nursery school," the rabbi said.

They were still comparing notes about the Negro families moving into the Fillmore, and the new parents from Central Europe and Shanghai, when Jacob and Tony rang the doorbell. The rabbi, having combed his hair, buttoned his sleeves and put on his suit jacket, ushered them into the office, where they joined Rachel.

"Hello, Mrs. Weiss," Tony said. "This is a pleasant surprise."

"Let's sit around the table," the rabbi said. "What's this all about?"

Jacob looked at Tony. Tony took the cue and explained the crime scenes they discovered at the Ferry Building and the Ital-ian Cathedral.

"We don't understand the 'Grynszpan Group' signs," Jacob said. "I've never heard of them, and neither has the Bureau in Washington, D. C. The killer seems to have left the signs in order to take credit for the murders. Does any of this make sense to you?"

"I'm afraid not," the rabbi said. "As you know, Rabbi Zalich and I support the Zionist movement. We make it a point to know about all its militant backers, including some that advocate vio-lence. Mind you, we don't endorse them, but we know who they are. This is completely new to me."

"We just came from talking to Rabbi Zalich," Tony said, "and he's never heard of this group either."

"So, Rabbi Seifert," Jacob said, "Rachel and I both wanted to talk with you about an idea we had regarding this." He turned to Tony. "And you too," he said.

"It took us a long time to get David back to sleep the other night," Rachel said, "so we made a pot of coffee and talked about the signs."

"Remember, Tony, when you first told us about it, we said we don't know anybody who would consider Grynszpan a hero," Jacob said.

"But what if the killer wasn't Jewish at all?" Rachel added. "What if he's somebody who wants the public to *think* that Jews are responsible?"

"The reason we thought of this," Jacob said, "is because the Communist Party's trying to outdo everybody else in being patriotic, right? And they're criticizing anybody who's not one hundred percent in favor of the war. So, if the Communist Party thought that Brown and Haber opposed the US fighting on the side of Russia, then they might consider them traitors to the Allies, right?"

Rabbi Seifert frowned. "This reminds me of how the Nazis tried to blame the Reichstag fire on the communists. That seems like just yesterday to me."

"Of course," Tony said, his eyes lighting up, "they executed that Dutch man. They said he was a communist, but I remember there was a lot of talk about how the Nazis themselves may have started the fire in order to give Hitler an excuse to grab his special powers! In the case of Brown and Haber, it might be the communists trying to blame an imaginary Jewish organization."

"We'll probably never know the truth about the Reichstag fire," the rabbi said, "but there've always been 'false flag' operations in wartime."

"I think we need to tell Ruthie about this," Rachel said. "She knows more communists than anybody else." She gave Jacob a smile and said, "Except for you, of course."

She stood up. "Come on, Jacob. We have to walk over to *Oma's* house and collect David."

"Thanks for inviting me to join you here, Rabbi," Tony said. "I sometimes think we Catholics and Jews ought to know each other better. I'm glad to meet you."

Seifert smiled. "The pleasure is all mine, Commissioner. You should join us at a service some Saturday."

Tony laughed. "I'm not sure my archbishop would allow me to do that, but we'll see."

## TUESDAY, MAY 12, 1942

# The Cliff House, Ocean Beach

## 2:00 P.M.

Dr. Albert Smith was eating red snapper with grilled potatoes at his favorite table by the window at the Cliff House. Monsignor Peter Fuchs, who had invited him to lunch, had ordered the abalone steak with scalloped potatoes. They shared a loaf of sourdough bread and were enjoying their second bottle of Wente Pinot Chardonnay. They could see the shiny black wet creatures cavorting on the famous Seal Rocks below. Two shades of blue met where the sky and the ocean came together on the horizon. Not even a single cloud could be seen.

"This is one of my favorite places," said Albert, "but even out here by the ocean there are more new faces than old regular customers."

"It's even worse downtown," the monsignor replied. "Everywhere you go, hordes of Negroes are strutting about."

Albert nodded. "They're blighting the city with their bad habits, boisterous behavior, and degenerate jazz music."

The monsignor made a disgusted grimace. "The Negroes probably didn't know how to read the ads the Chamber of Commerce placed in newspapers all over the country, 'Don't Come to San Francisco Now.'" They both laughed.

Albert was surprised when Fuchs blurted out, "You look at least ten years younger with your new haircut. Did you decide to show your solidarity with the troops, is that it?"

"It's just a haircut," Albert replied, sharply. "It means nothing." He was surprised at such an inappropriate remark from

Fuchs. They had known each other more than ten years, first at meetings of the Friends of the New Germany, then at summer camps, rallies and shooting competitions of the German Bund, and most recently at the goodbye party at the Whittier Mansion hosted by the consulate after President Roosevelt ordered all German diplomats to leave the country. *Maybe*, he thought, *the man is showing his age – forgetting his manners like this.*

"So, Monsignor, you telephoned me that you wanted to meet, that you had something to tell me in person."

"Indeed," Fuchs said. "Besides, I've always enjoyed discussing world events with you and I know you like seafood and good California wine."

"So what is it you wanted to talk about? I don't have anything to do with our former colleagues from the Bund days."

"I don't either," Fuchs said, being equally disingenuous. "The archbishop has prohibited us from making statements that could be considered even remotely sympathetic to the German side in the war. He was pleased when Archbishop Mooney in Detroit ordered Father Coughlin to discontinue all his America First and anti-Semitic political activities last week."

"I know, but that's not surprising, is it?" Albert asked.

"No, I suppose not. What's surprising is how the archbishop seems to be going out of his way to be sympathetic to the Jews – saying on the radio that it's unfair for them to have to suffer. Now he's assigning several priests to work with the refugees who have come here to live. And now Father Oppenheimer is cooperating in some murder investigation led by a Jewish FBI agent. I thought I'd better tell you about this."

"What is the name of this agent?" Albert asked. "Who was murdered? How is the Church here in the city cooperating in the investigation of this murder?"

"I don't know the name of the agent, and I don't know who was murdered," Fuchs said. "I overheard some talk about all of this but I didn't get all the information. I do know for certain that Father Oppenheimer told the Jew agent he would help him by sharing the Church's information about German organizations. I was always opposed to Oppenheimer collecting this kind of information, but it's outrageous that the Church should be helping the FBI in a Jewish project."

"We both know how devious they are," Albert said, "so this doesn't surprise me either. At least the Zionists are unpopular with the Jews here in San Francisco, where they brag about being One Hundred Percent American. And the archbishop hasn't let up on his crusade against the communists, has he?"

"No sir! But like everybody else he can't say much against Russia now because we're allied with them."

"Well, thank you for telling me about this, even though now that I'm just a private citizen, I don't have anything to do with public life. But it's pleasant to see you and enjoy lunch with you in this nice restaurant. Let's get some coffee. Then I must be on my way."

### TUESDAY, MAY 12, 1942

## St. Francis Wood and the Mission District

### 3:00 P.M.

*I should have already taken care of this*, Albert thought to himself, as he drove up Sloat Boulevard from the Ocean Beach to his home in the St. Francis Wood neighborhood. The house on San Anselmo Avenue was much too big for one person, but he kept it after his wife died over ten years ago. Having his medical office attached to the house was convenient. His well-to-do obstetrics and gynecology patients liked the privacy. They could park in front of the office at the end of the long winding driveway, where the mature eucalyptus and oak trees shielded them from the view of anyone going by on the street and the sidewalk. Albert's occasional trips to a Pacific Heights establishment provided him the necessary female company. A housekeeper came once a week to clean and dust. A gardener kept the lawn and the grounds trimmed and watered.

He parked his Packard in the two car garage, went into the house and changed into dungarees, an army style slipover sweater, a leather jacket, and work boots. He slipped his Colt 1911 pistol into his jacket pocket before returning to the garage. He took a canvas tarp and a large leather duffel bag out of one of the lockers that lined the wall and loaded them into the bed of his five-year-old Chevrolet pickup. He added a coil of rope and a tool box, checking to see if the short wrecking bar was in its place, at the bottom. The lock pick set was on the removable top shelf. He put it into his other jacket pocket.

*Tuesday happens to be a good day for this*, he thought, knowing that his sister Hannelore did her weekly shopping at the Crystal Palace Market in the late afternoon. Rain or shine. Year in and year out. His sister modeled commendable German appreciation for *Ordnung*.

He could do what he needed to do in less than an hour, so he would be gone well before Hannelore returned. He needn't worry about Kurt being at home.

Traffic was light, both uphill on Portola to Twin Peaks and downhill on Market Street all the way to the Cassel house. He found a parking place in front.

Albert deliberately allowed the pickup to stay dirty. He never fixed the nicks and dents. That way it would never stand out. He left the tarp and the rope in the bed of the truck. With the lock pick set he had the door unlocked in under three minutes. He picked up the duffel bag and toolbox and went inside.

There was no foyer or entry hall. He locked the door and entered the living room, carrying his things down the hallway. He passed a bedroom and a bathroom on the left and a kitchen on the right before reaching the back bedroom, where he knew Kurt Cassel kept his desk.

He unzipped the bag, opened the door to the coat closet, and went inside. He came out with two Lee-Enfield rifles and a Springfield M1903 which he put in the extra-large duffel bag. Two more trips into the closet yielded a half dozen hand guns and ten boxes of ammunition. He filled the duffel bag and zipped it.

According to his wristwatch, he'd been in the house for twelve minutes, so he was right on time.

He opened Kurt's briefcase, which was on the floor next to the desk, and started emptying the contents of the drawers into it. *I'll simply take everything,* he thought. *That way nothing will remain that contains a reference to our activities in the Bund.* He frowned, thinking about the accident. He wouldn't miss Kurt that much, but his death meant he could no longer assist in the work of the organization.

Just then he heard the unmistakable sound of a door closing. Footsteps followed, going from the front door down the hallway and into the kitchen. Hannelore was putting the bags of groceries on the kitchen table.

When he heard her coming down the hallway, he realized he'd turned on the bedroom light. She must have seen the light. There was no time to gather his things and leave by the back door.

"Albert!" she said, walking into Kurt's office. "What are you doing here? How did you get in the house?" Albert saw her looking at the open briefcase and the papers on the top of the desk.

"Don't get upset," Albert said. "Let's go into the living room and I'll explain. Why don't you make us some coffee?"

"Why are you going through Kurt's things? Don't get upset? I'm already upset – he left early to go with you on Sunday and he never came home. What's going on, Albert?" she said, walking into the kitchen. She brewed them a pot of coffee and poured two cups. They took the coffee into the living room and sat down on the sofa.

"I have some very bad news, Hannelore," Albert said. "You need to be brave now. I'm counting on you not to get hysterical. Kurt is dead. He had too much to drink and fell off the boat."

She sat, seemingly immobilized, as the color drained from her face. She took a drink and set the cup and saucer on the coffee table. Albert saw her eyes turn stony as she turned and stared at him. "This is *your* doing, isn't it? What *really* happened? Where is he, really?"

Albert finished his coffee and set the cup aside. He stood up, folded his arms over his chest and gave her a stern look. "I'll explain it all, but you must remain calm. It won't do you any good to become emotional."

Hannelore sprang up from the sofa and stood in front of Albert. Her fists were clenched and her face was turning red. "I told Kurt a long time ago not to get involved in your projects," she shouted. "He would never listen to me. Now you say he's dead? I don't trust you or anything you say!"

Albert unfolded his arms and reached out to embrace his sister. She drew back as if she was afraid of him, but then she raised her right hand and slapped him, hard, across the face.

"Stop this!" Albert said forcefully. She drew back her hand to slap him again. Albert pushed her away, harder than he meant to. Her head hit the edge of the brick hearth in front of the fireplace.

She moaned, started to get up, and then fell to the floor.

"Hannelore, I'm sorry," Albert said. He walked over to her and bent down. There was a deep gash on the right side of her head. "Hannelore?" he cried, but there was no response. The wound was bleeding heavily and she was unconscious. Her pulse was weak. *This may well be a fatal hemorrhage in the brain*, he thought. Albert told himself to ignore a wave of nausea. He had to move forward and adapt to the new situation.

He washed the coffee pot and cups and put them away after wiping them dry. He left the grocery bags on the kitchen table, then finished emptying the desk. He went into the bedroom and pulled out the dresser drawers throwing the contents on the bed. He put Hannelore's best jewelry and Kurt's gold pocket watch in his pockets. He went through the kitchen cupboard where Kurt kept emergency spending money and put the money in his pocket, dropping the money tin on the floor.

He returned to the living room. Hannelore had not moved. There was no pulse at all now. Albert got the briefcase and tool-box, took them out the back door and put them on the porch. He made a second trip with the duffel bag. After he carried every-thing to the back door of the garage he opened his toolbox, took out the wrecking bar and pried off the padlock hasp. He found the box of dynamite under a dirty painter's drop cloth.

He carried everything to his truck, covered the load with the tarp, tied it down and checked his watch. He hadn't anticipated the trouble with his sister, but the entire job had taken only thirty minutes.

## TUESDAY, MAY 12, 1942

## India Basin near Hunters Point

## 3:00 P.M.

The Pacific wind blew the sweet sickly smell from the slaughter houses in an easterly direction, over the placid waters of India Basin. Jerry Fogarty didn't love the smell, but he was used to it. Besides, he'd smelled worse in France back in 1918.

Jerry was born in the Mission and schooled at St. James. When the war came, he fought with the 77th Infantry Division in the Meuse-Argonne Offensive. When he returned home, he married his high school girlfriend at St. Teresa of Avila. After experiencing the horrors of his "Lost Battalion" days, living in Dogpatch with his wife and children and walking back and forth from his tidy house to his job at Bethlehem Steel always seemed to him like a full-time vacation. Now that his beloved Vivian was gone and buried in Holy Cross, he lived for his four grandchildren and fishing on the bay.

He rowed his homemade twelve-foot boat far enough from shore to cast out to the deeper waters. Fourteen large gray-painted seagoing navy and civilian ships anchored further out. Maybe today he'd get lucky and land a striped bass.

He shipped the oars and reached for the two-pound concrete-filled Hills Brothers Coffee can in the bow. He tossed the homemade anchor into the bay, grabbed his fishing pole and baited his hooks with fish heads from yesterday's catch. After he cast his line out, he sat down and lit his pipe.

He got several good bites but failed to hook whatever it was, so he reeled in his line to see if he needed fresh bait. About halfway through, he felt a strong drag. He knew it wasn't a bite – he didn't register a hit, just weight.

Figuring he'd snagged something, he shook his fishing pole up and down and sideways, hoping to throw off whatever it was. That didn't work, so he kept reeling in. It was heavy and he was getting tired.

After a few minutes, he saw something large, just below the surface of the bay. He kept reeling in until he realized it was a man's body, floating face down, dressed in what looked like a brown suit.

Dead bodies didn't bother him, not after the Argonne forest. Sometimes those memories came back so vividly it felt like yesterday. He put his fishing pole down and started pulling the body toward the boat hand over hand on the fishing line. When he got it close enough, he used his gaff to pull it to the side. He secured the gaff to the boat then reached over and uncoiled the rope he kept on the boat, making a large loop at the end. He worked the loop around the dead man's head and tightened it. Allowing about fifteen feet of slack, he tied the rope securely to the seat in the stern before unhooking the gaff and putting it back in its place. He pulled up the anchor and slowly rowed to the boat landing, where he used the telephone booth to call the police.

**TUESDAY, MAY 12, 1942**

## Bayview District Police Station,
## Newcomb and Newhall Streets, 4:00 P.M.

"What should I do with this guy?" asked Sergeant Mathew Kincaid. He held his hand over the telephone's mouthpiece and looked at Lieutenant Tom Johnson.

"He went fishing and hooked himself a floater. Should I tell him to call the Fire Department, or the Hall of Justice?"

"Where was he fishing?" asked Johnson. "Here, give me the phone." He walked over to Kincaid's desk and took the phone from him. "Hello, sir, I understand you hooked a body, not a fish."

"Yeah, hello," the man answered. "I snagged the guy and towed him in to where I keep my boat. You know, the Portuguese guys' little boat yard over here. I guess I should stay with him until you come pick him up, right?"

"So who am I talking to?"

"I'm Jerry Fogarty. I fish out in India Basin. Can you send a wagon over here and pick this guy up? I have to get home and make dinner for one of my granddaughters."

"Okay, Jerry, sit tight, we'll get on this right away. Where exactly is this John Doe right now?"

"He's tied up to my boat, and the boat is in its usual place next to the pier. I can see it from here. Don't worry, he's not going anywhere. How soon can you be here? And who am *I* talking to?"

"Jerry, this is Lieutenant Tom Johnson. I can't tell you for sure how long it will take. I've gotta check to see who gets to pick up this guy, us or the G-men. If you pulled him out of the bay, the FBI or the navy might want to horn in on this job. You know, because of the war and the navy's in charge of Hunters Point now."

"Look, Lieutenant, I been in a war, but I've got a daughter who will be bringing my granddaughter over at five o'clock. The kid will mutiny if she doesn't get dinner at 5:30. How about you just pick him up now – your place is only a ten-minute ride from here – and then you and the other guys can fight over who gets him later?"

"Ah, Jerry, so you're a veteran. God bless you. I can tell you're also pretty 'battle hardened' with the mothers and the daughters. God love you, my boy. We'll send our Black Maria over there right now, that there's a grand idea."

**TUESDAY, MAY 12, 1942**

## The Weiss Home, Webster Street,
## Fillmore District, 8:00 P.M.

"I don't often eat a sandwich," Tony Bosco said, "or pastrami for that matter. But I don't mind saying that this pastrami on Jewish rye bread is delicious!"

"Langendorf makes the best bread in the Fillmore," Rachel said. "I really missed it when I went to London. I couldn't believe how terrible the bread was in England."

Jacob nodded. "I agree," he said. "They can't have eaten that back in the olden days or they could never have built an empire."

Rachel joined them at the dining room table. "David's gone to sleep but he was kind of excited. He's not used to having the attention of so many people. It took me forty-five minutes to calm him down."

"I may be even more excited than your boy," Dennis said. "The material Ruthie and I found in Father Oppenheimer's files shines a whole new light on this case. He let us borrow a whole bunch of clippings from newspaper stories, too.

"Look at this," Dennis said, laying out three pages of notes and a clipping on the table from folders he and Ruthie had marked "Charles Brown" and "Father Fritz Haber."

"According to this clipping from the *San Francisco News*, Charles Brown came to San Francisco in 1935 and established his Hatzfeld Enterprises. He imported all kinds of German products for restaurants and homes, seemingly specializing in those hand-made beer steins with lids and little figurines of people from German folktales and history."

"That must have been a prosperous business," Tony said, "I'm sure there are almost as many Germans around here as there are Irish! I know they outnumber the Italians."

"Well," Ruthie said, "the clipping is from an interview with Brown that the paper published after he became an American citizen, just over a year ago. It says that he was born Karl Braun in a town called Hatzfeld, which is the name of his company. It quotes him as saying he joined the America First Committee for two reasons: he opposes America going to war again, and he loves the United States *and* Germany."

"So in other words," Rachel said, "he was trying to be loyal to his original country and he thought if he supported the America First Committee and it was successful, the United States wouldn't have to fight Germany. His native home would be safe from us."

"Well, that was not so unreasonable in early 1941," Tony said. "That was before Germany declared war on us. A person could be born in Germany, be an American citizen, and love his native homeland as well as his new country. The same goes for Father Haber. Now everything is different for people like them and me.

"I was born in Italy and have great affection for the land, the people and the culture. But I'm 100% American in my loyalty as a citizen. I would never consider turning my back on my new country in favor of Italy."

"That whole question of being loyal to America and loving your homeland – that's not a problem for Jews here," Jacob said. "Rabbi Seifert is a Zionist, and Rabbi Hirsch at Temple Emanu-El opposes Zionism. But they agree that American Jews should be one hundred percent loyal to America."

"Let's get back to Brown and Haber," Tony said. "What could be the significance of the 'traitor' signs? That they were traitors to

Germany because they became American citizens? Or traitors to the United States because they were involved in America First, like Brown or Italian classes, like Father Haber?"

Jacob shook his head. "Father Oppenheimer told us that Brown and Haber were both active in the Friends of the New Germany and the Bund. The Nazi government directly supported those American organizations. So it doesn't seem reasonable that anybody in Germany would have considered them disloyal, does it?"

Rachel chimed in, "I agree. Isn't it more likely that it was the communists who killed them wanting to make a point about patriotism?"

"That would seem reasonable, but Ruthie and I have already talked to all of our Communist Party contacts," Jacob said. "They all agree that they never thought Charles Brown or Father Haber were important enough to even pay much attention to, let alone kill."

"And what I have to show you changes things completely about Brown," Dennis said. He showed them a handwritten letter. "Father Oppenheimer told me and Ruthie that Brown gave this letter to him because he was Brown's confessor. Brown didn't want to just tell this story in the confessional, though. He wanted his relatives in Germany to know the truth if anything ever happened to him."

He read the letter.

*To whom it may concern:*

*I am guilty of having helped my government in Germany expel the Waxman, Jelinek, Sandel, and Meinberger families from their homes and businesses in Hatzfeld, and the confiscation of their property, wealth and assets, in my capacity as Kreisleiter in July, 1934. I was told they were all sent by train to Berlin, to be resettled in Pomerania. Only later did I discover that they were instead put into a concentration camp in Dachau. I am profoundly sorry that I cooperated in this. I believe the Jews will need to learn to serve Germany in new ways in the New Order. But I do not believe they deserve to be slaves in factories or labor camps, or be killed just because they are Jews. That is a profoundly un-Christian act. When I learned the truth, I tried to make amends. I helped four other Jewish families obtain the necessary documents to leave Germany and find new homes in France and Holland. I then left my relatives and came to the United States. I shall continue to support the New Germany, hoping that the Führer will cancel all programs that involve camps and slavery for Jews or other inferior peoples. I realize that the German government may want to punish me for helping Jewish families keep their wealth from the Reich and leave Germany. I am sorry if any of my relatives will suffer on my account.*

*Charles Brown (Karl Braun)*

No one at the table spoke after Dennis put the page down. Tony looked at his hands. Jacob took Rachel's hands in his and they sat like that for what felt like a very long time. Dennis's face was red.

"So, Charles Brown helped some Jews escape," Rachel finally said.

"After seeing this," Jacob said, "we have to go back to Father Oppenheimer's files and start running down everything we can find about Father Haber and the other people on his lists."

"Including everybody who attended that going away party at the Consulate last June," Tony added.

"Pretty much anybody who was a high muck-a-muck in any pro-Nazi or pro-Fascist activities," Ruthie said.

Jacob looked at each of them for a moment. "We also need to find out how my name got into Brown's diary."

**WEDNESDAY, MAY 13, 1942**

## The Bosco Home, Filbert Street

## Pacific Heights, San Francisco, 9:00 A.M.

"That must be Dennis Sullivan. He's picking me up this morning," Tony shouted to his wife. She was on the utility porch and he was in the breakfast nook having his second cappuccino.

He opened the front door and was surprised to see an emaciated-looking five-and-a-half-foot-tall man in a faded gray suit that had seen considerable wear. His gray hair was thinning and his pale white face was marred by the redness of his nose and cheeks, signs of a habitual drinker.

"Mr. Bosco? Mr. Anthony Bosco?" he asked.

"Yes, I'm Tony Bosco. Can I help you?"

"Yes, sir," the man said, pulling an envelope out of his inside pocket. "This is for you, sir."

Tony reached out and took the envelope without thinking. "You have been served," the man said, with a smile.

Tony just stood there, envelope in hand, watching him turn on his heel and walk to the sidewalk without saying goodbye.

"Is Dennis here?" Flora asked from the porch.

"Nobody's here," Tony replied, opening the envelope and reading the document inside. "That was a man serving me with a subpoena. It looks like I've been summoned to testify to the Tenney Committee of the state legislature in two weeks. They're going to have public hearings about Fascism and Communism, what they're calling 'Un-American Activities.'"

Flora walked into the living room with a shocked expression. He handed her the summons. "Why do they want you to do this?" she asked. "Do you have to go to Sacramento?"

"They'll probably call Angelo, and the publishers of our Catholic Italian language newspapers. I'm a logical person for them to call – former police commissioner, draft board president, and president of the Italian Chamber of Commerce. It says that the hearings will be here, at the St. Francis Hotel."

"But surely no one would imagine that Mayor Angelo Rossi has anything to do with 'Un-American Activities'!" Flora said. "That's laughable! He's the most patriotic person I know. He actually overdoes it, I think."

"That's for sure," Tony said. "I've criticized him for years for going along with those 'Get the Communists out of San Francisco' vigilantes."

"Does Eddie Sarno have anything to do with this?" Flora asked.

"That wouldn't surprise me at all. And even if he doesn't have a connection to Jack Tenney's committee, they could have read *La Voce del Popolo*. It's full of attacks on me, calling me an evil puppet dancing to the tune of the even more evil Fascist pope."

"I've heard that Eddie Sarno attended a seminary in Naples but dropped out when he failed his courses. He's hated the Catholic Church ever since."

"Well, I don't know about that kind of gossip," Tony said. "What I do know is that this is probably just the beginning of a battle to protect my reputation and our good name."

**WEDNESDAY, MAY 13, 1942**

## The Mayor's Office

## San Francisco City Hall, 10:30 A.M.

Jacob Weiss thought that Angelo Rossi personified a type: the man of the world who spares no expense to own and enjoy the best things in life. Pink-cheeked and smiling, rotund and robust-looking, a carnation in his buttonhole, Rossi shook the hands of Jacob, Tony, Dennis, Ruthie, and Chief of Police Gerald O'Reilly in turn, inviting them to sit in the chairs arrayed in front of his carved teak desk.

"Chief, it's good to see you again," Rossi said. "With you over at the Hall of Justice and me in City Hall, we don't see as much of each other as we should. Tony, thanks for getting us together. Dennis and Ruthie, I've heard good things about your work and I'm glad to meet you in person."

"Angelo, thanks for seeing us on short notice," Tony said. "Chief, I appreciate your dropping what you were doing and coming over here. I'll make this short and sweet because we are all busy." He turned to Dennis, Ruthie and the chief.

"This morning the mayor and I were subpoenaed to testify before Jack Tenney's California state Un-American Activities Committee two weeks from now. We discussed this on the phone and we decided that it would be best if I quietly dropped into the background in the Brown and Haber investigations. Jacob and the FBI have already agreed to take overall responsibility, so my dropping out shouldn't harm the investigations."

The chief looked worried. "Tony, I don't mean any disrespect, but I've been having second thoughts about the FBI overseeing these killings. Everybody knows they leak like a sieve!"

"Chief," Jacob said, "the FBI has an excellent record of keeping secret investigations secret. I assure you that my assuming overall responsibility for this case won't in any way jeopardize our mutual interest in keeping it undercover."

"Tony," the chief said, "have you and Dennis and Ruthie all agreed about you 'dropping into the background' as you call it?"

The mayor leaned back in his leather armchair as though he were enjoying the latest play at the Curran Theater.

"Yes," Tony answered. "I'm going to spend the next two weeks getting all my files in order. I don't know exactly what Tenney will ask me – actually his attorney will do the questioning – but I want to review all the records of my Italian government and cultural work and that's time-consuming. I can't do it if I'm spending full time taking care of this Charles Brown case."

"Plus," Rossi said, looking at the chief, "you know that Tony is my personal attorney. That means he has to help me prepare for my testimony by helping me review all of the records that relate to Italian government activities and Italian activities here in the city."

"And," Jacob said, "it's a complicated case. We've already made good progress but we're going to have to put in the hours next week in order to track down the leads we've developed so far."

"The three of us have already gotten to know each other and we're working well together," Ruthie added.

"And Tony promises to be available by phone anytime of the day or night if we need his advice," Dennis said, "so it's not like we're starting all over."

"All right, all right," Gerald O'Reilly said, putting his hat on.

"I'm outnumbered here, and besides I get the feeling if I don't agree, you're just going to order me to go along, aren't you, Angelo?"

The mayor burst out with a musical laugh from deep in his belly. "Ah, Chief, you don't disappoint me." He got up from his chair. "All right you all," he said. "Get out of here and go to work."

**WEDNESDAY, MAY 13, 1942**

# Federal Bureau of Investigation Office
# 111 Sutter Street, 11:00 A.M.

Jacob introduced Ned Piper to Dennis and Ruthie and explained that they would need access to his office and files during the investigation. "Where's Bosco?" Piper asked. "I thought he was going to be working with you."

"He is, but he's been pulled away for some other pressing business," Jacob answered. "Speaking of which, I'm hoping that Noreen can organize all of this material in my files." He handed Piper a stack of folders, each thick with typewritten and handwritten pages and newspaper clippings.

"You know Noreen," Piper said, "she's never heard of a job too big. By the way," he turned to Dennis and Ruthie, "I'll have her make up IDs for you two and keys for the office so you can come and go after hours if you need to get access to the files. This is pretty darn irregular, but we're at war, right?"

As they were talking outside Piper's office, Angus Ferguson approached with a suspicious look. Piper called him over and introduced Dennis and Ruthie. "And where is the famous Commissioner Bosco?" Ferguson asked. "I presume you've seen that he's become a celebrity now. His name is in the headlines of the *Chronicle* and the *Examiner* – 'Anthony Bosco named as leading Fascist on the Pacific Coast.'"

"You know damned well those Republican papers are gloating about Bosco and Mayor Rossi getting called before the anti-subversive committee," Piper said. "Republican papers love anything that throws a bad light on our mayor."

"Jack Tenney and his boys have been going up and down the state looking for ways to capitalize on everybody's anxiety," Dennis said. "Tony Bosco's no more a Fascist than Franklin Roosevelt."

Ferguson had been eyeing Ruthie, but she'd been ignoring him. Now, giving a look of unalloyed innocence, she turned and said, "Why, Agent Ferguson, I would have imagined that the FBI prided itself on making judgments based on evidence. How is it that you seem to be trafficking in gossip and innuendo?"

"Well, young lady," Fergusson replied, his face a mask of outraged righteousness, "perhaps I know some things that are beyond your ken. And I don't need any girl fascist sympathizers in *my* office!"

"Okay, Fergus," Piper said, his voice icy, "first of all, apologize to Miss Fuller for that ungentlemanly remark. Second, as far as I recall, this is *my* office, not yours, and I'll thank you to keep that in mind in the future!"

Ferguson, red faced and sullen, stammered out an apology and stepped back.

Jacob noticed that Dennis Sullivan had been working hard to keep from making a remark. His normally placid, friendly features had hardened. Before Dennis confronted Ferguson, which Jacob figured he was about to do, Jacob said, "Dennis, Ruthie and I have to be somewhere at noon, so we'd better be on our way. Thanks for everything, Ned." He put his arm around Dennis, who was about the same height and build, and headed with him to the front door.

"Jacob, do you trust that guy?" Ruthie asked. "I get a funny feeling about him."

"I've always thought he was harmless," Jacob answered, "but

now that you mention it he's always been way too interested in what I'm doing."

"I get the same feeling as Ruthie," Dennis said. "If I were you I'd be careful to keep our work far away from him."

**WEDNESDAY, MAY 13, 1942**

## Schroeder's Café, Front Street
## Financial District, 12:00 P.M.

Jacob tried to hurry, to be on time, but he found it difficult to walk quickly. Men in suits and women in skirts and jackets had spilled out onto the sidewalks of Sutter, Market, and Front Streets, joined by men in uniform, excited to be out of doors and freed from their typewriters, adding machines, and telephones. Their voices accented the rumble of cars and the blasts of horns.

Dennis kept up as Jacob threaded his way to Schroeder's Cafe. Ruthie was not far behind. "Slow down, you apes," she yelled out, her voice getting lost in the hubbub. Jacob looked back and saw her laughing, so he laughed as well and kept up his pace.

He opened the door to the venerable café and held it until Ruthie caught up. They made their way to Henry Schroeder, the manager, who stood at a podium located where the long bar ended and the restaurant section began.

"Ah, Mr. Weiss," Schroeder said, in his sharp-edged Berliner accent, "it's good to see you again. Your guests have already arrived. Come with me."

They walked to the rear of the large dining area to the back wall, which was lined with booths. All but one of the booths were occupied, their diners enjoying the privacy afforded by heavy burgundy-colored drapes. In the booth with open drapes, two men were sitting across from each other, watching them approach.

Schroeder bowed and left them. Ruthie and Dennis sat down next to the two men. Jacob pulled over a bentwood chair, placed it at the head of the table, pulled the drapes closed and sat down.

"Dennis and Ruthie, meet James Maguire and Mario Duranti. This is Dennis Sullivan and Ruthie Fuller." They reached across the table and shook hands.

"James and Mario, I'm hoping you will be willing to help us with a difficult investigation of two murders. I'll pay you the usual consulting fee as private investigators. I need a promise that you'll tell no one about the cases."

"Of course," Maguire said in an evident Irish accent. "I'm always glad to work with you." His accent fit naturally with his pale complexion, square jaw, high cheekbones, blue eyes, and thick black hair. Maguire was in his forties – a big man, noticeable even when he was sitting down. Not too many other men's hands fit perfectly with Jacob's in a handshake.

"The same here, Jacob," Mario Duranti echoed. "I'm with you." It was clear he was learning English, not a native speaker. He was about five foot four, wiry and strong looking, with excitable black eyes, black hair and an olive complexion. "You know I never give up a secret," Duranti continued, "and money, it's not a question. You people," he looked at Dennis and Ruthie, "maybe you are born American, then you are lucky people. Me, I'm lucky to be now a citizen. Many of my people, back in Italy, not so lucky. Anything you want, Jacob, I'm helping."

"Let me explain," Jacob said, looking at Dennis and Ruthie. "Mario got on Mussolini's black list, but his movie star cousin convinced her boyfriend to let him leave Italy. The boyfriend happens to be a pal of the *Duce*."

"Huh," Ruthie said, "Everybody should be so lucky!"

"I depend on Mario to be my eyes and ears in North Beach, keeping me in the know about actual fascist sympathizers. That's how I know that the charges against Tony and the mayor are politically motivated baloney."

"Me, I have friends – communists, socialists, anarchists – you know, they want cut the Church down to size," Mario said. "Say Rossi and Bosco, good Catholics, just fascists in disguise, but is not true."

"Eddie Sarno came to me hoping I'd pay him for peddling this stuff," Jacob said, "I kicked him out of my office."

"Giacobbe," Mario said, "about my cousin's boyfriend – big Fascist bastard is what he is. But my cousin Doris, she's a good talker and she told Mussolini, 'Hey, is better Mario's in America, not here to make trouble!' So," he spread his arms like an actor receiving applause, "here I am."

"James, Mario, and I hit it off," Jacob said, "because we all actually enjoy going behind enemy lines."

"How so?" Dennis asked.

Ruthie blurted out, "He's talking about how he was spying on the extremist Arab nationalists for the Special Night Squad, right, Jacob?"

"You said it." Jacob turned to Maguire as though he was about to ask him about his own story for the benefit of Dennis and Ruthie.

"And I suppose you want to know about me," Maguire said. "Well then, what you need to know," he smiled, looked at Dennis and winked, "is that I fought with Michael Collins in the Easter Rising in '16. But after that IRA bastard killed Michael in '22 for making peace, I gave up on the IRA. The thing is, see, I left them far behind. If they want to kill each other, I say, let them go ahead. But now they're hooking up with Hitler against England and bringing their bloody-minded business here. Well, sure and they'll have to deal with James Maguire. They *think* I'm one of them, see, and by the saints I'm a patriot, sure. But I'm not one of *them* anymore and never will be."

The waiter had arrived just before Maguire finished talking. He waited patiently, pad and pencil in hand, like a member of the congregation during a sermon. After he took their orders, Jacob explained the case and told Maguire and Duranti what he wanted them to do as part of the team.

The waiter returned with their lunches. They enjoyed the generous servings of Sauerbraten, Weiner schnitzel, and roast duck, followed by apple strudel and coffee.

"It's been great to meet you guys," Ruthie said, smiling at Duranti and Maguire. "But Jacob," now she laughed out loud, "don't you think we ought to stop eating in German restaurants for the duration?"

**WEDNESDAY, MAY 13, 1942**

## Saint Boniface German Catholic Church
## Golden Gate Avenue, 1:00 P.M.

"What's so important that we have to meet here?" Dr. Albert Smith asked Monsignor Peter Fuchs. "We just had lunch yesterday."

They were sitting in the last pew in back. The church was dark except for low wattage lights in the chapels and the votive candle on the altar. An old woman wearing a thick gray coat despite the mild weather was kneeling and praying at the rack of candles in front of the altar rail. Two men in uniform were sitting together about halfway to the front of the church on the other side of the aisle. An old man was lying down in one of the pews, sound asleep.

"Never mind that, Doctor," Fuchs replied. "This can't wait. Besides, I don't trust the mail. You shouldn't either. You know as well as I do that everything has changed since the *Reich* declared war on the United States."

"I don't need a priest to tell me how things have changed," Albert said. "And I don't have a lot of time. Coming down here now is a nuisance. The Tenderloin has gotten crowded with all the servicemen and war workers, and there are parking meters everywhere. The worst thing is all the Negroes walking around acting like they own the place."

"I'll get right to the point, then," Fuchs said. "Remember, the last time we met, I told you Father Oppenheimer was working with an FBI agent on a murder case. I found out the identities of the victims: it was Charles Brown and Father Fritz Haber. I also found out that the FBI agent's name is Jacob Weiss."

"What? How do you know about this?" Albert said. "I haven't seen anything in the newspapers."

The priest frowned. "We made an agreement back in '36 that I would keep you informed of developments in the Chancery Office. You agreed that you would never ask me to reveal my sources. Maybe the war's changed a lot of things, but it's not going to change how we work together."

"Yes, Father, I know. Forgive me. It's a shocking development."

"It certainly is," Fuchs said, "and so is the other thing I have to tell you. Apparently Chief O'Reilly has decided to have Commissioner Tony Bosco investigate the murders. The shocking part is that Bosco has agreed to work with that Jew in the local FBI office."

Albert paused a minute. "That's damned outrageous, Father, pardon my language. It's bad enough that an Italian would be investigating the murder of good Germans, but a Jew? Shocking is an understatement."

Fuchs stood up, and said, "That's what I had to report. I can't imagine who would have disliked him, or Haber for that matter, to the point of killing them, but I thought you would want to know."

They both started moving to the end of the pew and into the aisle. "It certainly is a troubling development," Albert said. "Thank you for informing me. But in the future please just send me any new information by mail. Use the code I taught you. You still have the code book, don't you?"

"Yes, of course."

The men genuflected, dipped their fingers into the holy water font and made the sign of the cross. They walked together through the swinging doors into the vestibule and then down the stairs, where they parted ways, disappearing into the crowds walking up and down Golden Gate Avenue.

•

Albert walked to his Packard, which he'd parked on McAllister Street across from the City Hall in the zone reserved for members of city commissions. He unlocked the car, sat down, took his war bond commission placard off the dashboard and placed it on the seat next to him.

*The good monsignor is right,* he thought to himself, *the Reich's declaration of war makes everything different. Things have to change.*

Instead of driving straight home, he drove west on McAllister Street past the junk dealers and Jewish bakeries, to Baker Street. He shook his head in disgust at the Negro children playing in the schoolyard of Fremont School. He turned left on Baker and drove to the entrance of the block-wide "Panhandle" of Golden Gate Park, before parking in front of the hospital for employees of the Southern Pacific Railroad.

He took a notepad out of his glove compartment, opened to a blank page and wrote a note with the Parker fountain pen he carried in his suit pocket. He folded the note in half and then half again before placing it into his suit pocket, along with a piece of chalk from the glove compartment. He closed the glove box, got out of the car and locked it.

At this time of day, with school in session and during the week, the Panhandle was deserted. He walked past the thirty-five-foot-high monument honoring the assassinated President McKinley to a grove of tall eucalyptus trees. He went to the fifth tree on the right, reached down to a hollow place among the roots, and slipped the note deep into the opening. Afterwards, he covered the area with eucalyptus leaves and walked back across the street, making a small chalk mark on the fire hydrant at the corner of Baker and Fell. He returned to his car and drove back to his house in St. Francis Wood.

**WEDNESDAY, MAY 13, 1942**

## Federal Bureau of Investigation Office
## 111 Sutter Street, Room 1729, 6:00 P.M.

Wearing her coat, Noreen Scanlon walked into Jacob's office, where he and the two detectives were still busy filling out the index cards with personal information from the files she had organized for them. She was getting ready to take the K streetcar back to Ingleside Terrace, where she lived with her parents. She was still single, just past her thirtieth birthday.

"Jacob, I'm leaving for the day. Is there anything else you need before I go home?"

"Noreen, you're a life saver," Jacob said. "No, we're fine here. Thanks for starting on this while we were at lunch. We'll be able to finish today."

"It just seemed logical," Noreen said. "I remember when you first joined us and you told us about the Director's special personal file of 'dangerous characters.' You were so proud that Mr. Hoover had shown you his secret file. You said you wanted a San Francisco version. Do you remember?"

"Sure," Jacob said. "It seems like just the other day, doesn't it? Anyway, we're almost finished here."

"Fergus, Ned and the typists are already gone," Noreen said, "so you can just lock up when you leave."

Ruthie stood up and stretched. "I don't usually sit down for almost three hours at a time like this. I can't say it's my cup of tea."

"Same here," Dennis said, taking a cue from Ruthie. They had been working at the table at the other end from Jacob's desk.

Oak-fronted file drawers with labels sat on the table and the desk.

Jacob looked up. "Law enforcement is about ninety percent paperwork and ten percent field work."

"By the way," Dennis said, "I see some of the city's leading Catholic businessmen, doctors and dentists in these files of the America First Committee and the German Bund. I'm not surprised that Charles Brown is here, but there are also files for Dr. Albert Smith, Father Haber, Monsignor Fuchs, and Kurt Cassel. Cassel is the city's chief electrical inspector."

"Oppenheimer told me that Cassel is married to Smith's sister," Jacob said. "And I met Monsignor Fuchs when I met with Oppenheimer at the archbishop's mansion the other day."

Jacob picked out one of the cards from the drawer labeled German Bund.

"Here is the card for Monsignor Peter Fuchs. Along with his address and telephone number, here's all the information about his German Bund work – when he joined, what duties he had. And at the bottom you can see he also was a member of America First and that he subscribed to Father Coughlin's magazine *Social Justice*."

Dennis stretched again and sat down. "Let's get this finished, shall we? Jacob, you probably need to get home, and Ruthie and I have a reservation for dinner at Henry's Fashion down on Market at 7:30."

**THURSDAY, MAY 14, 1942**

Lincoln Park Golf Course, near Hole 17

34<sup>th</sup> Avenue, 6:30 A.M. – 10:30 A.M.

*This has got to be my most scenic assignment so far*, thought Francis "Dutch" O'Malley. A wiry man in his forties, with light blue eyes and dirty blond hair, he was the proud son of Irish parents, but he'd always looked so German he'd answered to the nickname "Dutch" since he was a boy. The other jobs he'd done for Mr. Morley had gone well, without complications. Except for the last one, the priest. Francis had told himself that killing Monsignor Haber was a good deed because the priest supported the Nazi-lover Father Coughlin. But now he couldn't shake the awful sense that he'd stepped over some line he shouldn't have crossed. He had trouble sleeping, and the few times he did, he dreamt of his late mother. What would she have thought of him? Had he condemned himself to an eternity in hell, without the hope of ever being reunited with her?

At least Morley paid well. All Francis had to do was check the drop in the Panhandle just after dark every day. It was only a couple of blocks from his house. If he got a note, he called a number, let it ring three times and hung up. He called a second time and let it ring six times. The third time he called, he let it ring once. Then, Morley answered and gave him instructions. When the job was done, someone deposited his fee into his account at the Divisadero-Hayes branch of the Bank of America. Usually he had a day or so to plan the job, but Morley was in a hurry this time, so he had to get up early and drive out to Sea Cliff. He arrived before dawn.

Francis wore his favorite Irish tweed cap and a windbreaker jacket. He parked on 32<sup>nd</sup> Avenue, next to the golf course, took a golf bag and a knapsack out of his trunk, and walked up the road that bordered the golf course. He'd played the course with his uncle Joe many times.

He walked to a spot about three hundred yards from the 17th hole where he knew a grove of pine trees clustered together that would give him good cover and good visibility. He selected a tree, took the pole-climbing gear he got from his cousin in the Pacific Gas and Electric Company out of the knapsack and used it to get up to where the branches were thick. He used the rope he'd attached to pull the golf bag up and settled in to wait.

Mr. Morley said the subject played every Thursday and was part of the first group of players on the course. He would be the only golfer in his group of three who had pure white hair and never wore a hat.

Francis checked the sights on his Springfield M1903 rifle several times as the fog started to lift and the wind lessened. A trio of golfers made their way to the tee off for the 17th hole. Through his scope he had no trouble identifying the subject.

The men seemed to be discussing who would tee off first. Finally, a man in a red sweater and a matching tam o' shanter led off. Then, a second man, in a tan golf jacket and an Irish flat cap, followed. The second man teed off, with the white-haired man standing by himself to the right of the tee off spot. He was dressed in gray trousers, a white shirt, and a navy-blue cardigan sweater. Francis lined up the man's head in his sights and squeezed the trigger. The subject jerked backwards, dropped his golf club, and fell to the ground.

Francis put on the knapsack, put the rifle into the golf bag, lowered it to the ground, and then shinnied down the tree using the climbing gear. He exited Lincoln Park, returned to his car, stowed the golf bag and the knapsack, and drove away.

**THURSDAY, MAY 14, 1942**

## Federal Bureau of Investigation Office
## 111 Sutter Street, 9:30 A.M.

Dennis and Ruthie walked into the office together, but Jacob resisted making a comment. Rachel had told him, once again this morning over breakfast, that she refused to pry into Ruthie's and Dennis's "situation" – as she called it. She had told Jacob to mind his own business.

He held up the first section of the *San Francisco Chronicle* and said, "Look at this." A bold headline ran across the top of the page: "CITY ELECTRICAL INSPECTOR DROWNS" and below that in smaller letters "Body of Kurt Cassel discovered in the bay near Hunters Point."

"We... I mean I, haven't read the paper yet," Dennis said. Jacob noticed with amusement that the man was actually blushing.

He took the paper from Jacob. "It says here that his death is at this point considered an accident. Police are asking anyone with knowledge of Mr. Cassel's activities in the last week to come forward."

Ruthie took the newspaper from Dennis to read it herself.

"I was planning to go to the morgue to talk with the pathologist about Father Haber's body," Jacob said. "Now we have two bodies to deal with. Both of them were Bund members, right? We need an autopsy to make sure there wasn't any foul play in Kurt Cassel's death."

**THURSDAY, MAY 14, 1942**

# City Morgue, County Hospital
# Potrero Avenue & 22<sup>nd</sup> Street, 10:00 A.M.

"Welcome to my little kingdom," Martin Stanford said, extending his hand. They shook hands and Jacob asked the city's chief pathologist if he was related to "the railroad guy."

The doctor laughed. He was shorter than Jacob and much wider. He had a large head, bald on top, with a carefully trimmed fringe around the sides like the monks Jacob remembered from the pictures in his Austrian schoolbooks. Stanford wore a bow tie. You could tell from the lines on his face that he laughed a lot.

"Come with me," he said, motioning for Jacob, Dennis and Ruthie to follow. He turned and walked away from the door into a room that smelled of disinfectant. "As far as I know, my people did nothing with railroads except ride them from New Haven to Boston and back. Much to my shame, but alas not theirs, their fortune came from buying and selling Africans, not from building the Central Pacific Railroad. From what I've heard about them, they'd probably still be trading in human cargo today if the world hadn't abolished slavery."

"Except for everywhere that Hitler has taken over," Jacob said flatly.

"I'm afraid I haven't a clever reply to that, my boy," Stanford said. "My two sons are somewhere out there right now in harm's way doing their best to help bring a quick and hopefully painful end to Hitler."

He stopped next to a zinc-topped table. "*This* man, Cassel, died when the waters of the San Francisco Bay filled up his lungs.

It's hard to live when that happens."

"Is there any evidence of anything that contributed to his death? Any wounds at all, bruises, cuts – anything?" Ruthie asked.

"No, nothing like that." He pulled back the rubber sheet so they could see the body. No bruises were visible.

"Well, there is something," Stanford said, "but there's no way of knowing whether or how it might have contributed to his death."

"And what is that?" Dennis asked.

"His blood alcohol level," Stanford answered. "It was about 0.10%. He was a big man, but still that's a high score. He may well have been feeling the effects of drunkenness. He may have simply slipped and fallen off a boat. If he did fall, he apparently didn't hit himself anywhere on the way down. We don't even know if he knew how to swim, but he was wearing a full suit of clothes and that, plus being drunk, would have hampered even just staying afloat."

Jacob asked Stanford if he had contacted the man's wife, or family.

"That's the business of the detective in charge," the pathologist replied. He looked at Dennis. "Detective Sullivan, you can check with your colleague Melvyn Andersen at the Hall of Justice. He has the man's belongings as well, including his wallet and keys."

"What about Father Haber?" Jacob asked.

"I can show you the body if you wish," Stanford said. "He was shot in the head at close range with a .45 caliber hollow point bullet."

"We don't need to see the body," Jacob said. He was feeling unsettled. He'd had to look at several dozen bodies since he saw his parents and sister laid out in the Jerusalem morgue. But it still bothered him. He decided to keep his feelings to himself.

Stanford ushered them out of the morgue and they took a cab to the Hall of Justice. They walked upstairs to the third floor detectives' offices. Andersen, a slight man who also wore eyeglasses, had gone through the police academy in the same class as Dennis. They greeted each other like old comrades, and Andersen said, "Hi, Ruthie, how ya doin these days?" Dennis introduced Jacob.

"Mel, you know that Ruthie and I are doing some special work for the chief. Now we've got the FBI working with us, too. The chief wants us to take over the Kurt Cassel case. He's a person of interest in our investigation and we need everything we can get to help us. Did you contact Cassel's wife or family?"

"I was going to break the bad news this morning," Andersen said, "but do you want to do it? That's a job I hate. I'm happy to pass it off."

"We can take care of it," Dennis said. "Can you get us his belongings?'

"Sure, Dennis, sit tight and I'll be right back." They sat down on the chairs next to Andersen's desk. He came back ten minutes later with a canvas bag. "All his stuff is in here – his clothes, shoes, his wallet, keys, some money. We didn't dry it all out thoroughly, you know the drill, so it's probably still damp. Take this with you if you want."

He looked at Jacob. "So you guys are working with the FBI? I haven't seen you around here much," he turned to Dennis, "not since, what, around Easter?"

"Yeah, well, you know, it's wartime now. And you know the saying, 'Loose lips sink ships.' See you around, Mel."

**THURSDAY, MAY 14, 1942**

# Federal Bureau of Investigation Office
## 111 Sutter Street, 11:30 A.M.

Eddie Sarno was standing with his hands in his pockets in front of Noreen's desk when Jacob, Dennis, and Ruthie walked back into the office.

He flashed a transparently insincere smile at Jacob, revealing a row of crooked yellowed teeth. "*Dottore*! It seems we are meeting again."

"Hello, Sarno," Jacob said. "Did you think of something after we visited you at home?"

"I do have something new for you about that murder you came to see me about. Please don't come to my house again, but call me. I'll tell you." He handed Jacob a business card.

"Today, I'm meeting Agent Ferguson," Sarno said.

"Dennis!" Ruthie said, "This is the guy I told you about. He's the person who insulted me and Tony last month, when we were investigating the murder of Harlan Winthrop."

"The famous *La Voce del Popolo* editor," Dennis said. "Goes around making insinuations and then hides behind his Commie friends instead of facing the consequences like a man!"

Ruthie put her hand on Dennis's arm. "He's harmless, Dennis," she said. "Don't let him ruffle your feathers."

"You're right." He turned to Sarno. "Why are you here?" he asked.

"And what have we here, a convention?" the voice of Angus

Ferguson boomed out as he walked up to the four of them.

"*Dottore*," Sarno said to Ferguson, "I'm happy to come here to tell you my information." He walked past Jacob, Ruthie and Dennis.

"Come with me, Mr. Sarno," Ferguson said and they both walked into his office. As Sarno passed Dennis, he said out of the side of his mouth, "So she dropped old *Signor* Bosco and now she's got a big young stallion?"

Ruthie rolled her eyes. Dennis got red in the face. Jacob watched them, thinking they were a good looking couple.

He broke the spell when he said, "Come into the office and we'll get Kurt Cassel's address. We know he has a wife. Somebody has to break the news to her and she might be able to help us eliminate him as a person of interest."

"And, Ruthie," he said, smiling, "since you get on so well with Sarno, call him tonight and find out what 'new information' he wants to tell me." He handed her the business card.

**THURSDAY, MAY 14, 1942**

# The Cassel Home, San Carlos Street,
# Mission District, 1:00 P.M.

Jacob rang the doorbell. When no one answered, he rang it again. They waited almost a minute, then Dennis knocked hard.

"Let's go around to the back door," Ruthie said. "She might be in the back of the house." She led the way through the alley between the two houses. When they reached the backyard, they went up the three stairs and Dennis knocked again. Once again, no one answered.

"Maybe she's in the garage," Dennis said. "It looks like the door is unlocked."

They walked over to the garage behind the house. "This door isn't unlocked," Dennis said, "somebody has ripped the hasp off and it's just hanging here." He opened it enough to look inside. "She's not in here," he said, holding the part of the hasp that was hanging off the door. "This is bent. It looks like somebody pried it off with a crowbar or a large screwdriver. Let's knock on the back door again."

"Hey, what the hell youse doing down there?" The loud voice was coming from the house next door. An elderly man in a sleeveless undershirt and suspenders, his jowly face full of white whiskers, was leaning out of a second floor window. "Get da hell outta here or I'll call da cops!"

Dennis pulled out his SFPD badge and flashed it at him. "I'm Detective Sullivan and these are my colleagues Detective Fuller and FBI Agent Weiss. We're looking for Mrs. Cassel. Have you seen her today?"

"Huh," the man grunted, "Youse da cops? Okay, then. I ain't seen Hannelore today or yesterday either. Nice lady. Last I saw her I says hello when she's coming back from the Crystal Palace Market. Every week, same time, you could set your watch on it, she goes back and forth to that market. Me, I'm on my way over to the Eight Ball over on Guerrero. Every day I have me a little walk over there, ya know, around 5:00. Ya know, when the whistle blows. I'm going down my stairs, and she's goin into her house. I ain't seen her since then, Mr. and Mrs. Coppers. Come to think of it, I ain't heard her either. Usually Kurt and her plays them damned German opera records every night after dinner. Loud. I told em, 'ya should turn those damn things off, we're fightin them Krauts again,' but they doesn't seem to give a damn."

"Okay, thanks for your time and the information," Jacob said impatiently. "You can go back inside now."

The man moved back from the open window and closed it. After knocking one more time, Dennis took out his lock pick tool and unlocked the door. He stepped aside and Jacob walked in. "Wait there," Jacob said. He pulled out a handkerchief to cover his nose and mouth and walked further inside. He discovered the body in the living room.

"Stay on the porch," he said sharply. "We've got a dead body, and it's been here a while. You two go find the closest call box and get ahold of the chief. Tell him we have a body. It could be related to our investigation. Tell him to get somebody over here to take the body to the morgue, and do it on the QT – somebody he trusts who will keep this quiet."

"There's a call box on Valencia and 18th," Dennis said. "Are you going to wait here?"

"Yes," Jacob answered. "I don't want Mr. Eight Ball next door getting curious and coming over. I'll wait outside and see you when you get back."

In thirty minutes, Kevin McCarthy and George Bonn from the county hospital parked their ambulance in front of the Cassel house. Dennis had told them they would need to be quick, so he and Jacob met the two white-coated men wearing surgical masks at the front door. McCarthy carried the rolled-up stretcher and looked at Dennis as he walked into the living room. He nodded and said, "We met at Coit Tower, right?"

Dennis nodded back. "Yes, but there's no time for talk here today. We need you in and out quickly."

"It's your show, Detective," McCarthy simply answered. "You can come see this one at the morgue." He and Bonn picked up the body and placed it on the stretcher. Hardly skipping a beat, they picked up the stretcher, took the body to the ambulance and drove away.

Dennis, Ruthie, and Jacob worked quickly. The smell was lingering. "It looks like a cyclone hit this place. Somebody pulled out every drawer in every room of the house," Dennis said. Jacob checked the closet in what must have been Cassel's office. At the back, behind several men's topcoats, he discovered what he thought could be the door of a safe. It was flush with the wall and painted the same color. Unless you knew it was there, you could easily overlook it. The only giveaway was a circle on the left side, less than an inch in diameter, with a place to insert a key in the center.

"Dennis," Jacob called, "bring your lock pick over here."

"If a burglar did all this, he was sloppy, or maybe in too much of a hurry to find the safe," Ruthie said.

"Well, it's pretty well camouflaged," Dennis said. He unlocked it, stood back and the door swung open. He took his pen flashlight out of his jacket pocket and shined it inside. "Very interesting," he said to Jacob and Ruthie, who were standing behind him. "Come take a look."

Jacob traded places with Dennis, who stood to the side while shining the flashlight into the safe. Jacob unfolded his handkerchief, put it over his right hand, and reached inside, taking out two objects, one after the other. He walked over and placed them on the desk: a pistol and a military medal on a ribbon with the black, white, and red colors of the German flag in the Great War. "I think I know what the medal is," Dennis said. "An Iron Cross Second Class. Do you know, Jacob?"

"Yes, that's right," Jacob answered. "Awarded for bravery in the Great War. And what have we here?" He picked up the pistol using the handkerchief. "Here's one of the newest German weapons, a Walther P.38. I wonder how Cassel got hold of a gun they only started producing in large numbers a couple of years ago!"

**THURSDAY, MAY 14, 1942**

# Federal Bureau of Investigation Office
## 111 Sutter Street, 2:30 P.M.

Jacob, Dennis and Ruthie stopped at the office to call Tony Bosco about the latest developments and to update Ned Piper.

Noreen waved several pink memos from a telephone message pad at Jacob as he walked in. She told him that Father Oppenheimer from the Catholic Chancery called twice, saying it was urgent.

Jacob took the memos and walked to his office, joined by Dennis and Ruthie. They had just sat down when Ned Piper stuck his head inside. "Jacob, I need to talk to you," he said. He nodded to Ruthie and Dennis. "You two might as well hear about this too, so come along."

"I have to return an urgent call," Jacob said, holding up the pink memos. "As soon as I'm done, all right?"

Piper nodded and returned to his office.

"You can stay here if you want," Jacob said. "I'll make this quick." He dialed OR 6767 and asked to be connected to Oppenheimer's office.

"Hello, Father, this is Jacob, what's the urgent matter? I have two messages here." He listened, then said, "I'll come to your office. I'll be bringing the two detectives with me, so tell Guido. We'll get a taxi and be there as soon as we can."

He put down the receiver and turned to his colleagues.

"That was Oppenheimer," he said. "Monsignor Peter Fuchs

appears to have been assassinated this morning at the Lincoln Park Golf Course. His body was taken to the morgue, so we have two bodies to examine."

"Good God," Dennis said, "what's going on?"

"But first," Jacob continued, "we have to stop at the Chancery Office. Oppenheimer has something he wants to show us. He thinks it could be related to our investigation."

"I think we should tell Tony about all this stuff," Ruthie said. "I can call him right now. Is that okay, Jacob?"

"Sure, you do that. I'll go tell Ned we have to talk later. Dennis, call us a Yellow Cab?"

"Right away," Dennis answered.

Thursday, May 14, 1942

San Francisco Catholic Archdiocese Office

1100 Franklin Street, 3:15 P.M.

They all got out of the Yellow Cab. Jacob paid the driver and they walked up the stairs into the Chancery Office. Guido Molinari met them inside, flashing a big smile. "Dennis Sullivan!" he said. "My old rival, how ya doin?"

Dennis smiled. "Jacob and Ruthie, this is Guido Molinari. He and I fought it out on the football field many afternoons when he played quarterback for St. James and I quarterbacked for Sacred Heart."

"Hey," Guido said, laughing, "not just afternoons. Don't forget that night we beat you in the semi-finals at Kezar Stadium!"

"Don't remind me," Dennis said. "A field goal in the last minutes. Pure luck!"

"Agent Weiss!" Guido said, giving Jacob a mock but not unfriendly salute, "Father Oppenheimer is waiting for you."

They walked past "the prelates of the past," as Father Oppenheimer called the portraits lining the long hallway, to his office. He greeted them and they sat down.

"So what exactly do you know?" Jacob asked.

"Monsignor Fuchs plays every single Thursday morning with two other golfers. He was waiting to tee off at the 17 thole this morning when somebody shot him dead. A bullet in the head. They went to the office and called the police, who came with an ambulance and took him to the city morgue."

"Did you hear anything about who could have done this?"

Dennis asked.

"No. The police called the archbishop and he came down and told me in person," Oppenheimer answered. "I haven't told the archbishop about your investigation, and I'd like to show you something I just discovered."

Oppenheimer got up and led them to the office next door.

"This is Monsignor Fuchs's office," he explained, motioning them inside.

He stood behind the desk. "When I heard the news, I told the archbishop I would take care of putting the monsignor's things in order, so I got the key to his office and came in here to collect his personal things."

He turned to Dennis and Ruthie. "You all know that I've been working to keep the archbishop informed about anti-Semitic, pro-Nazi and pro-Fascist activities," he said. "And we all know that Monsignor Fuchs was one of the most outspoken supporters of Father Coughlin in the Bay Area."

Oppenheimer picked up a photograph album from the desk, opened it, and pulled out one of the photos. He handed it to Jacob.

"Fuchs wrote at the bottom, at least this looks like his handwriting, 'Clear Lake, August 1938, Bund Brothers' and if you don't recognize these men, I'll tell you who they are."

"That's the monsignor on the right," Ruthie said, "but I don't recognize the others."

"From left to right," Oppenheimer said, "Charles Brown, Dr. Albert Smith, Kurt Cassel, Father Fritz Haber, and Monsignor Peter Fuchs. We know Brown's story, and Haber came from Northern Italy about ten years ago. But he was born and raised in and went to school in Germany. Cassel came here from Germany after the Great War. He was married to Smith's sister."

He handed Jacob another photo. "And one more thing," he added. "This one is labeled, 'The Bund and the FBI' but I don't know the man who is standing with the monsignor."

Jacob took the photo and looked at it with Ruthie and Dennis. "Well, well," he said, "there's my colleague Fergus in a bathing suit with one of the Bund brothers."

**THURSDAY, MAY 14, 1942**

## City Morgue, County Hospital
## Potrero Avenue & 22nd Street, 5:00 P.M.

"My dear," Martin Stanford said, bowing to Ruthie, "we had better stop meeting like this or people will start talking."

"Wow, that's an old one, Doctor," Ruthie said.

"So where's the monsignor's body?" Dennis asked. "Maybe *you're* used to the way this place smells, but the sooner I'm out of here, the better!"

"It's highly unusual for me to see three detectives twice in one day, looking at four different bodies," Stanford answered. "We'd better get started."

He took them over to two of the zinc-topped tables and pulled back the rubber sheet to expose the priest down to the waist. The monsignor, who many had regarded as larger than life because of his overbearing manner, was now diminished and shrunken.

"I won't need to autopsy him. The cause of death is obvious, and the archbishop dislikes having the bodies of his priests disfigured before burial." Stanford picked up a scalpel laying on a nearby shelf and walked to Fuchs's head. "Here is the entry point," he said, placing the blade next to a hole near the top of the forehead. He turned the body over. "You can't see an exit wound. That's because the bullet never left his body."

"It's still inside?" Dennis asked.

"The bullet never left the body at the scene," Stanford clarified. "I extracted it here. It must have been shot from well above him, and the trajectory was downward until it hit his head. It buried itself near his spinal cord just below his neck. He wouldn't have felt a thing."

Stanford walked over to the shelf. With a large tweezers, he picked up the bullet out of a metal dish. "This is a thirty-aught-six," he said. "I saw these in 1918, when I was in France. I was still a medical student when I served as an army doctor in the field. I had to extract the same cartridge from soldiers who accidently shot themselves with their Springfield rifles. One poor devil did it on purpose, hoping to go home wounded. The army would have none of it. They declared him a deserter, and executed him." He shook his head at the memory.

"Whoever put this into Fuchs's head could have shot from a long way off," Jacob said. He told them that the rifle was effective even at five hundred yards. "We used the Lee-Enfield in Palestine, and we used to say it was the best in the world, with an even better range, but we had respect for the Springfield."

"You men and your guns," Ruthie said. "The point, I guess, is that whoever did this was far away, right? That's how they could have gotten away."

"Exactly," Jacob said.

"And here," Stanford said, gesturing at the table to his left, "is, shall we say, our exhibit B." He pulled back the rubber sheet and exposed the head of an older woman, brown hair turning gray, with an ugly gash on her forehead.

"Our Mrs. Cassel here," he said, "died from a massive trauma to her head, as you can see. She could have fallen and hit her head or she could have been hit by something hard. Either way, the impact, and the loss of blood that followed, was fatal."

"Well," Jacob said, "let's leave Dr. Stanford to his work and be on our way. I doubt that Ned Piper is still at the office, but we have even more to tell him now."

"I told Tony I would call him later, because we had to leave the office," Ruthie said. "Let's go back to the office, Jacob. I'll call Tony and Eddie Sarno. We can stop on the way and get a cup of coffee and a sandwich."

"Good idea," Jacob said. "Two of the former Bund brothers appear to have been assassinated. Cassel drowned, and his wife seems to have been killed by a burglar. Maybe it's coincidental but I don't believe in coincidences. As far as we know, Dr. Smith is alive and well but we'd better contact him. His sister and her husband are dead and we need to break the news. If the assassin is targeting former Bund members, Dr. Smith might be in danger."

**FRIDAY, MAY 15, 1942**

## The Smith Home, San Anselmo Avenue,
## St. Francis Wood District, 10:00 A.M.

"This looks like the house in *Gone with the Wind*" Ruthie said as they got out of the car. They had parked in the spacious area between the house and the garages. Jacob rang the bell under the columned portico and the door was opened by a clean-shaven man wearing a gray military style pullover sweater, faded dungarees, and black canvas basketball shoes. He'd slung a towel over his shoulders and his face glistened with perspiration. The man was as tall and muscular as Jacob despite being perhaps twenty years older. His "crew cut" made it hard to tell his age.

"Good morning," Jacob said. "Dr. Smith?"

"Yes, I'm Dr. Smith," said the man, his lively blue eyes quickly taking in Dennis and Ruthie as well. "Excuse my informality, but I've been exercising. What can I do for you?"

Jacob introduced them all and asked if they could come in to chat for a few minutes. "It's about a case we're working on," he said.

"Yes, yes, by all means," Smith said, ushering them into a large entry hall. "Please, come into the living room and be seated." He waved them into a room that Jacob figured was larger than his living and dining rooms combined.

After they sat down, Smith asked them if they'd like coffee. "I've just made a pot and was about to have a cup. I like a good cup of Vienna Roast after my morning workout. You're welcome to join me," he said.

"I'd love a cup," Jacob said. Dennis and Ruthie said they'd enjoy one too. "Do you serve it Vienna style with whipping cream?" Jacob asked. "That's one of the best memories from my childhood."

Jacob noticed that Smith's blue eyes sparkled at his mention of Vienna. "You're a long way from home, too, Agent Weiss. I think I knew some Weisses in Vienna."

"Perhaps," Jacob said, "It's a common name. Actually, I was born here, but I grew up in Vienna. But that was a long time ago."

Smith nodded. "Of course, of course. I'm afraid I have no whipping cream, but I can offer you cream from the best Marin County cows."

They all laughed and Smith went away to get the coffee.

Jacob got up and walked around the room, noting the framed pictures of European scenes: oil paintings of landscapes, watercolors of the bridge over the Neckar River at Heidelberg and the ruins of the castle high above the city. A framed photograph stood on the closed lid of the grand piano. It depicted a younger Dr. Smith in a military uniform alongside his bride.

The doctor returned with a tray and handed them each cups of coffee with cream. "I don't serve sugar," he said, "I don't believe in encouraging unhealthy habits." He took a sip and nodded, as if he approved the flavor.

"I saw you looking at our wedding picture," he said to Jacob. "The world was a very different place when that photo was taken. I don't think of myself as sentimental, but I make an exception for that memento of my marriage to my dearly beloved late wife Marie."

"I'm sorry for your loss, sir," Jacob said. "Do you mind my asking, has she recently passed away?"

"No, no, I don't mind telling you – she died some ten years

ago. She had a terrible case of the Spanish flu while I was serving in France in '18. She recovered but was sickly all her life."

"I'm very sorry, sir," Dennis said. "That must have been difficult for you. Three of my mother's five siblings died during that epidemic."

"The hardest part," Smith said, "was the loss of our little one. I was in France, Marie was sick, and the flu took our infant boy, Hans. But never mind," he seemed to be forcing himself to change the subject, "millions died from that affliction."

"I agree," Jacob said, "but I can't imagine how painful that must have been for you. I suppose Hans would be about my age now." He sighed, then got straight to the point. "Dr. Smith, I'm afraid we have some distressing news. We're here because we are concerned about your well-being."

"That's a rather somber statement," Smith said.

"Can you promise me you'll keep this meeting confidential?"

"Yes, of course, if that's necessary."

Jacob waited a moment. "I'm sorry to inform you that your sister and her husband are dead," he said in a quiet voice.

Smith blanched and put down the coffee cup so hard it rattled against the saucer. "What..." He seemed to be rendered speechless.

"Your sister died in her home. There seems to have been a burglary at her house and she may have been killed when she discovered the thief. She seems to have been hit on the head, though we don't know the details."

Smith was sitting, looking shocked, and saying nothing.

"Her husband drowned in the bay. He was found in India

Basin."

"Do you think there could be any connection between their deaths?" Smith asked, looking at Jacob, his voice shaking.

"I'm sorry, sir," Ruthie said. "And there's more bad news. Your friends Father Haber, Monsignor Fuchs, and Charles Brown are also dead."

Smith had gotten up from the sofa, agitated, and was pacing the room. "This is all such terrible news. I read about the monsignor in the paper," he said, "but Brown? Father Haber? What's going on?"

"Do you know if your sister and the others had enemies? Had any of them mentioned anything to you about being worried for their safety?" Jacob asked.

"No, nothing like that," Smith said.

"We know that you, Brown, and Haber belonged to the Friends of the New Germany and the Bund," Jacob said. "Have you been bothered because of your membership in those groups?"

"No, never," Smith replied. "Many of us who moved to the United States from Germany joined those organizations – social clubs really. My sister, her husband, and I were members. I knew Charles Brown back in the old country. Hannelore, Kurt and I socialized with Father Haber, but I didn't know Monsignor Fuchs well. He enjoyed our activities, especially the music and the dinners. It was all good fun, keeping the old customs alive."

"Lots of Italians who came here joined similar groups," Ruthie said. "But things changed. Now celebrating your old country is getting people into trouble."

"Dr. Smith," Dennis asked, "do you have any enemies at all you can tell us about?"

"Well, Charles and I are on the city's war bonds and waterfront security committees," Smith said. "But I can't imagine anyone would object to our doing our duty."

"What about any former patients who would want to hurt you?" Jacob asked.

"Good heavens, no, Agent Weiss."

Jacob pressed on. "What about those committees? They're only just getting started, right?"

"Yes. Mayor Rossi said he valued our civic work in the German American community. I suppose I'll be the only representative now."

"Dr. Smith," Jacob said, "would you like us to arrange someone to be posted here from the police department?"

"No, that won't be necessary. There are times when we just have to carry on in the fact of danger. Don't you agree?"

"Of course. I learned that when I lived in Vienna and Jerusalem," Jacob said.

Smith nodded, and stayed silent.

Jacob stood up. Dennis and Ruthie responded to his cue. "We won't take any more of your time, Dr. Smith," he said. "We appreciate the excellent coffee."

•

After they left, Albert congratulated himself on maintaining his composure in the face of all of the "bad news" from the detectives. He hadn't expected to be so impressed by Jacob Weiss. He smiled when he thought about how the Jewish FBI agent clearly had no idea that he'd been under observation ever since he arrived in San Francisco.

**FRIDAY, MAY 15, 1942**

# El Portal Café and Cocktail Lounge
## 3200 Fulton Street, 12:00 P.M.

Jacob drove from St. Francis Wood to Nineteenth Avenue, took Nineteenth and crossed Golden Gate Park. Then he drove east on Fulton Street to Eighth Avenue and parked around the corner from the café. They had all skipped breakfast, and the El Portal was on the way to Pacific Heights.

The owner seated them in a booth with a view of the park across the street. The waiter came and they all ordered hamburgers and Cokes.

"Dr. Smith seemed shocked," Jacob said. "If he's in danger we have a duty to protect him. What do you think?" He looked at Ruthie and Dennis.

Ruthie nodded in agreement. She looked Jacob in the eye, "The question is, how would you feel about protecting a Nazi sympathizer?"

"Ruthie, I took an oath to defend the people of this country. My feelings don't enter into it."

"You're downplaying how your feelings could bias you," Dennis said. "But you're savvy enough to handle that. What's more important to me is that it feels like Smith is taking us for fools when he says that the Friends of the New Germany and the Bund were just social clubs."

"Actually, you have a good point," Jacob said. "It's common knowledge that down in LA they were collecting arms and ammunition and explosives. They wanted to do real damage to our military preparedness."

"And what about up here?" Dennis said, "The consulate in Pacific Heights was spying on the military bases and the port here in San Francisco. According to Father Oppenheimer's files, Dr. Smith was a regular visitor to the consulate."

"Yes," Jacob replied, "and Smith was here in San Francisco when the consulate was secretly moving arms and ammunition across the border from Mexico into Arizona, New Mexico, and Texas. That stuff was meant for pro-Nazi saboteurs."

Jacob took a drink of his Coke. "Ned Piper can't prove it, but he believes that the Berkeley woman and her daughter who were murdered in the desert in Texas in 1938 were hostages in a Nazi operation. The woman's husband, who was the head of the Atlas Powder dynamite company, refused to give the saboteurs the dynamite they demanded, so they shot the women in cold blood and left their bodies to rot."

Ruthie perked up. "That was in all the papers. It was a horrible story. I remember that. Hazel Frome and her daughter Nancy. My mom got all my friends and me worried about Nazi kidnappers after that happened."

"Well," Jacob said, "Ruthie, you asked me about my feelings. I think the doctor is downplaying the political side of those German organizations, but I feel sorry for him. He did seem really upset. I'm not ready to put him on an enemies list."

"Speaking of an enemies list," Ruthie started, "I called Eddie Sarno last night. He told me about a woman named Luisa Arzano. She's obsessed with what she calls 'traitors' in San Francisco, and she's going around with a gun in her purse."

"I never heard of her," Jacob said. "Her name's never shown up on any of our 'ABC' lists."

"Eddie said she's kind of gone crazy since her husband got

killed a few weeks ago. He's afraid she's going to shoot somebody."

"Does he think she might have killed Father Haber?" Jacob
asked.

"He didn't say that, no, but he said she called Tony and the
mayor traitors and showed him her gun in a restaurant."

"Let's see if Tony knows her," Jacob said. "We need to make
sure she doesn't hurt anybody, if she hasn't already."

## THURSDAY, MAY 14, 1942

## The Bosco Home, Filbert Street

## Pacific Heights, San Francisco 1:30 P.M.

"That's a beautiful picture, Tony," Ruthie said. She was standing in front of a large, framed painting in the Bosco living room. In the foreground were olive trees, perched on the slopes of a hill. Men, women, and children were picking olives and putting them in baskets. In the background, at the top of the hill, stood a gray stone church topped with a cross.

"That's my hometown, Castelnuovo d'Asti, in the Piedmont region of Italy," Tony said. "A local artist there painted it. I like it because it reminds me of the home I left behind."

"Actually," Flora said, setting down a tray with small espresso cups. "We have three homes now, this one in San Francisco, a little ranch down on the Peninsula, and one close to that church in the picture. The house Tony was born in was passed down to us and his brothers and sisters. Oh dear, that sounds boastful, but I don't mean to brag. A lot of our friends who can afford it like to spend time back home in Italy."

"We can't go there because of the war," Tony explained, "but we used to gather there with relatives almost every summer since the Great War ended. We haven't been back for the last three years."

"Let's hope the Allies defeat the Fascists quickly," Jacob said. "I have friends in Palestine and relatives in Austria, but now I don't know if they're alive or dead."

Flora handed Jacob, Ruthie, and Dennis cups of the strong coffee. Tony took a sip. "Tell me about your visit with Dr. Albert

Smith," he said to Jacob.

"Before we do that," Jacob said, "do you know a woman named Luisa Arzano? Eddie Sarno told us she's possibly dangerous. She's going around calling out you and the mayor by name and she's carrying a loaded gun in her purse. Sarno thinks she's gone crazy."

"So Eddie is cooperating? Saints be praised," Tony said. "Yes, she and her husband are communists. They made speeches against me and the mayor during his last campaign, but I can't imagine her as an assassin."

"Sarno says her husband died and she's lost her mind. We can pick her up today and question her."

Tony nodded. "That's good," he said. "About Smith, you called to tell me he was on the list of people you planned to interview. I certainly know him."

"Why is that?" Dennis asked. "Have you had dealings with him in the past?"

"Yes, I have," Tony answered. "Smith publicly called me and Mayor Rossi 'war mongers' because we campaigned for President Roosevelt two years ago. He donated a lot of money to Thomas Dewey's isolationist campaign before Dewey lost to Wendell Willkie at the Republican Convention."

"But a lot of Republicans here in the Bay Area were critical of Roosevelt's running for a third term," Dennis said.

"It's possible that Smith really does hate war," Ruthie suggested. "He told us he was a soldier in France. Maybe he came here to get away from all that bloody European business."

"We need good solid evidence before we judge somebody a potentially dangerous person," Jacob said, looking at Tony. "Do you have anything for me besides Smith's political preferences? That 'war monger' language was used by all kinds of people, from senators on down."

"You told me you arrived in '39, right, Jacob?" Tony asked. "So you weren't here in May of '38 when the German Bund rented the auditorium in California Hall for a huge rally. People came from all over, a lot of the men wearing their Nazi Bund uniforms, carrying their swastika flags. Smith was one of the organizers."

"I remember that," Ruthie said, "matter of fact, I was there, with my friends Esther, Larry and Barbara! We were outside protesting!" She turned to Tony. "We were mad as hell with your friend Mayor Rossi. He let them meet and even gave a welcome speech."

Tony shook his head. "Yes. That was a big mistake. Not just a mistake – a moral black mark. The archbishop and I urged him to refuse the Bund the right to meet there, but he insisted they had 'freedom of speech.' Then I told him not to appear, but he claimed he had a duty to welcome them."

"I was in Europe," Dennis said. "When I heard that the Bund marched in San Francisco I was ashamed for my city. My friends and relatives didn't join the communists that night, booing the police and making a big fuss outside." He gave Ruthie a look. "But my uncles on the Labor Council voted for the resolution demanding they be barred from meeting in the city."

Ruthie blushed scarlet and her green eyes blazed. "Protesting Nazis is standing up to Fascists, not making a fuss, Dennis," she said forcefully. "We booed the police because they just stood there when the Nazis attacked us outside the auditorium. If you're going to start denying communists freedom of speech, you can find yourself another girlfriend."

Dennis laughed, and Ruthie joined in. She looked around, appeared to realize what she'd said, and got a sheepish look on her face. "Well, it's no secret is it?" She grinned, stood next to Dennis, and put her arm around his waist.

Flora turned to Tony. "Ah, Tony – you were right after all." She clapped her hands. "We need all the love we can get these days. We're happy for you two."

Jacob grinned. "I suspected something, too, but Rachel refused to discuss it. I think it's great, but let's keep focused on business, okay? Can you two separate business and pleasure enough to work effectively on the same team?"

"Sure, boss," Ruthie said.

"It's not an issue, Jacob," Dennis replied.

Jacob turned to Tony. "Ruthie and I have checked with all our informants and haven't found any evidence that communists are behind The Grynszpan Group. But it makes sense that the Communist Party *could* be after Smith because of his previous Bund work. Who *are* these people? At this point we have theories but no evidence.

"We need to know more about Dr. Smith," Jacob said. "And if it's necessary to protect him from a Zionist assassin, we'll have to do that. I'm going to get James Maguire and Mario Duranti to use their contacts to find out more about Smith. And I've already put a twenty-four hour watch on him."

**THURSDAY, MAY 14, 1942**

## The Weiss Home, Webster Street, Fillmore District, 11:00 P.M.

Little David was the first to hear the telephone ring, and his wailing woke up Rachel and Jacob. "That's your special FBI line," Rachel said, rubbing her eyes and getting out of bed to calm the boy.

"I'm sorry," Jacob said. "I wonder who this can be." He walked into the kitchen, where a black telephone was mounted on the wall next to a framed photograph of the Old City in Jerusalem.

"Hello," he said.

"This is Maguire," said the voice on the other end. "Can you meet me at the usual place? I have some important news to report."

"I'll be there in fifteen minutes," Jacob said. He told Rachel he had to go out for a couple of hours. He dressed in dungarees and a work shirt, and slipped his .38 into his waistband. He took his denim jacket from the coatrack by the back door, smoothed his hair back and put on his well-worn white dockworker cap. He kissed Rachel and the toddler goodbye, went out the back door and drove their 1939 Graham Model 97 to 22nd Street. Two young men coming out of Seamus Clooney's saloon whistled as they passed Jacob locking the car. "That's one of those supercharged 'Sharknose' models, right?"

Jacob smiled and nodded as he walked into the saloon. He sat down next to Maguire. Clooney came over and said, "Mr. Weiss. The usual?" Jacob said yes and Clooney brought him a pint of Anchor Steam beer from which Jacob took a small drink. "Well,

James," he said, "this better be important, you woke up the kid."

"I figured you'd want to hear about this since it's already in the paper." Maguire picked up a folded newspaper and handed it to Jacob. "Look just below the fold there, I've already opened it to the second page."

Jacob saw the article describing how Monsignor Peter Fuchs was shot in the head at Lincoln Park that morning. According to the story, the police had no leads.

"I already read the afternoon papers," Jacob said. "Besides, I know about this. I've been to the morgue. Why did you think this was worth waking me up about?"

"I had the idea of checking in with some of my pals, you know, IRA veterans. To see if anybody had heard anything about the Brown, or Haber, or Fuchs murders. I went down to Bill O'Keefe's bar, just a block from my house on Rhode Island Street."

Jacob took a long drink.

"Lots of us boys from the old country, we like Bill's place, see, and he pours Jameson's and the good local beer." Maguire paused to take another drink.

"Every once and a while, mind you, one of the boys from my Dublin days shows up. Tonight, who should it be but Francis O'Malley. Francis, you see, was with us the day they killed our leader Michael Collins, and it quite knocked him sideways. Damaged his mind, it did. He and I left all that behind and came here to San Francisco. But the boy's never been the same since. Some days he's fine, but you can never tell what crazy stuff he'll start doing. One thing for sure, he went all cynical, gave up on everything. He was one of the most devoted republicans, but he said, 'to hell with 'em all.' And since then, he's been making lots of money doing what he does best – 'just taking care of business'

– he calls it, killing for cash, not for Ireland and Irish liberties. And that's God's truth."

"What?" Jacob asked. "You mean he's a hired gun?"

"Exactly what I mean. And listen to this. He's there at Bill's when I come in, and he's in a bad way. I tells Bill right away, this boy's had enough, he has. But Francis slapped the bar and said his money's good and he'd have another whiskey and another pint."

"You have to know, Jacob, that Francis and me, we're like brothers. After his parents died, The Cause gave him a family. And I saved his life once, back there in Dublin.

"Anyway, I says to him, 'Francis, I've never seen you like this, boy, what's going on with you?' He says to me, 'Ah James, what'll I do? I can't eat or sleep. I work for this guy, you know, odd jobs, I calls 'em. There was this one job, a priest. Well, okay I thought, he's a Father Coughlin Nazi lovin fascist, so I took care of him. Afterwards it started to bother me, you know – a man of God. And then I did another job for the same guy. Another priest! He didn't tell me it was a priest. I swear I didn't know, but its right here in the paper! James, this job's done something to me head. How can I have this on me conscience?' Then, Jacob, he shows me this newspaper and there's the story, see?"

"*This* was worth getting up for, James," Jacob said.

"What do you want to do?" Maguire asked. "Are you going to ask me to bring in Francis? In me younger days, I would never be an informer like this, but times has changed."

"We can't just forget we know what he did, when we have it from himself that he shot Fuchs," Jacob said. "But I'm not for taking him off the street right now. I'd rather watch him and see if he can lead us to whoever he's been working for."

"In Dublin," Maguire said, "we used say 'tis better to catch the puppet master than the puppet.' I'll try to get the boy to give up whoever's pulling his strings."

**FRIDAY, MAY 15, 1942**

## Federal Bureau of Investigation Office
## 111 Sutter Street, 9:00 A.M.

Jacob, Ruthie, and Dennis waited for Ned Piper to sit down before they pulled up their own chairs. "What's going on, boss?" Ruthie asked. "Pardon me saying so, but you look like the devil. Did you get any sleep last night?"

"I had too many things on my mind," he answered. "I got up at 4:00 and went to the gym at the YMCA."

"Well, that's two of us who didn't sleep all that well," Jacob said. "What's going on?"

"It's about Tony Bosco," Piper said. "Ferguson went over my head and called the Director yesterday morning after he talked to Eddie Sarno."

Jacob started to reply, but Piper stopped him. "Hold on, it gets worse. The Director called me, mad as hell, and wanted to know how come I've done nothing about a Fascist traitor in the second most important city on the West Coast. Hoover is furious. He called up Walter Winchell and told him that Tony is 'the number one Fascist in California' – yes, those were his words – still in charge of Draft Board 100 and allowed to walk around freely. Winchell's going to do a radio broadcast about Tony."

Jacob shook his head. "Boss, that's straight out of Sarno's attacks on Mayor Rossi and Tony, who Sarno calls 'the brains behind the throne' of City Hall. Sarno's been peddling this stuff in his Italian language paper for over three years. It was old, stale, baloney when I first came to the city. The communist paper publishes the same stuff. Actually, they get it from Sarno. They even had a picture of Sarno on the front page like he's some kind of heroic patriot. I hope you set the Director straight. I can't believe Fergus would have the nerve to go over your head like this."

"Well, he did. He resents you, Jacob. He told me he thinks I've favored you over him ever since you arrived. He even told the Director that you and I are not taking our responsibilities seriously. Hoover ordered me to interview Tony personally and send Washington a full report addressing all the charges against him."

"This is ridiculous," Ruthie said, "Tony's getting treated like he's guilty – without a trial or anything. Jacob, you know the Director! Can't you call him and back up Ned?"

Before Jacob could reply, Piper said, "That's not going to work. Hoover's worried, I could hear it in his voice. If the president hears about this, it could damage the Bureau's claim that it can do a better job keeping us secure than the army. So he's going all out to show he's got the West Coast covered when it comes to possible sabotage and subversion."

"Poor Tony," Dennis said. "I'm beginning to think Eddie Sarno is behind the subpoenas that were sent to him and the mayor."

"I'm sure of it," Piper said. "I'm sure Tony and the mayor are preparing their testimony for the hearings, but I wanted you three to break the news to Tony personally. He has to be ready for the worst, which could be as bad as an order to report to an internment center. Same with the mayor."

"Where is that Ferguson?" Ruthie said, "I want to give him a piece of my mind."

"The one bright spot in all of this," Piper said, "is that Ferguson is gone, at least he's out of my sight. I told the Director that we already knew about all those charges against Rossi and Bosco. That we'd already taken action, contrary to what Fergus said. I got the Director to agree that ignoring the chain of command the way Fergus did is something the Bureau can't tolerate."

"That was good thinking, boss," Jacob said. "The Director is a stickler about respecting the chain of command, from the field offices all the way to what he likes to call 'The Seat of Government' in his personal office."

"Exactly," Piper said. "I formally reprimanded Fergus for insubordination, and sent a telegram to the Director demoting him. The Director signed off on my action and I got a telegram back right away. I'm making Fergus clear out of his office. Starting today, he's working in the storefront we set up down in Monterey. Now he's in charge of the paperwork connected with confiscating the boats of those Italian fishermen who had to be moved to internment camps."

"Well," Dennis said, "he wanted action with the Italians, so now he's got what he wanted. But it's a shame that Tony's going to have to get caught up in all this."

Jacob told Piper, Dennis, and Ruthie about his meeting with James Maguire and about Francis O'Malley taking credit for shooting Monsignor Fuchs.

"O'Malley's working for someone and we need to figure out who hired him," Jacob said. "We know that Cassel, Fuchs, Haber, Brown, and Smith vacationed together at Clear Lake four years ago. Fuchs called them 'Bund Brothers' and kept a photo as a keepsake in his album. He also posed at Clear Lake with Ferguson."

"So there's a Bund connection to the Catholic Church and the FBI," Piper said. "Those men are all dead now except for Fergus and Smith. Fergus can't do anymore harm, but I'm going to put some heat on him now, you can count on it."

"Smith told us he doesn't want any protection," Jacob said, "but I've already arranged for it. Besides, I'd like to know what he's doing."

"What about the communist angle you were going to investigate?" Piper asked. "What have you found out about that?"

"We're not finished checking out the communist shooter theory," Jacob said. "Also, we're not going to arrest O'Malley right away. Maybe he can lead us to whoever paid him to shoot the monsignor."

"And," Ruthie said, "we have a new lead from Eddie Sarno."

**FRIDAY, MAY 15, 1942**

# The Arzano Home and City Jail

## 2200 15th Avenue & Kearny Street, 3:00 P.M.

Luisa Arzano was listening to *One Man's Family* on KPO when the doorbell rang. She put down the glass of sherry. She and George had always enjoyed sherry during their favorite radio drama. When she opened the door, she saw a tall man in a suit, a police officer in a uniform, and Tony Bosco.

Tony showed her his badge. "Mrs. Arzano, we need to speak with you. Can we come in?"

Luisa turned without a word and started down the hallway, heading for a large purse on the stool next to the telephone niche. The officer quickly caught up to her, pushed her up against the wall, pulled her arms back, and snapped handcuffs on her wrists.

"Check the purse, Dennis," Tony said.

Dennis opened the purse and held up a .45 caliber Colt M1911.

"You fascist bastard!" Luisa shouted at Tony. "How dare you come into my house like some Gestapo agent?"

"We have a warrant to search your house," Tony said, "and I'm afraid we're going to have to take you to the Hall of Justice."

They took Arzano to the city jail. While Dennis busied himself calling people Luisa said could confirm her whereabouts over the past week, Jacob questioned her about her .45 and the threats Sarno had told them about. Tony had called Jacob to do the questioning when Luisa said she would not say a word if "the fascist" was in the room.

She claimed she'd learned to shoot at home. When she and her husband George moved into their new Sunset Heights house on Fifteenth and Rivera, the first thing George did was mount a straw-filled target on the back wall of the garage for shooting matches with their two boys. When Luisa complained that she felt left out, George taught her to fire the .22 caliber pellet gun. Before long, she was the best shot in the family.

Two days after the Japanese bombed Pearl Harbor, Luisa and George dressed up and took their sons Philip and Alexander to breakfast at the Cliff House. They'd been among the first to sign up and were leaving for Basic Training.

After breakfast they stopped at the house, the boys loaded their duffel bags into the Ford, and they drove to the Southern Pacific Station, where they said goodbye. She described how she and her husband were both quiet on their drive back home. They changed into everyday clothes and walked two blocks up to the barren hilltop at the end of Rivera Street, where George started teaching her how to use the .45 caliber M1911 pistol he'd brought back from the Great War.

By Easter Sunday, Luisa was out-shooting George once again. As they walked back down the hill after target practice, they admired the panoramic view of the Pacific Ocean glittering all the way to the horizon.

"If the Japs invade us and land down there at Ocean Beach, this .45 won't do us much good," George had said to her.

"Maybe not," she'd replied, "but if they get close enough, I'll sure as hell take one or two of them with me before I go."

The very next week, the war came to her, but not the way she or George could have expected. He was working in the hold of the *J.B. Flood*, a freighter bound for Hawaii docked at Pier

35. A large crate full of truck parts was being lowered into the hold. The hook holding the load broke. The crate fell, landing on George. It broke his neck and severed his spinal cord.

Luisa knew her atheist dockworker husband would have "turned over in his grave" if she acted out the old country Sicilian wailing widow customs. She didn't intend to sit around mourning, wearing ugly black clothes like some old lady in Catania. Since she was a crack shot, and there were fascists in the city government, she wanted to do something to help win the war.

Jacob left the room, and when he came back Tony was with him. Luisa scowled at him. "Luisa," Tony said, "we have somebody out there killing our leading citizens. I sincerely hope it's not you, but we're going to have to keep you here for a while. At least until we find out who's responsible for these murders."

**FRIDAY MAY 15, 1942**

## Francis "Dutch" O'Malley's Cottage
## Baker Street, Panhandle District, 7:00 P.M.

Francis opened the gate from the sidewalk to the cottage he rented at the back of the old lady's lot. The gate was never locked. She liked to go in and out of her house by her back door and often forgot her keys. She seemed to enjoy telling people that the neighborhood was so safe, nobody had to lock their doors anyway.

Francis unfolded the note he'd found in the hollow root of the eucalyptus tree and read the one-line message. He'd already decided what to do, so he walked back into his small brown shingled cottage and dialed a number he knew by heart. After the third set of rings, a voice said, "Mr. Morley."

"I'm outta this business, okay?" Francis said. "Don't leave me any more messages."

There was a pause. Then the stern voice with a strong accent said, "It's not up to you. The arrangement is I give you an order, and you carry it out, yes? You are paid very well, are you not?"

"This isn't about money." Francis said, "I got no complaints. I just decided to get out. This isn't the army, you know."

"We shall not debate what this is, Mr. O'Malley," said the person on the other end. "You don't just decide to retire."

"Listen," Francis retorted, "this is America, see? I'm a free man. I decide on what work I do, understand? I'm not some lifer in your army."

"You're making a big mistake," the voice said. "And you've already wasted too much of my time." The man hung up the phone.

Francis would not be intimidated. He didn't care what happened anymore. Besides, he could take care of himself. He felt hungry, so he slipped his .38 into his waistband and put on his lightweight leather jacket and his Irish tweed cap. The evenings were cool and he would need a jacket when he walked back up McAllister after supper at his favorite diner on Fillmore Street.

**FRIDAY, MAY 15, 1942**

## The Smith Home, San Anselmo Avenue,
## St. Francis Wood District, 7:30 P.M.

Something about Jacob Weiss kept Dr. Albert Smith thinking about his visit. He supposed it was the FBI man's saying that Hans would have been about his age now. He had a nerve to say such a thing.

On second thought, it was perfectly logical. Who wouldn't want such a son? Weiss was obviously healthy, athletic, with a good constitution, a confident manner – obvious good breeding. The man's father would undoubtedly be proud of him. There was absolutely nothing about him that seemed Jewish. In fact, Weiss looked and sounded more Aryan than Joseph Goebbels.

He looked like some of Albert's former comrades in the Freikorps. Like tall, handsome, Otto von Wächter, back in the SA days, when he helped organize the assassination of Dollfuss. Those were glorious days of changing the world by acting on it. Forcefully. Decisively. Ridding the future *Reich* of the likes of Matthias Erzberger, Walter Rathenau, and Engelbert Dollfuss.

He enjoyed recalling when he and his comrades punished the betrayals of such traitors to the *Volk*! He missed those days. He was grateful to Manfred von Killinger, who had helped him flee the authorities. He'd never forget von Killinger saying, "It's better to live to fight another day." But he wished he could have stayed at home and built a career like Manfred. Funny how a Jewish FBI agent reminded him of the good work he had done with Manfred in San Francisco. He laughed to himself recalling how the gullible Americans let them operate a network of agents out of the consulate.

He realized those days were over. Von Wächter and von Killinger were helping to build the New World Order. Governor of Galicia. Ambassador to the new Slovak Republic. Both would soon be free of Jews. Albert didn't believe in self-pity, but he felt stuck out on the edge of nowhere.

He wondered why he couldn't contact Ferguson. He also had to talk to the Irishman who wanted to walk away from his duties with impunity.

He changed into his exercise clothes, put his Colt M1911 in the pocket of his old hiking jacket, and put on a faded brown fedora.

He drove to the Baker Street address that Francis O'Malley had listed on his America First Committee membership application. The address was on a gate next to an old house. Since the gate was unlocked, he just opened it and walked inside. A sidewalk ran alongside the house to a yard and a separate small cottage in the back, with O'Malley's address on the door. The cottage was dark, but he walked to the front door and knocked. No one answered, so he went to the back and knocked on the back door. After waiting ten minutes, Albert decided that, since he didn't know when the Irishman would return, he would visit him another time. Besides, the drive to the Panhandle from St. Francis Wood had relaxed him, and confronting the Irishman in person was beginning to seem like a bad idea.

# Part IV
# Saturday, May 16, 1942

**SATURDAY, MAY 16, 1942**

## The Weiss Home, Webster Street,

## Fillmore District, 8:00 A.M.

Jacob was standing, drinking a cup of coffee, so he answered the telephone on the kitchen wall after the first ring.

"It's Maguire," said the voice on the other end. "Tis early, I know. I don't want to wake yer little one but I just got off my shift at the doctor's house. Mario is on duty now, and I need to sleep, you see. But you need to know this."

"I just got back from my run in Golden Gate Park, and everybody's already up and about," Jacob said. "So what's up, James?"

"I think I earned me money last night, or maybe ye owe me a bonus. I was sitting in my Chevrolet up the hill from the doctor's 'little mansion' eating a sandwich and thinking I'd rather be in my pub. Out goes the doctor in his pickup truck. So I followed him all the way over Twin Peaks until he parked by that old wooden school on McAllister. I didn't park, see, I just waited to see where he'd go. Sure as me mother's name is Kathleen, he walked past the drugstore there on the corner and went in the gate to O'Malley's house. I went to the corner and made me a U-turn in front of that Native Son building, you know, and I took a space right on the corner. So I checked my watch and after about fifteen minutes, the good doctor came out and walked back up the hill to where he parked. I gave him a minute and drove up and watched. He went to Fulton and up to that grand church, there, then took Stanyan and went over the Twin Peaks. I followed him all the way back to his house."

"This is big, James," Jacob said. "I have to ask, of course, are you sure he didn't know you were following? Did you use all the procedures I taught you?"

"Ah, Jacob, course I did. I even drove some of the way with me lights off. Always made sure one or two cars were in between me and his banged up pickup."

"Excellent! Now we have evidence that Smith knows O'Malley. But that doesn't prove Smith hired him to shoot Fuchs."

"Jacob, here's the thing, and then I need some sleep: So one night at O'Keefe's place, we're having a right good time and Francis, he's goin on and on about how he's living the good life, ya know – 'there's the park three blocks away, and I can walk to Mass at St. Agnes in fifteen minutes, and the Lucky Market is right on me corner.' Tis enough to make a man weary, all the braggin and boastin."

"You're rambling on," Jacob said. "Perhaps you *should* get some sleep. How is this important?"

"Ah but, Jacob, Francis said, like he should get a prize, like, 'me bank is right on Divisadero next to me movie house and right across the street, like, is where I get me car serviced.'"

"There's a Bank of America right there, I know it, on the corner near the Harding Theater," Jacob said. "So you're thinking that if it turns out O'Malley has a bank account there, we could find out if he's making suspicious large deposits. If we could prove the money came from Smith, we'd be closer to having proof that Smith is involved in the murders. Maybe I'll be able to get you a bonus for this, man."

"I'll take a bonus if ye offer me one. And anyway, 'twill be a good deed to catch a guy that's goin around payin us to kill our priests. And say a prayer, if that's what ye do in yer synagogue there, for poor Francis, will ye?"

"Right you are. We do say prayers," Jacob said, smiling. "Remember, Jesus was a Jew! Now go get some sleep so you can be ready for your shift after Duranti's done. And thanks for the good work, my friend!"

## SATURDAY, MAY 16, 1942

## Federal Bureau of Investigation Office

## 111 Sutter Street, 9:30 A.M.

Ned Piper was pacing back and forth in front of his desk. It was one of his "thinking out loud" sessions.

"I'll approve your application to get access to Francis O'Malley's Bank of America records, but even if we find large deposits, we can't prove that this Dr. Smith paid O'Malley to shoot Monsignor Fuchs."

"Unless we can prove that the money in O'Malley's bank account came from Dr. Smith," Ruthie said.

Dennis looked skeptical. "Why would he let himself be caught making a payment that would go into a killer's account?"

"He could be so full of himself that it wouldn't occur to him that he had anything to fear from clerks in a bank," Ruthie replied.

"Well," Jacob said, "if we do find big bank deposits, we'll question O'Malley. He's already unraveling and it probably wouldn't take much to get him to confess."

"The problem is," Dennis said, "what if O'Malley doesn't know who paid him? There could be somebody Smith paid who then paid O'Malley."

"Yeah," Ruthie said, "It makes sense that's what he would do. He'd either hire somebody else to hire the killer, or use a false name. He'd never let the actual killer see him or know who he really was."

"That's all true," Jacob said. "But people can get too confident and make stupid mistakes. I learned that back in Palestine when we tracked down one of the masterminds who hired the actual terrorists in Nablus and Jerusalem. When we caught him, he said 'I underestimated you Jews.'"

"Think about Fuchs making those photo albums," Jacob said, "even the smartest people fall victim to hubris. Fuchs must have gotten so full of himself it never occurred to him that he ought to keep those kinds of activities quiet."

"In any case," Piper said, "looking at those bank records is a first step. Noreen can telegraph the request to Washington, and we'll say it's urgent. We should be able to get an approval right away."

### SATURDAY, MAY 16, 1942

# Bank of America, Divisadero–Hayes Branch
## 560 Divisadero Street, 11:00 A.M.

The customers at the tellers' windows turned and looked at them when they walked into the lobby – Jacob and Dennis in their expensive suits and ties and Ruthie in her fashionable downtown attire. The customers were mostly older men in work clothes or housewives in everyday cotton dresses and sweaters or light coats, some with children.

The manager, a middle-aged man in a suit and tie that Jacob figured was from Sears Roebuck, immediately sensed that something was wrong. He stood up at his desk behind a glass partition in the rear of the lobby and walked toward them across the marble floor. "Good morning," he said. "My name is Edward DeMatei. How can the Bank of America be of assistance today?" He offered his hand.

Jacob introduced them all and took out the FBI order authorizing their access to the bank records of Francis Xavier O'Malley. "We would like to examine these records right now, please. Do you have a private room where we can do so?"

"Yes, of course. You can use the room we reserve for our customers to examine their safety deposit boxes. Please come this way." They followed him to a door across from the manager's desk on the other side of the bank. After he unlocked it, they went inside and sat down at the table in the middle of the room.

"We'd also like to interview the bank tellers who have served the owner of this account, Francis O'Malley," Jacob said. "Can you please send them in?"

"I'll be happy to oblige," said DeMatei. "It should not take long. I'll have our head teller, Gertrude Clark, bring the account records to you." He walked out, closed the door and they waited.

After some ten minutes, they heard a knock. "Come in," Jacob said. A middle-aged woman wearing plastic frame eyeglasses with short curly hair and a friendly looking face introduced herself. She was holding a folder. "Who shall I give this to?"

Jacob held out his hand. "Mr. DeMatei told me you wanted to talk to any of us who have served Mr. O'Malley," Clark said. "I have, and you can start with me if you want."

"Well, we wanted to look at the records first, but as long as you're here, can you tell us if anyone in addition to Mr. O'Malley ever deposited or withdrew money from this account?"

"Oh, yes," Clark said, smiling again, "that nice well-dressed gentleman with an accent. I know that because I have to approve all deposits or withdrawals over one hundred dollars. I'd have to look at the records there, but I remember that he made several large deposits to Mr. O'Malley's account."

"Let me see," Jacob said, opening the folder and beginning to page through the transaction forms. Dennis and Ruthie got up and looked over his shoulder. "Here are four deposits of $1,000 each."

"Can you remember anything else about the man who made these deposits?" Dennis asked. "Would he have had to sign a deposit slip?"

"Well," she answered, "I remember that he put cash into the account. He only needed a deposit slip, and since it was cash, my approval was pretty much just a formality, you see."

"Can you remember what he looked like?" Ruthie asked.

The teller looked at Jacob and Dennis. "The last time he came in – just a few days ago, actually – he looked different. He has one of those short haircuts that the boys are getting before they go into the service."

"Do you remember how tall he was, or what color were his eyes, or anything?" Dennis asked.

"Oh, he's a big man, like you two boys," she said. She looked at Jacob and laughed. "He's probably old enough to be your father."

### SATURDAY, MAY 16, 1942

## The Smith Home, San Anselmo Avenue,
## St. Francis Wood District, 11:00 A.M.

Albert finished reading the *S an Francisco C hronicle* over breakfast. He turned on KGO for the morning news broadcast. The local news was interrupted by a breathless announcer's staccato voice: "This just in from the Associated Press. The ten-thousand-ton tanker ship *Virginia* with 180,000 barrels of gasoline on board has been torpedoed and sunk by a German U-boat near the mouth of the Mississippi River. Only thirteen of the twenty-seven crew members survived the attack."

*Well, well,* Albert thought, *this is good news.* He wondered if his cousin Heinrich Schmit had sent this one to the bottom. Heinrich might be hunting in the Gulf of Mexico.

He felt envious. His cousin was able to distinguish himself on the frontlines of the naval war. Albert felt like he was stuck in a backwater. The jobs of sabotage and eliminating traitors and hangers-on of questionable future loyalty were beneath his talents. And now he'd have to improvise in order to adjust to accidents and avoid being exposed by the stupidity of others.

He would miss Charles Brown. It was a shame he had to die, but it was his own damn fault. He'd never understand why Brown told him about rescuing those Jews back home. What an outrageous betrayal of everything they were fighting for. Brown must have realized he'd made himself a traitor to the fatherland.

Kurt Cassel, for all his faults, had done excellent work. He could be annoying, but he couldn't be replaced. Now he'd have to scrap the plans to continue the sabotage work Kurt had carried out for him, from the Bay Area all the way to San Pedro.

Even if his brother-in-law were still here, the declaration of war made everything harder. *The monsignor was right about that*, Albert thought.

The monsignor. Well, he and Father Haber had always been just hangers-on. Fuchs had never done much to help and was starting to make a nuisance of himself. Haber had turned into a sanctimonious holier-than-thou. True, he supported Father Coughlin, but he betrayed the cause when he criticized *Kristallnacht* and wrote those recent columns about the poor, desperate, Jews.

Thinking about Fuchs and Haber reminded Albert that he still needed to do something about Jacob Weiss, the Jewish FBI agent. The police must be keeping Brown's and Haber's murders out of the papers. He'd hoped to cause some disruptive scandal that would discredit both the FBI and the Zionists – what the Americans called a double play.

He kept thinking about his sister. If only she'd stayed calm and listened to him she would never had died. He didn't mean to push her so hard, but after all *she* slapped *him*. The memory of her lying on the floor with a deep gash on her head, blood seeping from the wound, kept coming back. He'd never had trouble sleeping at night before. But it was an accident, and in any case there was nothing to be done about it now.

**SATURDAY, MAY 16, 1942**

## The Smith Home, San Anselmo Avenue, St. Francis Wood District, 12:00 P.M.

*No one will look twice at a middle-aged tourist with a Kodak Retina around his neck getting in and out of his new Packard,* Albert thought to himself. But might they pay attention to a man putting a large Wilson brand duffel bag into his trunk? Unlikely, he decided. Just another visitor to San Francisco rearranging the things in his car.

After his early morning exercise followed by a healthy vegetarian breakfast – a weekly ritual he enjoyed every Friday, in homage to the *Führer* – Albert found himself still thinking about his response to the recent, unexpected events. He didn't regret ordering the death of the monsignor. That was an entirely rational response. But he now realized that it was a good thing the Irishman had not been at home. He would have shown the man his identity if he'd reprimanded him. Wanting to lecture him about duty would have been irrational – an understandable but overemotional reaction to feeling disrespected by an underling.

*Important work remained unfinished,* Albert thought. Cassel's death meant he didn't have the personnel to carry out the explosive work planned before the declaration of war. And there's no way the organization could supply him with money, arms, ammunition, or people to work with him.

He'd need to improvise. Turn a negative into a positive. When he was the young Albert Schmitz, he changed history by punishing traitors to the German people with each pull of the trigger. Now, isolated and on his own, he'd need to use the resources available to weaken the enemy's morale. He'd need to make the

Americans feel that nobody was safe from attack. It could come anytime, anyplace.

He knew where to start, because he'd prepared ahead for such an eventuality. He'd make it necessary for the mayor to convene a meeting of the waterfront security people, and then he'd launch his long-planned *Aktion*, a bold move to instill fear all up and down the West Coast. Every major newspaper in the country would put it on their front page.

Energized by his exercise and breakfast, and recommitted to his duties after his *Selbskritik*, Albert prepared for the day's work. He went to the garage and selected the Lee-Enfield rifle with a 3.5x sniper scope. He oiled it and loaded it in his large duffel bag along with a box of cartridges. The duffel bag went into the trunk of the Packard.

He went back into the house, showered, shaved, and dressed in gray slacks, a sports shirt, and a dark blue windbreaker jacket. He decided to wear a dark blue flat cap made in Italy. Perfect tourist attire.

He picked up his Retina camera, left the house, locked the door, and walked to the garage.

As he drove down the driveway he noticed a car he'd never seen in the neighborhood before: a black Ford, parked on the other side of the street about a block away up the hill.

Instead of heading toward Nineteenth Avenue, he turned right toward the St. Francis Wood Association office. As he passed the Ford and headed the other way, he noticed that the driver seemed surprised.

By the time he was almost two blocks away, Albert saw the Ford making a U-turn to follow him. He accelerated beyond the informal fifteen mph speed limit that residents used, then took a well-practiced, seemingly random trip through the maze of neighborhood streets. After five minutes, he began monitoring his rearview mirror. When another five minutes went by with no cars at all visible behind him, he figured he'd shaken the Ford that might be tailing him. He headed for Playland at the Beach.

## SATURDAY, MAY 16, 1942

# Federal Bureau of Investigation Office
# 111 Sutter Street, 1:30 P.M.

Mario Duranti's long hair was uncombed and flying about as he rushed into Jacob's office. Never a fancy dresser, he was in clothes more suited to warehouse work than sitting at a desk. "The summbitch got away from me, Jacob," he almost shouted. "He's old guy but good driver. I couldn't keep up, my Ford, his Packard." He was waving his hands as he talked. "I got feeling he knew exactly where he's going – and fast, fast! Maybe he practice how to lose somebody."

"Well," Jacob said, "I wouldn't be surprised at all. What time was this, anyway?"

"Between 11:00 and Noon," Duranti answered. "I can't tell you way he was going, I lose him in first five minutes. He could be anywhere now."

"You said he was in a Packard, right? So we need to put out an alert. We can get his license plate number. Dennis, can you do that?"

Dennis nodded. "Right, and we have to just hope he didn't change his license plate after we visited him yesterday."

"Why would he do that?" Ruthie asked. "We just asked him some questions for his own safety."

"There's no telling," Jacob said. "At this point, we can't assume anything. I can't imagine he could just pay somebody four thousand dollars out of his own funds. On the other hand, we know from breaking the New York spy ring that four thousand dollars was just chicken feed for German agents back east."

Ned Piper walked into the office. He looked at each of them. "You have to be very careful here," he said. "Dr. Smith is a prominent citizen and a member of both the Waterfront Security Committee and the War Bonds Committee! You can consider him and O'Malley prime suspects in the Fuchs murder, but you don't have anything linking him to the other murders. Hell, when it comes right down to it, we can't even prove that the money he deposited was for killing the monsignor, can we? So, go get him, and let's question him, but go easy."

**SATURDAY, MAY 16, 1942**

## Sutro Heights, near Point Lobos Avenue
## Above Playland at the Beach, 1:30 P.M.

Only two tourists were strolling on the grounds of the old Adolph Sutro mansion. The city had razed the house and turned the grounds into a park. Atop a hill, overlooking the beachfront amusement park, the place was out of the way, but the views always attracted a few hardy visitors. Today he only saw two, and they were both in uniform.

Albert realized that he disliked having to smile at them. They were, after all, enemy soldiers.

After they left, he waited ten minutes but saw no one else. He walked to the very edge of the cliff. Checking again to make sure no one was watching, he looped the strap of his duffel bag over his head and onto his shoulder, stepped carefully over the barrier, and half walked, half skidded down to several massive boulders. They screened a large bush growing out of the stony cliff.

He lifted the branches and slid into a hiding place designed and built to accommodate a standing person of his height. Once inside, he took off the duffel bag, took out the Lee-Enfield and quickly attached the scope in the dim light allowed by the cover – bush branches carefully tied with wire to a stiff wire mesh that perfectly fit the opening of the hiding place.

The idea for the sniper's nest had come to him one sunny afternoon when he and Manfred von Killinger were hiking along the cliffs at Lands End. They decided to walk to Playland at the Beach to watch the carefree Americans scream on the roller coaster and careen off one another in the bumper cars. They both won first prizes in the shooting gallery and gave the teddy bear and

cherubic doll to children waiting their turns. As they walked up
Point Lobos Avenue and headed back to the Whittier Mansion,
Albert had made von Killinger laugh. "Look there," he pointed
up at the top of the cliff, "A skilled marksman could hardly find a
better place from which to wreak havoc down in the amusement
park."

At that point, the consul general was flush with *Reich* dollars
meant to be spent on projects that would, as they liked to say,
"benefit the future prospects of the *Volk*." Building the sniper's
nest took one man three weeks. He was a fellow Bund member
with experience in mining camps. By day, he was foreman of
the city crew that maintained the Sutro Heights Park. By night,
accompanied by a trusted lookout, he worked for the *Reich*. The
work didn't attract attention because the debris from the exca-
vation was simply added to what came from one of his daytime
projects. He was digging holes to bury the old statues of Greek
gods and goddesses that he was removing from the parapet
above the edge of the cliff. Albert paid him a handsome sum for
his labor, as well as a one-way train ticket to New York City for
himself and his helper. He agreed to submit the names and addresses of his family back in Leipzig, which were checked for
accuracy, then made a solemn promise never to return to San
Francisco. He understood that should he break his promise, his
family would be punished in an appropriate fashion.

Albert had hoped to put the facility to use during an open car
tour of the ocean beach and Lands End area by a high ranking
official. Perhaps even President Roosevelt and his wife. But no
such event had taken place, and today, he thought, the targets
would be ordinary servicemen.

The range was perfect, and the view through his scope was
unobstructed. It would be easy to choose men in uniform. Even
better if they were Jewish men. *Americans are sometimes rather*

*thick*, he thought, *but speeding one or more Jews home to their Hebrew God ought to send a clear message.*

The first subject was a short, stout man in an army uniform. He was definitely Jewish. Albert squeezed the trigger and the man seemed to be driven to the ground by an invisible hammer. The second subject was a tall Marine. Thin and wiry, he looked like he'd been flung backwards by an unseen force. He knocked over a bystander as he fell.

Albert worked quickly. He stowed the rifle and scope in the duffel bag, looked out to make sure no one was observing him and heaved himself up out of the hole.

He replaced the bush cover and sat down on one of the boulders that hid it, snapping some pictures with his camera. To anyone who happened to see him, he was just a tourist enjoying the view of the ocean, the Great Highway alongside the ocean beach, and Playland, with Golden Gate Park in the background.

He timed himself. After ten minutes, he climbed to the top. A man in an army uniform watched him clamber over the low barrier and said, "Wow, did you climb all the way up? You must be in good shape!" His lady friend and another couple looked over, friendly and interested.

"Ha," Smith said, trying to sound like James Cagney in the movies. "Thanks, I does the best I can."

They all laughed. "We heard something that sounded like shots," the other man said. Did you hear anything?"

Albert shrugged. "Maybe a car backfired," he said.

SATURDAY, MAY 16, 1942

## The Mayor's Office
## San Francisco City Hall, 3:00 P.M.

Mayor Rossi took the call from Chief O'Reilly twenty-five minutes after the two servicemen were shot dead outside the Fun House. Military police on patrol had covered the dead men, dispersed the frightened bystanders, called city police, and guarded the scene. Uniformed officers from the Park Station had arrived in ten minutes, loaded the bodies into their patrol wagon, and sped them to the morgue. Chief O'Reilly had heard about the "assassination-style shooting" from the patrolmen at the scene, and he had called him on his direct line.

"I know, I know," the mayor said to O'Reilly, "you want to keep this out of the newspapers. I agree, but with so many people who saw this happen, nobody can guarantee we can keep it quiet."

"We've got to try, anyway," O'Reilly said.

"Of course. I'll call the papers and the radio stations and try to muzzle them when we're done here," the mayor said. "The other thing we need to do is call an emergency meeting of the Waterfront Security Committee. The Ocean Beach area is not technically part of the waterfront, but since we don't have any security committee for the Westside beachfront and Lands End, we need to expand the duties of the existing one."

"We should have done that in December," the chief told him. "I said so at the time but you were against it. What just happened shows that I was right all along."

"Well, that's water under the bridge," Rossi said. "I'll have my secretary contact all the committee members."

"Another thing," O'Reilly said, "we need to have the FBI and the army there. We already have Agent Weiss looking into several suspicious killings – Charles Brown, Monsignor Fuchs, and three others."

"That's a good idea. I'm going to call General DeWitt first. If I know him, he'll want the meeting to be in the Presidio anyway. We can just let him think it was his idea."

"So you'll tell the papers to stop any reporter who wants to do a story about shootings at Playland? And the radio stations?"

"I already told you that," Rossi said. "I'll suggest to DeWitt that the committee members should arrive at the Officers' Club for a meeting at 7:00 P.M."

### SATURDAY, MAY 16, 1942

## The Smith Home, San Anselmo Avenue,
## St. Francis Wood District, 4:00 P.M.

Albert approached his house from the top of San Anselmo Avenue so he could check to see what cars were parked nearby. The Ford was gone, but a black Chevrolet was fifty yards from his driveway. As he passed it he saw a man wearing a fedora sitting in the front seat. He didn't know if the FBI was assigning men to protect him or if he was being considered a suspect. Either way, he decided that he had no reason to be concerned. The trees and long winding driveway shielded his coming and going from prying eyes.

He went inside, put away his things, mixed a martini and turned on KGO to see if there was any news of his work. The afternoon *San Francisco News* had three articles about shootings – in Chinatown, North Beach, and the Fillmore. Nothing surprising there, he thought. Inferior races like the Chinese, the Negroes, and even the Italians, have always killed each other, usually over gambling and women, and they probably always would. He reflected on how the city was changing for the worse with all the Negroes moving into the houses and apartments left behind by the Japanese. But there was nothing in the paper or on the radio about Playland at the Beach.

He got up when the telephone rang. A woman's voice said, "Dr. Smith?"

"Yes, this is Dr. Smith," he answered and the woman said, "please hang on for a moment, this is the mayor's office."

After a few seconds, Albert heard the familiar voice. "Hello, Dr. Smith, it's Angelo Rossi."

"What can I do for you, Your Honor?"

"I'm convening the Waterfront Security Committee for an emergency meeting."

A smile ghosted over Albert's lips. "What happened, Your Honor?" he asked.

"All will be made clear at the meeting. Also, and I know you are a busy man, Doctor, but I need to stress that we need every member of the committee to be there, no exceptions. General De-Witt will be there, as well as a representative of the FBI, and of course Chief O'Reilly will join us. We will meet at 7:00 P.M. sharp in the Officers' Club at the Presidio. Enter through the Lombard Street gate. The sentries will have your name and will provide you with a pass. I must go now and call the other committee members." He ended the call.

•

Albert enjoyed a glass of 1941 Inglenook Cabernet with his grilled steak. He liked the vintage and imagined it would be remembered long after he was gone. He might soon be, as the Americans said, "not long for this world." But if he was success-ful, his work would be remembered. He'd never taken seriously the motto on his old belt buckle, *Gott Mit Uns*, but he smiled to himself, thinking that his plan seemed to be working well.

After dinner, he went to his garage workshop and unlocked the cupboard where he had stored the materials he'd brought from Kurt Cassel's house. He picked out two of the sticks of dy-namite they'd purchased with *Reich* funds from the Atlas Powder Company. He put the dynamite and components into a wooden box that once held apricots from an orchard in the East Bay. He locked the cupboard and took the box to his workbench.

Assembling the bomb was done quickly and from memory.

He'd done it so many times it was almost automatic. The finished product fit comfortably in the false bottom of the large briefcase he would carry into the meeting at the Officers' Club. Since he would be on the list of attendees for the mayor's meeting, he didn't expect the sentries at the gate to inspect his briefcase. Even if they did, he'd explain that doctors always carried a medical emergency kit. They'd find nothing in the briefcase but that kit and the file with minutes of previous meetings of the Waterfront Security Committee.

Albert realized that two sticks of dynamite probably wouldn't kill *everyone*, but that didn't matter. The killing of General De-Witt, Mayor Rossi, and Chief O'Reilly would be in the headlines all over the country.

As he closed the briefcase and put it in the Packard he found himself with an odd and troubling thought. It would be a shame if he killed the young FBI man who was the same age as his Hans would have been. Although he was a Jew, the boy looked and acted Aryan. He dismissed the thought and went into the house to make a telephone call and get dressed for the meeting.

**SATURDAY, MAY 16, 1942**

## The Cisco Hotel, Divisadero Street, Pacific Heights District, 5:45 P.M.

Emma Mosert, the proprietor of one of the city's most exclusive establishments, was on the veranda enjoying the view and savoring her daily martini when the telephone rang. She was wearing a silk kimono with red cranes on a black background. Customers complimented her for being "a young fifty-five."

She had to put down the cocktail and hurry inside to the telephone reserved exclusively for medical calls. "Hello, Dr. Smith, this is a surprise! If I'm not mistaken this is only the second time you've ever called *me.*"

"Yes, yes, I'm sure that's correct, Mrs. Mosert," Smith said, "but I'm in rather a hurry so let's forego the friendly chat, shall we? I have a favor to ask."

"Why certainly, Doctor. After all the good deeds you've done for me and my girls over the years, I'd welcome an opportunity to, shall we say, retaliate." She laughed heartily at her own joke.

"Very funny, Mrs. Mosert, I'm sure. The favor is very simple, just a telephone call. It will probably take no more than five minutes."

**SATURDAY, MAY 16, 1942**

## Foster's Cafeteria

## 555 Sansome Street, 5:30 P.M.

Ruthie sensed that James Maguire and Mario Duranti felt shy in her presence. They had met outside Foster's and now they were standing inside with her and Dennis, waiting to be served. "So how come you guys are not in uniform?" she asked, trying to break the ice and get a word out of the two men.

"Ah, but dear girl, we're 'old men' you see," James replied. "We fall under 'The Old Men's Draft' for guys our age and older."

"Who are you calling old," Mario said with a look of feigned indignation. He laughed and pushed his tray another twelve inches toward the servers.

"So you both registered for the draft just a couple of weeks ago, right?" Dennis asked.

"Sure," Maguire said. "We're ready to do our duty, old men or not. After all, we're both veterans, just not of this here American army. Right, Mario?"

"Yeah, you in Ireland and me in Italy. But I never expected to be deputy sheriff!"

"So you were surprised when Jacob said he wanted the sheriff to deputize you?" Ruthie asked.

"Surprised?" Mario said. "Me, I was, how you say in American language, flabbergasted."

"Same here," James said. "If the chief of police wanted me in the city jail, that wouldn't surprise me, but for the county sheriff to want me to be a deputy, well, that's a good one!"

Ruthie was up to the server and asked for the roast beef and mashed potatoes. Dennis, James and Mario ordered the same. They agreed that Foster's gravy was famous for a reason. They all ordered coffee. Ruthie asked for lemon meringue pie; the men ordered apple pie.

They found a quiet table, sat down and quickly consumed their meals. As they ate dessert, James looked at Dennis and Ruthie. "So what exactly are we supposed to be doing, anyway?" he asked. "Jacob was in a hurry and said you would tell us everything."

"Jacob arranged for you to be sworn in as sheriff's deputies," Dennis said. "You'll now be legally authorized to assist the police department and the FBI. You can back us up in case the prime suspect declines to cooperate."

"So now that Sheriff Monaghan has deputized you," Ruthie said, "you are official representatives of the city and the county of San Francisco. The Presidio is an army base, but the Chief of Police and the Sheriff are allowed to work with the military police if the suspect in a crime goes into the Presidio."

"Okay, that's clear as mud," Maguire said. "I like to keep things simple, see, so how about this: Dennis – and pardon me, Ruthie dear – you're the boss. You lead and we'll follow. Just let us know what you want us to do."

"Yeah, that's good for me, too," Mario said. He patted the left front of his leather jacket and smiled. "We both followed Jacob's orders to bring our old .45s along with our new badges."

They noticed people waiting for an empty place at a table, so they finished their coffee, deposited their utensils and trays, and walked outside.

"I have my car today, so we can walk over to where I parked behind the produce market, get the car and drive to the Presidio," Dennis said.

As they walked, the rail cars that served the piers and warehouses shuttled by on their right while the rocky cliff face of Telegraph Hill loomed over them on their left. Dennis explained how they would operate once the meeting began.

## SATURDAY, MAY 16, 1942

# The Officers' Club, Moraga Avenue
# The Presidio of San Francisco, 6:35 P.M.

Albert handed his California driver's license to the uniformed military police officer on sentry duty at the Lombard Street Gate. The MP looked at the license, bent down to look at Albert's face, then consulted the clipboard in his left hand. He handed the license back and walked to the front of the car, where he wrote down the license plate number. When he came back to the window, he said, "Thank you, sir. Do you need directions?"

Albert replied that he knew the way. He looked at the man's nametag. "Thank you, Lieutenant Beckmann," he said.

"And, sir?" the sentry added, handing Smith a VISITOR placard, "put this on your dashboard. You must use the parking lot directly across from the Officers' Club. You can't park anywhere else."

Albert nodded, put the car in gear, and drove along Presidio Boulevard toward the Officers' Club. His most recent visit was last summer. In the time since, the place had been transformed. He'd never seen it so crowded with vehicles and men in uniform.

He was early enough to find an empty parking space near the exit of the lot. He got out of the car, reached over and picked up the briefcase. He locked the car and walked across the street to the Officers' Club. A Jeep with small MP flags attached to the front fenders was parked in front.

"Good evening, sir," said the MP standing next to a table at the entrance. "I'll need you to open your briefcase for inspection. Place it on the table here."

Albert smiled. "Of course, Lieutenant Carroll." He opened the clasp and spread the two sides until they locked in place.

The MP looked inside, picked up the leather emergency kit, and held it out to Smith. "What's inside this, sir?"

"I'm a doctor. I carry this everywhere. I can unzip it for you if you like."

The lieutenant nodded. Albert opened the bag and placed it on the table. "What is this thing next to the stethoscope and the thermometer?" the lieutenant asked.

"That's called an otoscope, for examining ears and the nasal passages," Albert explained. "I also have bandages, Mercurochrome, and Aspirin there."

When the lieutenant finished paging through the file with minutes from the previous meeting, he put it back in the briefcase. "You can close your briefcase, sir. We're done here, thank you."

Albert thanked him, took the briefcase, and walked into the foyer, toward the Lounge.

He greeted the man in civilian clothes who stood at the podium at the entrance. "I'm Dr. Smith," he said, "I'm on call this evening and might be summoned. What is the number here if the hospital needs to reach me? If so, please send someone inside to let me know."

The manager gave him the number and said, "I'll notify you myself, sir."

Albert went to the telephone booth in the foyer, dialed a number and left a message.

He walked out and back into the Lounge.

"Dr. Smith! It's good to see you, sir."

It was Jake Oster, an older businessman who, Smith recalled, liked to regale him with tedious stories about his German grandparents.

"Mr. Oster," Albert replied, "I'm glad to see you, too. Excuse me a moment. I must use the men's room before the meeting starts. I'll see you afterwards."

Oster smiled. "Of course," he said and walked toward the meeting room. Albert went into the men's room at the far side of the Lounge and entered the first stall. He bent down and saw that neither of the other two stalls were occupied.

He opened the briefcase, put the bag and the file on the toilet seat, and pulled out the cover of the hidden compartment. He carefully took out the bomb, set the timer for 7:30 P.M. and then put it back in its place. Just then, someone entered, so he waited two minutes until he heard the door open and close. He flushed, walked out, washed his hands, and headed for the meeting room.

**SATURDAY, MAY 16, 1942**

# The Officers' Club, Moraga Avenue
# The Presidio of San Francisco, 6:58 P.M.

According to his wristwatch, it was just before 7:00 when he entered the meeting room. Mayor Rossi and Chief O'Reilly were sitting together at a large table that would easily accommodate the eleven members of the Waterfront Security Committee. General DeWitt was sitting next to O'Reilly. There was an empty chair next to the mayor, so Albert walked over, greeted him and took his seat, putting the briefcase on the floor.

He looked around, nodding to Jake Oster and several other businessmen. At the other end, he saw the young detectives who had visited his house, Sullivan and the woman Fuller. He was surprised to see them at the meeting.

Mayor Rossi stood up, and the chatter around the table slowed to a stop. "Good evening, gentlemen," Rossi said, "we're here because we need to consider extending our security to include the Western Lands of our city. You are here to advise me as to the most expeditious way to accomplish this task."

Albert was already finding it hard to listen, but he forced himself to appear interested. After six minutes that seemed like an eternity, he saw the young FBI man Jacob Weiss come in and take a seat to his left next to Jake Oster. Weiss nodded and locked eyes with him for longer than seemed appropriate. For someone so young, the man had an unsettling gaze.

Angus Campbell was making a belabored comment about the artillery emplacements along the cliffs at Ocean Beach when the manager of the Officers' Club walked into the room. He examined the people at the table. When he saw Albert, he walked over to him, bent down, and said, "Doctor, you have had a call. Your patient has gone into labor and you need to come right away."

Mayor Rossi looked alarmed. "Oh, Doctor, please do attend to your patient," he said, "We shall soldier on without you."

*What an idiot*, Albert thought, but he nodded and, in a low voice, said, "Thank you, Your Honor."

He pushed back his chair, stood and followed the manager out of the meeting room into the Lounge.

He walked quickly out the door and onto the sidewalk. He saw two men standing at the end of the sidewalk by the curb. They walked up to him with their guns drawn. They blocked his way, showed their badges, and started searching him.

"Who are you? What in God's name do you think you're doing?" Albert said, looking from one to the other. He checked his watch – it was 7:10.

He heard someone call, "Dr. Smith, you forgot your briefcase!" Albert looked over his shoulder and saw Jake Oster. He was running, with his right arm extended, holding the briefcase. "You forgot your briefcase! The mayor saw it on the floor after you left. Here you go!"

From the corner of his eye, Albert saw Jacob Weiss and the two detectives coming out the door. They brushed past Oster onto the sidewalk. Albert saw the agent take the briefcase out of the businessman's hand. They came toward him.

"Agent Weiss, what is the meaning of this?" he said. "I'm on my way to deliver a baby! Who are these men?"

"Dr. Smith," Weiss said, "we knew you would be at this meeting. We decided to meet you here rather than bother you at home again. If you need to deliver a baby, I'll meet you at the hospital. When you're finished we can sit down over coffee and you and I can get this business out of the way."

"Agent Weiss, there's nothing I'd like more than to chat over coffee again. Please tell these men to put away their pistols and I'll be on my way. You can meet me at St. Mary's Hospital and give me my briefcase then. Just be careful with it. That's a good man."

"Jacob," Maguire said, "look what we found." He held up a .45 and Duranti showed him a .38.

Weiss opened the briefcase, took out the medical kit and folder and dropped them on the ground. He looked at Albert. "Why does it still feel like there's something inside when it's empty?" he asked.

•

For an instant, Jacob's mind threw him back to a dark night in northeastern Galilee. He was riding in a bus packed with Arabs. Dressed as an Arab student, his hair blacked, his face darkened with makeup. His briefcase carried a bomb made of three sticks of dynamite attached to a timer. He got off the bus, did his job, and returned to his quarters. They read about it later in *The Palestine Post*: "Rebel arms cache destroyed by Yishuv patriots."

Jacob handed the briefcase to Dennis and stepped over to Smith. He grabbed him by the lapels and pulled him close. They were face to face. "How much time do we have?" he asked him through clenched teeth.

"Until 7:30," Smith said, grinning. "So you're running out of time, aren't you?"

Jacob threw Smith back to Maguire and Duranti. "Take this Nazi bastard to City Jail for now. Don't let him out of your sight. We want him alive for his trial."

**SATURDAY, MAY 16, 1942**

# The Officers' Club, Moraga Avenue

# The Presidio of San Francisco, 7:15 P.M.

Jacob looked at his watch and grabbed the briefcase out of Dennis's hands. He saw the MP watching them with increasing alarm. "Who has the keys for that Jeep?" Jacob shouted at the MP.

"I have the keys, why?" the man answered.

"Get over here. On the double! I'm FBI. We have to dispose of a bomb."

"Shouldn't we try to defuse it?" Dennis asked.

"That's crazy," Ruthie screamed. "Don't you remember those detectives at the New York World's Fair? They blew themselves to smithereens."

Smith was laughing.

"We don't have time for a discussion," Jacob said. He held out his FBI identification to Lieutenant Carroll and said, "We'll talk later, get your ass behind the wheel, soldier, and get us to the bridge. There's a bomb in here. If we don't get it into the ocean quickly we're both finished."

The MP went white, but he vaulted into the Jeep an instant ahead of Jacob. "Hold on," he said. He started the engine, slammed the Jeep into first gear, and it leaped from the curb onto Moraga Avenue. The MP took the curves so fast the Jeep went up on two wheels. They careened through the Presidio and onto the highway leading to the bridge. When they got to the toll plaza booths, he picked one that was empty and barreled through at top speed as the toll collectors gaped at them.

"Keep going until I tell you to stop," Jacob yelled. About a third of the way across, he spied an empty place down in the straits below. "Stop here," he shouted. As the Jeep screeched to a halt, Jacob jumped out, clambered up to the sidewalk, and yelled at several clusters of people, "Get out of the way!" He ran to the railing and looked below to make sure no shipping was about to sail under them.

The MP was right behind him, motioning with his .45 for people to get back.

Jacob finally threw the briefcase off the bridge and helped the MP keep back the pedestrians. When people stopped walking, wondering what was going on, he and Lieutenant Carroll went to the railing. He checked his watch: 7:29.

Just then, a large waterspout rose out of the Golden Gate straits. The sound of a muffled explosion barely registered, all but muted by the noise of the traffic.

# Part V:
# May 24, 1942

### SUNDAY, MAY 24, 1942

## The Bosco Home, Filbert Street
## Pacific Heights, San Francisco 5:00 P.M.

Rachel and Jacob stood side by side in the Bosco living room looking out the window at the bay and the Golden Gate Bridge. Their fifteen-month old little boy was sitting on one of the sofas next to Father Henry Oppenheimer. The priest was reading to the boy from a picture book of Bible stories.

Tony Bosco walked up to Rachel and Jacob and handed them each a martini. "Tony, do you know what those big ships are – the ones about to pass under the bridge?" Rachel asked.

"Oh, yes. They're the *Colorado* and the *Maryland* – battleships. The *Maryland* has been repaired after getting damaged at Pearl Harbor. I don't know whether to be reassured or afraid to see them heading out into the Pacific."

Rachel frowned. "What do you mean, Tony?"

"The navy intercepted secret Japanese navy radio transmissions. They plan to attack the West Coast to retaliate against General Doolittle's Tokyo raid. We're sending out a small fleet, including the *Colorado* and the *Maryland*, to defend San Francisco."

"I'm glad we'll be protected," Ruthie said, "but can we really stop a Pearl Harbor right here in San Francisco Bay?"

"Let's hope this show of force gets them to think twice about invading us," Jacob said.

Rachel turned to Jacob. "What's the latest news about Dr. Smith?"

Jacob explained that Smith confessed to working with the

consulate, doing spying and sabotage jobs, from the time Hitler came to power. When the Bund dissolved and later when the president shut down the consulate, he went to work for the Abwehr – the military intelligence department of the German army. He began to feel isolated, but he carried on anyway.

"He told us he was duty bound to kill Charles Brown after he learned that Brown had helped Jewish families," Jacob said. "And he had orders to eliminate anyone he considered disloyal or a risk to his own security. He has no remorse for killing Father Haber and Monsignor Fuchs.

"When I asked him about his sister and his brother-in-law, he just shrugged and told us that this is wartime, and sometimes innocent people die," Jacob said.

"He told me he was proud of organizing and managing his attacks," Jacob said. "Here in the Bay Area and in Southern California. He boasted about getting Ferguson to spy on our FBI office for him. He smiled when he told me he'd tried to make me a suspect in Brown's murder. Trying to blame Brown's and Haber's murders on a Jewish terrorist organization was also his idea. The false flag tactic was meant to get the public to think the FBI was conspiring with Jewish terrorists."

"I told you I had a bad feeling about Ferguson," Ruthie said. "What's going to happen to him?"

"He's been arrested and will probably be tried for treason," Jacob said. "Ferguson told Ned the FBI had treated him badly during his whole career. He wanted to get even, and Smith paid him very well. That's where he got the money to build his vacation cabin at Lake Tahoe."

Dennis joined them at the window. "Ruthie and I were sort of debating what should be done with Smith. He's admitted to killing Brown and to hiring O'Malley to kill Fuchs and Father Haber. He accidentally killed his sister, and he shot the two servicemen at Playland. And he tried to blow up the Officers' Club. He told us that Cassel's death was actually an accident. He was drunk and fell off Smith's boat."

"Smith should have a jury trial for each of his crimes the same way as any other American citizen in California," Tony said.

"But, Tony," Ruthie said, "he also admitted, even bragged, that he committed all of those crimes for his 'Fatherland,' for his 'Volk'. So why should we give him any right to a trial by jury?"

Flora Bosco came into the living room and walked over to the group by the picture window. The battleships had sailed into the ocean but smaller destroyers and other ships were still passing under the bridge.

"I heard some of what you were saying," she said, "but I can't help feeling sorry for the doctor. He's a misguided man who sold his soul to the devil. And I feel sorry for that Arzano woman. What's going to happen to her?"

"The chief and the district attorney had her committed to Napa State Hospital. She's a sad case, but she's not a danger to anyone now."

"I have trouble feeling sorry for Dr. Smith," Tony said. "He's expressed no remorse for what he did. The only thing he regretted was having hired Francis O'Malley. He told me he should have done all the work himself."

"Francis O'Malley, on the other hand, was so remorseful he shot himself," Jacob said. "We found him and a suicide note at Lands End. He felt that his murders could not be forgiven, that the worst was his shooting priests. He said he couldn't sleep and knew that if his mother was alive she would never speak to him again. He said he was going to hell and decided not to wait."

"He wrote that he'd enjoyed watching the sunset over the Pacific one last time. He was having his last drink of Jameson and then he shot himself with his .38 caliber pistol."

There was a long silence. "That's an awful story," Flora said. "But back to Dr. Smith, how does killing *him* do any good for anybody? It won't bring back his poor sister, or those boys at Playland. And good heavens, Father Haber and Monsignor Fuchs!"

Ruthie was shaking her head. She seemed about to respond, but Jacob said, "Trial by jury is a foundation for our American liberties. I've been studying the American constitution so I can pass the exam to attend law school at night. I've learned about the way wars have created fears that led the government to limit constitutional rights."

Tony nodded. "You'd be an excellent trial lawyer, Jacob. I certainly agree with you. I've been preparing a speech of my own, to defend my good name and my own citizenship rights. I don't accept the right of a state legislature committee to accuse me of being a traitor. Their so-called evidence is bogus. I'm not allowed any witnesses or a defense lawyer. There's no jury. They're just a bunch of publicity seeking politicians."

He looked at Jacob. "I won't back down, even if Hoover continues to pass on malicious gossip about me to people like Walter Winchell!"

"We're all on your side, Tony," Ruthie said. "The mayor and the archbishop and a dozen others have written to President Roosevelt, the Secretary of the Army, and the Attorney General to support you."

"I know," Tony said. "But General DeWitt believes what the Un-American Committee says." He laughed. "That's what I call it. They say I should be relocated because I'm a security risk."

"You ought to have an opportunity to defend yourself in a jury trial," Jacob said. "The charges against you are ridiculous. You'd quickly be declared innocent, and the public would see that this 'Un-American Committee' is politically motivated. Dr. Smith ought to be tried by a jury, too, but I'm afraid that's not going to be possible."

"Why do you say that?" Flora asked.

"My boss, Ned Piper, heard from Hoover that the President is going to issue an executive order about how traitors would be tried," Jacob said.

"You mean like his order to move the Japanese to camps?" Rachel asked. "You told us the FBI argued that it wasn't necessary. But Roosevelt wanted to lock them up in camps because he thinks they are untrustworthy. That's a betrayal of our American values!"

"And now," Jacob continued, "Roosevelt plans to order that anyone like Smith, accused of sabotage or other crimes on behalf of the Axis, would be tried by secret military tribunals. I believe strongly that we have to fight to protect the rights of the accused for a jury trial, *especially* when we're at war. If we don't take on this fight, then *we* could be traitors – allowing the subversion of the values of our constitution."

Flora looked at Jacob and smiled. "Such eloquence, don't you think, Tony? He sounds like he's summing up his case in court."

Father Oppenheimer walked over and joined them. He was holding little David Weiss in the crook of his arm. The boy had his right arm around the priest's neck. When he saw Rachel, his little face broke into a huge smile. He reached out to his mother with both arms. Oppenheimer lifted the boy over to his mother.

"Your son loved the story of David and Goliath," he said. They all laughed.

"Let's move into the dining room and have dinner," Flora said. "We can't fight on an empty stomach."

## Acknowledgments and Author's Note

I received valuable suggestions from Ben and Betsy Asen, Rodger Birt, Jeffrey M. Burns, Robert W. Cherny, Philip Jacques Dreyfus, Mary Claire Heffron, Constance Holmes, Charles J. Issel, David W. Issel, James G. Issel, Rhodri Jeffreys-Jones, Ava F. Kahn, Marjorie Penn Lasky, Zeese Papanikolas, and Charles Wollenberg. Special thanks to my editor, Andrei Cherascu, my copy editor DJ Hendrickson, and to Chris Carlsson, who designed and published the book.

For assistance in the research for this book, I thank Susan Goldstein and the staff of the San Francisco History Center of the Main San Francisco Public Library, Catherine Powell and the staff of the Labor Archives and Research Center of San Francisco State University, Linda Wobbe and the staff of the library and archives of St. Mary's College of California, Jeffrey M. Burns, former director of the Chancery Archives of the Archdiocese of San Francisco, and the Bancroft Library of the University of California, Berkeley.

For generosity and friendship while I lived in the West End and taught at the Polytechnic of Central London, I thank Hazel Brookeman, Alan Morrison, and Jane King. I regret that my good friend and colleague at the American Studies Centre, Chris Brookeman, my "boon companion" on our countless jaunts and excursions in and beyond London, did not live to read this novel.

This is a work of fiction inspired by actual historical events I discovered in declassified FBI files and collections of personal correspondence while researching "Jews and Catholics Against Prejudice," in *California Jews* (2003), *For Both Cross and Flag: Catholic Action, Anti-Catholicism, and National Security Politics in World War II San Francisco* (2009), and *Church and State in the City: Catholics and Politics in Twentieth Century San Francisco* (2013). Tony and Flora Bosco, Jacob Weiss and Rachel Bernstein, Ruthie Fuller, Dennis Sullivan, and their associates, Albert Smith, and his associates, and most of the other characters in this novel are products of my imagination. Actual historical persons, and events involving real persons, such as Orde Wingate in Palestine and London, the Winston Churchill birthday party, the work of Rabbi Harold Reinhart and the West London Synagogue with the *Kindertransport* children, the pro-Nazi work of Manfred von Killinger and the German Consulate in San Francisco, and the California legislature's Un-American Activities investigation of Angelo Rossi, and some others, have been fictionalized. The dates of all the significant international, national, and local developments in the novel are accurate, but most of the events and characters are my invention.

In addition to unpublished sources in the archives and libraries above, I would like to acknowledge the following published works.

*J. Edgar Hoover and the Anti-Interventionists by Douglas M. Charles (2007)*

*The Origins of FBI Counter-Intelligence by Raymond J. Batvinis (2007).*

*Hoover's Secret War against Axis Spies: FBI Counterespionage during World War II also by Raymond J. Batvinis (2014).*

*Fetch The Devil: The Sierra Diablo Murders and Nazi Espionage in America by Clint Richmond (2014).*

*Hitler in Los Angeles: How Jews Foiled Nazi Plots Against Hollywood and America by Steven J. Ross (2017).*

*Cosmopolitans: A Social & Cultural History of the Jews of the San Francisco Bay Area by Fred Rosenbaum (2009).*

*The Bad City in the Good War: San Francisco, Los Angeles, Oakland, and San Diego by Roger W. Lotchin (2003).*

*Orde Wingate: A Biography by Christopher Sykes (1959).*

*Fire in the Night: Wingate of Burma, Ethiopia, and Zion by John Bierman and Colin Smith (1999).*

*One Palestine, Complete: Jews and Arabs under the British Mandate by Tom Segev (1999).*

*Baffy: The Diaries of Blanche Dugdale, 1936-1947 edited by N.A. Rose (1973).*

*Marks of Distinction: The Memoirs of Elaine Blond with Barry Turner (1988).*

*Chaim Weizmann: A Biography by Norman Rose (1986).*

*Men of Vision: Anglo-Jewish Aid to Victims of the Nazi Regime, 1933-1945 by Amy Zahl Gottlieb (1998).*

*A Refuge from Darkness: Wilfrid Israel and the Rescue of the Jews by Naomi Shepherd (1984).*

*Never Look Back: The Jewish Refugee Children in Great Britain, 1938-1945 by Judith Tydor Baumel-Schwartz (2012).*

*The Kindertransport: Contesting Memory by Jennifer Craig-Norton (2019).*

*"Hurrah for the Blackshirts!" Fascists and Fascism in Britain between the Wars by Martin Pugh (2005).*

*Hitler's British Traitors: The Secret History of Spies, Saboteurs and Fifth Columnists by Tim Tate (2018).*

*Militant Zionism in America: The Rise and Impact of the Jabotinsky Movement in the United States, 1926-1948 by Rafael Medoff (2002).*

*The Jews Should Keep Quiet: Franklin D. Roosevelt, Rabbi Stephen S. Wise, and the Holocaust by Rafael Medoff (2019).*

*Nazi Spies in America by Leon G. Turrou as told to David G. Wittels (1938, 1939).*

*Sabotage! The Secret War against America by Michael Sayers and Albert E. Kahn (1942).*

*Under Cover: My Four Years in the Nazi Underworld by John Roy Carlson (1943).*

*The German Fifth Column in World War II by Louis De Jong (1956).*

*The Nazi Movement in the United States, 1924-1941 by Sander A. Diamond (1974).*

*Hitler's Spies: German Military Intelligence in World War II by David Kahn (1978).*

*Nazi Saboteurs on Trial: A Military Tribunal and American Law by Louis Fisher (2003).*

*Saboteurs: The Nazi Raid on America by Michael Dobbs (2004).*

*Swastika Nation: Fritz Kuhn and the Rise and Fall of the German-American Bund by Arnie Bernstein (2013).*

*Double Agent: The First Hero of World War II and How the FBI Outwitted and Destroyed a Nazi Spy Ring by Peter Duffy (2014).*

*Hitler's American Friends: The Third Reich's Supporters in the United States by Bradley W. Hart (2018).*

*The Nazi Spy Ring in America: Hitler's Agents, the FBI, and the Case That Stirred the Nation by Rhodri Jeffreys-Morley (2020).*

*Hitler's True Believers: How Ordinary People Became Nazis by Robert Gellately (2020).*

*Nazis of Copley Square: The Forgotten Story of the Christian Front by Charles R. Gallagher (2021).*

## About the Author

Bill Issel, professor of history emeritus at San Francisco State University, is the author of *For Both Cross and Flag* (Temple, 2009), *Church and State in the City* (Temple, 2013), *Coit Tower* (Carleton Street, 2019*)*, "Jews and Catholics Against Prejudice," in *California Jews* (Brandeis, 2003), and "Deutsche Einwanderer in San Francisco," in *California Dreams: San Francisco, Ein Porträt* (Bundeskunsthalle, 2019). He is the winner of the Distinguished Scholar Award of the American Catholic Historical Association, the Award of Merit of the San Francisco Historical Society, research and public history grants from the National Endowment of Humanities and the Rockefeller Foundation, and three Fulbright teaching grants, in London (1978-1979), Pécs (2008-2009), and Timişoara (2018-2019).